THE SISTERS GRIMM

BOOK NINE

THE COUNCIL OF MIRRORS

ALSO BY MICHAEL BUCKLEY:

In the *Sisters Grimm* series:

In the *NERDS* series:

THE SISTERS GRIMM

BOOK NINE

THE COUNCIL OF MIRRORS

MICHAEL BUCKLEY

pictures by Peter Ferguson

Amulet Books
New York

Library of Congress Cataloging-in-Publication Data has been applied for and may be obtained from the Library of Congress.

ISBN 978-1-4197-0186-3

Printed and bound in U.S.A.
10 9 8 7 6 5 4 3

Amulet Books are available at special discounts when purchased in quantity for premiums and promotions as well as fundraising or educational use. Special editions can also be created to specification. For details, contact specialmarkets@abramsbooks.com or the address below.

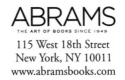

THE ART OF BOOKS SINCE 1949
115 West 18th Street
New York, NY 10011
www.abramsbooks.com

For Sylvie and Phoebe Sanders.
Thanks for riding this flying carpet.

ACKNOWLEDGMENTS

The Sisters Grimm would never have existed if not for my beautiful wife, Alison. She's as important to this series as Sabrina and Daphne, and her presence is written into every sentence. It's nice that she's my literary agent too. She's managed me through ups and downs, my insecurities, and temper tantrums and helped me grow this "silly idea" into a career.

There are three other people who have made outstanding contributions. The first is my editor, Susan Van Metre, who has been a friend and mentor to me. The second is my other editor, Maggie Lehrman, who came on board midway and has added a new layer to the stories. The third is Jason Wells—probably the hardest-working man in, well, anything. I have been blessed by his cleverness and understanding. They are backed by an army of talented and hardworking people at Amulet Books: Michael Jacobs, Chad W. Beckerman, Laura Mihalick, Chris Blank, and the sales and marketing departments. I am a truly lucky person to have such brilliant people helping me, holding my hand, and demanding the best from me. You have my undying respect, admiration, and loyalty.

I want to thank my family, Wilma and James Cuvelier, Michael and Kassandra Buckley, Douglas Lancaster and Beth Fargis-Lancaster, Paul Fargis and Rev. Dawn Sangrey, Chris

Fargis, John and Vida Fargis, Edwin and Maria Buckley, and all the nieces and nephews both here in the United States and in China. I want to thank my good friends Joe Deasy and Josh Drisko. Thanks to Autumn Heard and Jannelle Purcell at Starbucks as well as everyone at Ted & Honey's for the chair and the free Wi-Fi.

Many thanks to Peter Ferguson, who brought these books to life. At my house, Peter's drawings and paintings have always been received like Christmas presents. Thank you for your vision and inventiveness. Your pencil is forever linked to my laptop.

Thanks to Finn. I love you, son.

And to every teacher, librarian, student, professor, blogger, and kid who ever took a chance on this series. Reading takes time. I have appreciated all that you gave me. As Daphne would say, you are all very punk rock.

THE SISTERS GRIMM

BOOK NINE

THE COUNCIL OF MIRRORS

ONCE UPON A TIME *there was a sleepy river town called Ferryport Landing. It was nestled on the bank of the Hudson River in upstate New York, where mountains look over valleys and water runs down into the great river and on to the sea. Quaint little shops filled the town center, and trees freckled the landscape. The town's citizens bicycled along cobblestoned lanes and through community gardens. Apple pies cooled on windowsills, and few people locked their doors at night. If a person didn't know better, he might have suspected Ferryport Landing had been propped up on wheels and rolled out of a storybook.*

But that was a long time ago.

Now it was dead. Its demise wasn't slow, like so many other tiny dots on the map that rust and decay when the mill closes or the steel plant shuts its doors. No, Ferryport Landing was murdered. Its citizens tore it to pieces. They smashed shop windows and looted goods. They spilled great heaps of trash onto its streets. They lit fires whose hungry flames still lapped at the few buildings left standing. They tipped over cars, leaving them scattered on the streets like the forgotten playthings of a huge child. The little town was wrecked and then abandoned.

The Grimm sisters stood over Ferryport Landing's poor, broken corpse to pay their respects to a fallen friend.

"Is that it?" Daphne said. "Is that the end?"

Sabrina nodded. "Yes. And it's about time."

1

TWO WEEKS EARLIER

ctober 14

My name is Sabrina Grimm and this is my journal. My family has been bugging me to write in it for a while. I tried a few times, but to be honest I thought it was stupid. I never wanted to get involved. I wanted to be a girl who lived on the Upper East Side of New York City. I wanted to go to school and make friends and buy bagel sandwiches at the deli on York and 88th Street every morning. But that's not what happened.

If you're reading this, you're either Puck (stop snooping, stinkface!) or you're one of my descendants. If you're a descendant, then maybe you're like me and you kind of got dumped into this life where everything is upside down and nothing makes sense. Well, I need to fill you in on a few things, and you might want to sit down for this.

You know those bedtime stories your parents read to you at night? You know, the ones filled with fairies, giants, witches, monsters, mad tea parties, princes on white stallions, sleeping princesses, jungle boys, cowardly lions, and guys with straw for brains? They're not stories. They're history. They're based on actual events and actual people who are as real as you and me. They call themselves Everafters—real-life fairy-tale characters—and that's where our family comes in. We're Grimms, descendants of one-half of the Brothers Grimm, and we keep an eye on the Everafter community—which is no picnic. OK, I know you're probably thinking I've been sitting too close to the microwave, but I'm telling the truth.

Let me start at the beginning. Two years ago my parents, Henry and Veronica Grimm, disappeared. My sister, Daphne, and I were tossed into an orphanage and bounced around the foster care system for a while. For a long time we thought we had been abandoned, but it turned out Mom and Dad were kidnapped (long story). Enter Granny Relda, our long-lost and believed dead grandmother (another long story). Once she tracked us down, she brought us to live with her in a little town called Ferryport Landing. That's where a lot of the Everafters live.

You've probably never heard of Ferryport Landing. As I write this, the town is being destroyed. There's an angry mob of ogres, trolls, talking animals, and assorted creeps running down its streets, terrorizing everyone. Anyone with any sense has left or gone into hiding—but not us. Oh no! Our family has no sense to lose, which means we're knee-deep in trouble and things don't look like they're going to get any better.

But you still need to know about Ferryport Landing and what happened here. Which gets me to another of the Grimm family responsibilities. According to tradition it's our job to keep a journal of everything we see and hear that involves Everafters. The journals might just help you out, and your journals might help out the Grimms that come after you. So, take it from me: just bite the bullet and do it. I can't count how many times the journals have saved my sister and me.

Of course, there may not be any more Grimms after me. I might die and then no one will be reading this. Like I said, things are pretty bleak.

But that's enough backstory for today. I'll write more when I can. For now I have to go save the world.

Sabrina snapped her journal shut and tucked it into the folds of her sleeping bag for safekeeping. She rubbed the sleep from her eyes, then got to her feet, stretching the stiffness from her aching body. Sleeping on the cold, marble floor of her bedroom was no fun.

Not that where she and her little sister, Daphne, were sleeping could actually be called a "bedroom." A bedroom had a bed. A bedroom had a window. A bedroom had a place to put your clothes, a closet, a rug, and other things to make it comfy and homey. What the girls had was an empty space with walls of stone and an unforgivingly hard floor. Sabrina hoped the living situation was temporary, but to make sure, she knew she had to get to work.

Next to her sleeping bag she kept a rusty cowbell and a drumstick. She scooped them up and padded over to where her sister lay, still slumbering. First she called out to the little girl. She even gave her a few shakes, but Daphne could sleep through a tornado and rousing her meant Sabrina had to take drastic measures. She found that the most effective of those tactics was a cowbell ring to her sister's ear.

DONK! The cowbell clanged as the drumstick smacked its side.

Daphne did not stir.

DONK! DONK! DONK!

Nothing.

"Wake up! We're under attack. Monsters and lunatics and weird dudes with pitchforks! They'll be here any second!"

Still nothing.

DONK! DONK! DONK! DONK! DONK! DONK!

Finally, Daphne poked her head out from underneath the flap of her sleeping bag, as did the humongous brown snout of Elvis, the family's two-hundred-pound Great Dane. Both of them eyed Sabrina sourly.

"You are a terrible human being," Daphne croaked.

"Woof!" the dog agreed.

"C'mon. Get up. We've got to get to work," Sabrina said.

Daphne scowled but did as she was told. When she and Elvis were on their feet, they stretched and yawned in unison. Sabrina noticed a huge book hiding in the folds of her sister's sleeping bag, and she frowned. It was called the Book of Everafter, and it was a collection of magical fairy tales. A person could do more than read it, though. They could actually go inside and visit the stories they loved. It gave people powers, too—dark powers, like the ability to rewrite the past and entrap people in its literary prison.

"You shouldn't leave that lying around," Sabrina said. "I told you when we took it out of its room that you had to be careful with it. Haven't we had enough trouble without that thing falling into the wrong hands?"

Daphne snatched it up in her arms. "Sorry."

"Have you found anything in all those stories we can use to fight Mirror?"

The little girl shook her head. "There's a lot of stories—like thousands! I'm still reading."

"Let's see if anyone else is having any luck," Sabrina said, then led Daphne and the big dog into a huge hallway known as the Hall of Wonders.

Massive columns held up a ceiling as high as the sky. Beneath it were hundreds—maybe even thousands—of doors. No one knew for sure. Each opened into its own unique room, and even after many months, the closed doors still sparked the curiosity of Sabrina's inner detective. The Hall of Wonders was a magical place. She could spend a lifetime exploring it, but now there were more important concerns at hand.

The sisters stopped at a door that opened into a room not much bigger than their own, but its contents were quite a bit more unusual. Mounted on every wall were a number of beautifully ornate, full-length mirrors—twenty-five of them, to be exact. Of the twenty-five, only five were intact. The rest were broken, only their frames remaining, but Sabrina had collected their shards and carefully glued them onto the walls of a room much closer to the Hall's exit than the original

Room of Reflections. When the light hit the fragments just right, it created a dazzling play for the eyes, full of twisted reflections.

Moving the mirrors from their home at the far end of Hall had another advantage: other members of Sabrina's group could keep an eye on them. At the moment, two people watched the mirrors. The first was an elderly man resting in a chair. He had hair like a lightning strike—white and untamed. His suit was several sizes too big for his thin frame, and his arthritic hands trembled in his lap. His name was Mr. Canis. The second figure was almost his opposite. She was no older than Daphne, with amber curls that spilled down to her shoulders. She wore a red sweatshirt and hand-me-down jeans, and her face was full of possibility and hope. Everyone called her Red.

"You two look tired," Sabrina said.

"We're all tired," Canis said without taking his eyes off the mirrors. He was an old man, and recently his age had been catching up with him fast. He was prone to coughing fits and seemed to wince when he walked. Sabrina was very worried about him.

Red turned to the girls and smiled. "He won't sleep. He's been up for days."

"I will sleep when Mrs. Grimm is safe and sound," Canis

growled, then turned his attention to Daphne. "You two should really lock that book up where it belongs."

"Geez, the walk to its room is like three hours long. I won't let anything happen to it. See anything new?" Daphne asked.

"As a matter of fact, yes," Canis said, gesturing to the five intact mirrors. Instead of reflecting back Sabrina's image, they revealed a bird's-eye view of Ferryport Landing. Ugly purple and ebony clouds hovered in the sky—the same clouds that had appeared two days earlier, and now sat over the town, blasting lightning and ear-splitting claps of thunder. "We have found your grandmother. Mirrors, tell them."

The five mirrors suddenly glowed with otherworldly light. They shimmered and rippled like the surface of a wishing well recovering from a tossed penny, and when they calmed again, Ferryport Landing was gone and four strange faces materialized. In one mirror, a brutal barbarian named Titan appeared; the second showed a seventies-era nightclub owner who went by the name Donovan; the third was a West African with long dreadlocks named Reggie; and the fourth was Fanny, a roller-skating waitress with hair as alarmingly red as a fire engine. The fifth mirror remained empty but continued to glow.

"One of the reasons we couldn't find her is we were looking in the wrong places. She's still in Ferryport Landing," Fanny said. She stood in what looked like an old-fashioned ice-cream shop, complete with red counters and matching stools. Behind her, a milk-shake machine hummed and a jukebox waited for a nickel. Fanny chomped on chewing gum—she never seemed to run out—and could be very sweet, but she had a tendency to spin around on her roller skates from time to time, which made Sabrina dizzy.

"What? How?" Sabrina asked.

"He hasn't broken through the barrier," Canis said.

"But—why not? Mirror is in Granny's human body now. That was his whole plan," Sabrina said.

"Who cares?" Fanny cheered. "Let's just be happy Mirror is stuck here in Ferryport Landing with the rest of us."

"He can't be thrilled about that," Daphne said.

"You said it, kiddo. The light show outside isn't a storm. It's a temper tantrum," Reggie said. When he spoke, his long, thick dreadlocks shimmied like streamers at a New Year's Eve party. "He's as stuck as ever, and quite salty, if the storm's any indication."

Daphne slipped her hand into Sabrina's and gave it a squeeze. Sabrina knew her sister must be just as relieved as she was. Since Mirror hijacked their grandmother's body two days prior, Sabrina had feared his plan to escape the town had worked. If Mirror had gotten free, he could have gone anywhere, unleashing his magic on an unsuspecting and unprepared world and taking their grandmother with him. But now . . .

"Serves him right!" Titan roared, and Sabrina spun to face his mirror. He was a rugged man with long rust-colored hair and a scraggy beard. Everything he said came out in a blustery rage, turning his face the shade of his mane. He appeared in front of a medieval torture chamber filled with spiked weapons and boiling oils. Despite his fearsome appearance and strange living quarters, Sabrina could see his heart was in the right place. Now he cried, "If only I were a living, breathing man, I would put a painful end to our brother's atrocity!"

"He's no brother of mine," Reggie grumbled in his thick Caribbean accent. "The First is a scoundrel of the worst kind."

"The First?" Sabrina asked.

"That's what we've been calling him, sister. He was the first magic mirror the Wicked Queen ever made—you know, the prototype," Donovan explained.

"Anything is better than his other name," Red said. "'The Master' is—"

"Creep-tastic?" Daphne asked, pretending to shudder.

Sabrina didn't have to pretend. Every time anyone mentioned Mirror her blood cells flash-froze inside her veins. How could she have ever called him friend? How could she have confided all of her hopes and fears to him? He had played her like a child's toy, betraying her and her entire family, and now he had her grandmother, manipulating the old woman like a helpless marionette in his twisted puppet show.

"Whatever his name, our brother will pay! He has stained the honor of magic mirrors everywhere!" Titan roared.

"You mean, all four of us?" Donovan said. "We're all that's left of the original twenty-five."

Titan snarled. "All the more reason to respect our heritage."

"Calm down, sugar." Fanny applied another layer of ruby-red lipstick as she spun around like a top. "You'll get your blood pressure up again. Now that we know where our brother is, it's time to focus our energies on how to catch him and free Relda Grimm from his control."

"Please tell me you have some ideas," Sabrina said. Her plea was met with heartbreaking silence.

"What about you?" Daphne said to the fifth undamaged mirror. Its surface appeared empty. Was its guardian in there . . . listening? Daphne softly caressed its frame as if coaxing a shy puppy out from under the bed. "What do you think?"

"You're wasting your time," Canis said. "I haven't heard so much as a peep from that one."

Daphne turned from the empty mirror with a sigh. "Have you spotted Uncle Jake yet?" she asked.

Donovan shook his head. "He's harder to find than your granny. It's like he disappeared off the map. We can sense his presence but can't pinpoint it. Wherever he is, he doesn't want to be found, and I suspect he's using magic to make sure he stays that way."

"What about these broken pieces? Any sign of him in here?" Sabrina examined the shards. Most people would sweep a broken mirror into a dustpan and toss it in the trash, but these pieces were far too special to throw away. Though their guardians were long gone, these pieces retained powerful magic. One look and a person could peek through the reflections of ordinary mirrors all over the world. Now Sabrina glimpsed a man putting on a necktie in a department store, a woman washing the makeup off her face, and a high school student practicing a speech in a bathroom mirror. In other shards she saw people closer to home. One showed Sheriff Nottingham struggling to tie Mayor Heart's corset. His boot was planted squarely on her back for leverage as he tugged and tugged. In another, an ogre smashed through the bicycle store on Main Street. In yet another, dwarfs looted the local grocery.

Canis shook his head in disgust. "Nothing."

"Well, Uncle Jake can take care of himself," Sabrina said. "We need to focus on Granny. Now that we know where she is we can go rescue—"

"You and your sister are sitting this one out," a voice said from behind her. Sabrina spun around to find her father and mother along with her baby brother, Basil, standing in the doorway. Henry was a good-looking man dressed in a heavy jacket and hiking boots. Like Canis, he looked tired. "I can't put you girls into that kind of danger."

"But danger is my middle name," Daphne said.

"Your middle name is Delilah, young lady," Veronica said. Sabrina's mother was a true knockout, but her face also showed signs of weariness. "Some jobs are just for grown-ups. Besides, I could use your help with Basil."

"Babysitting!" Sabrina cried.

"He's having trouble adjusting," Henry said. "He won't eat or sleep. I'm worried."

As if to prove Henry's point, the boy fussed and struggled, his little fists pounding on Veronica's chest, and tears running down his face.

When Basil was just a newborn, Mirror had kidnapped him with plans to steal the young boy's body as a vessel for his corrupt soul. Poor Red had become entangled in the plot as well, and was forced by a manipulative Mirror to act as Basil's babysitter while struggling with her own demons.

"I'll take him, Mrs. Grimm. He knows me," Red said.

Veronica looked pained. Sabrina could tell her mother did not want to let the boy go, but Basil needed sleep like everyone else, and Red had a knack with him. Despite the sad circumstances of their life with Mirror, Red and the little boy had a bond that no one could break. Veronica reluctantly surrendered the little boy into Red's arms and his tears transformed into giggles.

"I'll get him something to eat," Red said.

Veronica watched them exit the room. The moment they were gone, tears fell from her eyes. She looked as if she might collapse, but Henry swept her into his arms and held her fast.

"It will take time, 'Roni. He doesn't know us yet. But he will," he assured her.

Veronica clung to him like he was a lifeboat in a stormy sea, but Sabrina could see her father's despair as well. If people could break in two from grief, Henry and Veronica were very close to cracking up. It frightened Sabrina to realize her parents were so fragile.

"So you have a plan to save your mother?" Canis asked Henry.

Henry shook his head. "No. But it can't hurt to take a look. That storm has been hovering over the southern end of town, so I assume he's near the rail station, probably on Route 9. I'm going to sneak over there and see what's what. Maybe I'll see something that can help us."

"I'll get my things," Canis said, and snatched the white cane that leaned against his chair. He struggled to his feet, using what looked like every ounce of his strength. The cane itself skittered across the floor, desperate to find purchase. Poor Mr. Canis looked like an old tree struggling to stay rooted in the face a hurricane.

"Mr. Canis, it would be best for you to stay here and keep an eye on things," Henry said.

Canis looked into Henry's face. "You have several babysitters already, Henry, and your mother and I shared important tasks and worked as partners. I was not her assistant and I certainly wasn't her wet nurse."

"I don't need you for babysitting. I need someone to help get things ready. What if I go down there and find a way to rescue Mom? She's going to be exhausted, maybe even hurt. We need to get a room ready for her if that happens," Henry said quickly, almost sheepishly. "Veronica's got her hands full with Basil, and I can't trust the kids to do it the right way. You're needed here."

Canis frowned. "Babysitting."

Sabrina braced for an argument. Staying put and preparing

bedrooms was not what Mr. Canis was accustomed to doing. Once he had been the family's fiercest and most intimidating ally. He sent tremors of fear into the wickedest of villains, wielding the full barely controlled savagery of the Big Bad Wolf. Leaping into action was more his nature, and Henry's request seemed to hit the old man like a sucker punch. But no fight came. Instead, Canis turned and exited the room.

"He wants to feel useful," Veronica said.

"He'll slow me down. If something happens, I don't want to have to worry about getting him back here," Henry said, though Sabrina could see he immediately regretted his choice of words. "Not that anything will happen, of course."

"I'd feel better if Jake was going with you," Veronica said.

"I would too," Henry said as he buttoned his hunting jacket. "But Briar's death is still fresh, and Jake always took loss very hard."

Losing Uncle Jake's girlfriend Briar Rose was a shock to everyone, but for Jake it set off an emotional typhoon. She was the second person he had lost to violence, after his father had been killed by a mindless monster known as the Jabberwocky fifteen years ago. Now the love of his life was dead. Briar was killed by a dragon controlled by some of Mirror's goons—members of a group called the Scarlet Hand.

Sabrina heard a fluttering of wings and then a voice above their heads. "Who needs Jake when you have the Trickster King?" Something wet and sticky landed on Sabrina. It dripped down into her ears and collected under her chin, smelling like the livestock tent at a state fair. Sabrina looked up, even though she didn't need to. She knew the slime bomb was from Puck, and sure enough his pink fairy wings beat furiously to keep him aloft. He held another balloon with funky green ooze sloshing around inside.

"What was in that balloon?" Sabrina growled as she tried to wipe the muck off her face.

"You know . . . I don't have a clue. I found it collecting in a pool near the sewage treatment plant. It was just sitting there—free for the taking! Can you imagine? Who would just leave this stuff around?" He tossed the second balloon and it hit her in the shoulder, splattering all over her face and neck. "This is Grade A filth—top of the line."

Sabrina clenched her fists.

Puck looked genuinely shocked. "Don't tell me you're angry! You should be honored. When I found this slop, you were the first person that popped into my head. How could I test it on anyone else? I didn't want to offend you. And now, because of you, I can go into battle confident that my crud bombs bring the right amount of stomach-lurching awesomeness. I couldn't have done it without you!"

Before Sabrina could snatch his leg out of the air her father called Puck's name, and the boy darted down the hall after Henry, toward the portal to the outside.

"You're really leaving us here?" Daphne cried, chasing them into the hallway. Sabrina and her mother followed.

"We are," Henry said.

"You can't keep us locked up in this mirror," Sabrina shouted, but Henry didn't hear. His body vanished as he stepped through a magical portal that led outside to the real world.

"Smell you later," Puck said, and flew after Henry.

"I just got put back at the kids' table," Sabrina said.

"I never left the kids' table," Daphne grumbled.

Veronica patted them each on the shoulder. "There's plenty to do around here. Go find Pinocchio and get him to help Canis with that room. It would be good for him to lend a hand. We are feeding him, after all."

Sabrina stalked away. "Fine!"

When the girls were out of earshot of their mother, the complaining began.

"They treat us like we're babies!" Sabrina said.

"Yeah, why not put us in diapers?" Daphne said.

"We've been in dangerous situations before."

"Very dangerous!"

"We've fought dragons and Jabberwockies and creepy guidance counselors covered in fur!"

"Ugh. He was creepy."

"I killed a giant once!"

"I ate 'fish surprise' in the orphanage cafeteria!" Daphne shouted.

The two stomped on until they came to Pinocchio's room. The odd little boy was largely responsible for the family's uncomfortable living situation. He had opened the doors in the Hall of Wonders and released the magical creatures that were locked inside. The chaos that followed destroyed the Grimms' home, so Sabrina was stunned when her father invited Pinocchio to stay with them. In her opinion he should have been locked away—or even better, sent out to live in the wilderness, possibly to be eaten by coyotes and rabid beavers . . . or whatever lived in the wilderness. But Henry wanted to give him a chance to prove himself. So far he had proved himself to be rude and lazy.

"He's going to laugh in our faces," Daphne said.

"I hope he does," Sabrina said, channeling all her anger at her father toward the little snot. She pounded on his door harder than she needed to.

"Whoever it is, please go away. I'm having some 'me' time!" the boy shouted from behind the door, his voice a high-pitched whine.

"Get out here! You know I have keys to this room," Sabrina shouted back. "Open the door or I will open it myself and kick your puppet behind!"

"I was not a puppet! I was a marionette!"

Sabrina growled and reached into her pocket for her set of keys. She sorted through them to find one that fit the lock and threw the door open so hard the force almost knocked it off its hinges. The girls stomped into the room and found Pinocchio lying on a king-size brass bed, flipping through an architectural magazine.

"Hey! This is private! You're invading my . . . what on earth is all over you? Oh, that smell! You are putrid!"

"What does putrid mean?" Daphne said.

Before Sabrina could answer, Pinocchio spoke. "It refers to something that is in a state of foul decay. You children have always lacked a sense of personal pride when it came to cleanliness, but your current state is a new low."

"He's saying I stink," Sabrina said.

"Actually, I'm saying you both stink," Pinocchio said.

Sabrina examined his room in astonishment. In addition to

the luxurious bed, he had a dresser, armoire, table lamp, Oriental rugs, an overstuffed chair, and a box of chocolate bon-bons. "Where did you get this stuff?"

"I discovered them in some of the other rooms." Pinocchio huffed. "Hey, you're getting that slop all over my things. Some of these pieces are antiques!"

Sabrina grabbed the boy by the collar and dragged him off the bed. He flailed and kicked and eventually freed himself from her grip.

"Did you ever think for a moment in that tiny little brain of yours that there might be other people who needed this furniture? Mr. Canis? My mother and father? My baby brother?"

"Not to mention me. Hello!" Daphne said as she stretched a cramp out of her back.

"We're all sleeping on the floor! You owe your lousy life to this family and this is how you repay us?"

"It's every man for himself now, Grimms," Pinocchio said, shooing them away like pesky flies.

Sabrina fought the urge to strangle him and nearly lost. Instead, she grabbed him, spun him around, and kicked him in the behind so hard he went flying through the doorway and into the hall. "Get out!"

"You're evicting me? You wouldn't!" Pinocchio said, straightening his clothes.

"I can and I will. We have a million major emergencies going on right now: a maniac is possessing my grandmother's body, my uncle's girlfriend was just killed, we're homeless, there are wild things running loose, and I have a worthless sack of nonsense hogging beds and being lazy. Which of those problems is the easiest to solve, puppet boy?"

"I WAS NOT A PUPPET!" Pinocchio shouted, and shoved his sharp little nose into her face. "Fine! What do you require?"

"Go back to wherever you found all this furniture and bring back whatever you find—if you spot a crib, take it to my parents' room pronto! Then get your stuff out of here. This is going to be my grandmother's room when we rescue her."

"I will not be ordered to do manual labor!" the boy said. "That kind of work is done by the uneducated classes."

"Get moving or when I'm done with you my foot is going to be filled with splinters!"

"I haven't been made out of wood in centuries," he grumbled.

"You better change that attitude, pal," Daphne called after him. "Next time we say jump, you better be in the air when you say 'how high?'"

Sabrina watched the boy disappear down the hall.

"Did that sound tough?" Daphne asked. "I felt tough."

"Get your jacket," Sabrina said.

"Oh, boy! I know that look. You haven't had that look since we were in the orphanage," Daphne said, grinning. "You're thinking about shenanigans!"

"Shenanigans?"

"It's my new word. It means 'fun troublemaking,'" Daphne explained.

Sabrina nodded. "We don't belong at the kids' table. We're going to help Dad rescue Granny Relda."

"Right after you take a shower," Daphne said.

Sabrina sniffed her glop-covered shirt. "Yes, right after I take a shower."

2

inocchio was just the distraction the girls needed. His grumbling and endless whining kept Veronica so occupied the girls were able to stash the Book of Everafter in a safe place and slip out of the portal unseen. As they passed through the surface of the mirror, there was a rush of air, a dramatic drop in temperature, and Sabrina, Daphne, and Elvis found themselves inside a heavy thicket, deep in the Hudson Valley forest. The bushes were the perfect place to hide the door to their magical home, but they were less than convenient when exiting.

The girls pushed free of the thorns and prickly vines and stepped into a chilly splattering of autumn rain. Drops dripped onto Sabrina's head and trickled down her face and neck, sending tingles straight to her feet. She leaned down and quickly zipped up her sister's sweatshirt, then did her own.

"It rained like this the day we came to Ferryport Landing," Daphne said, catching some of the drops on her tongue. Sabrina remembered the gray sky, icy drizzle, and brisk chill that had greeted them when their caseworker Ms. Smirt shoved them down the train platform to meet their grandmother for the first time. She could even recall declaring that she and Daphne weren't going to stay with a crazy old woman who believed fairy tales were real. Funny how life got in the way of plans. Now she couldn't imagine her life without Granny Relda. She had to rescue her from Mirror, even if her father tried to stand in the way.

"We have to be patient with them," Daphne said, seemingly reading her sister's mind.

"Now you're on their side?" Sabrina said. "Five seconds ago you were shouting about how unfair they were."

"When Mom and Dad went to sleep, I was six and you were ten. I was obsessed with princesses—"

"You still are."

"Don't interrupt. What I'm saying is, to them, one day we were little girls, and then all of a sudden we weren't. They need time to catch up."

"But they need to understand that Granny never treated us like little girls. She would have had us leading the rescue," Sabrina said.

"Actually, she would have made us stay home too. It was just easier to sneak out when she was in charge."

Sabrina sighed. She knew Daphne was right, but it was still frustrating. "So are you saying we should go back?"

Daphne laughed. "No way!" She leaned down and gave Elvis a wet kiss on the snout. "Find Granny, buddy."

The dog gave himself a shake and water went everywhere. He sniffed the air and trotted into the wet brush. They watched him leap up a steep incline and they followed, trudging through spongy mounds of brown leaves and across slick black rocks. It wouldn't be long before they were both soaked to the bone, but Sabrina didn't mind. It felt good to be in the outside air without feeling the careful eyes of disapproving grown-ups on her. It infuriated her that her father couldn't see potential in his daughters. He kept them locked away like porcelain dolls. What did she and her sister have to do to prove they could take care of themselves?

After an hour of walking and losing the dog half a dozen times they realized that Elvis's nose wasn't really necessary. All they had to do was walk in the direction of the tremendous storm rumbling across the sky. Lightning slashed the horizon, followed by explosions so loud they rattled Sabrina's teeth. A normal person might have rushed to the cellar, fearing an approaching tornado, but if the mirrors and Mr. Canis were right, this was no ordinary storm. It would lead them to Granny Relda.

The girls stumbled out onto a deserted road and walked along its edge, despite the fact that neither of them had seen a car in weeks—not since the Scarlet Hand took over the town. It felt to Sabrina as if she and her sister were the only two people left in the world. She took Daphne's hand, not only to assure her that they would be OK, but to calm her own anxiety as they walked on toward the storm. Eventually, they found Elvis waiting by a bend in the road. He looked frightened, pacing in circles and panting. Daphne rubbed his neck to calm him down, but it did little to soothe the giant dog.

"Granny's nearby," Sabrina said.

Daphne nodded and turned back to the dog. "You stay here, OK?" Elvis clamped his teeth down on Daphne's sweatshirt, but she pulled away. "We'll be careful, Elvis. You stay."

The girls left him and continued to follow the road around a tight turn. Whatever lay ahead was blocked by trees, but the very tops of their branches glowed as if the sun were hovering right behind them. Once they were on the other side they saw their first glimpse of their grandmother in three days.

It was not a happy sight. The old woman was engulfed in an intense light so bright that it hurt to look directly at her.

Her hands were held high above her head and glowed like two giant torches. Rockets of energy exploded from her fingertips and streaked into the sky, leaving in their wake plumes of smoke and magic. The rockets' target was Wilhelm Grimm's invisible wall, built long ago to keep Everafters from leaving Ferryport Landing.

Sabrina had never seen so much raw power. It was almost too horrible to watch, and yet, despite the earth-shattering intensity of the demonstration, it was nothing compared to the ancient and unyielding strength of the barrier. Each magical attack slammed into its surface, exploding into a million vivid colors that spread out over the dome's surface. Aftershocks sent tremors into the earth and air. One attack was followed by another, and then another and another. Granny Relda's heaving body exploded with magic, and as Sabrina watched, a terrifying truth filled her mind—her grandmother was not in control of herself. Mirror was inside her, forcing her to move as he wished. Sabrina wanted to run at him and demand that he set the old woman free, or at least try to communicate with Granny and encourage her to resist Mirror's control, but the power and heat from the explosions were too strong. If she stepped forward, she might catch fire.

And then Sabrina heard a voice behind them and nearly

jumped out of her skin. "I'm soooooo telling." Puck stood behind her. "You two disobeyed your parents! I'm both shocked and really impressed."

Sabrina tried to compose herself without giving away that he had scared her enough to almost make her lose control of her bladder. "We're tired of being under house arrest in the Hall of Wonders."

"Yeah! We've fought lots of monsters," Daphne said.

"Actually, you've done a lot more 'running away from monsters' than actual 'fighting' of said monsters," Puck said. "I've seen it myself and it is always hee-larious. I love this big turnaround. It seems like only a month ago you were complaining about your family responsibility, and now you can't wait to get out there and beat up the bad guys. Well, I'm all for it. The whole 'I don't want to be a Grimm' thing was getting a little tired."

Daphne nodded. "He's right. You were getting kinda lame."

Suddenly, their father, Henry, raced out of the woods, snatched the children by the arms, and dragged them back within the trees. Sabrina had never seen someone's head explode, but she thought she might see her father's. He looked like an erupting volcano, and she felt like a panicked villager frozen in fear at the sight of the angry lava god.

"Get back to the mirror right now!" he demanded.

"Granny had us do these things all the time, Dad," Sabrina explained. "She trained us to be brave and take action."

"And look where that got her!" he roared, then spent the next ten minutes in a breathless rant about respect, trust, and sneakiness. When he finally came up for air, he said, "You're grounded."

"You can't ground us. We're homeless," Daphne said.

Henry was momentarily befuddled. "Fine! But once we get a home you are going to be locked inside it until you are very old and very gray! Come on, I'm taking you back myself."

"What about the old lady?" Puck asked.

Henry shook his head. "We didn't come out here to save her. I wanted to make sure she was OK and see if there are any obvious weaknesses in Mirror's power over her."

"And what did you learn?" Sabrina asked.

"That an all-powerful monster has control over my mother and if we confront him, especially now, when he's angry, he'll incinerate us with his magic."

"So we're just going to give up?" Puck said.

"You don't just go running headfirst into a fight. No, we're going to get some help. We need to find the Wicked Queen," Henry said. "She made Mirror. She has to know how to stop him."

Suddenly, Elvis raced to join the group. He was even more

frantic than before, whining and growling as he raced about in circles.

"Something's wrong," Daphne said, doing her best to ease the dog's panic.

"It must be the storm," Henry said.

But a crunching noise drowned him out. It came from within the woods and was followed by the sound of a tree falling over—a very big tree. When Sabrina turned to face the sound, she saw something so grotesque and terrifying she nearly fainted. Its body was mammoth and covered in thick, matted hair. Its arms were long and spindly, but its legs were thick with muscles and tendons. A ridge of raised spikes poked through the stretched skin covering its spine and trailed upward to its head, which was both shocking in size and shape. The head was nearly as big as half of the rest of its body, but it was also lumpy like a pumpkin that had fallen off a truck. Its eyes and nose were not where they should have been—almost as if it were a toddler's Play-Doh creation. But its most eye-gouging feature was its fang-filled mouth that came unhinged at the jaw when it roared. It opened so wide Sabrina could have stepped inside with no trouble.

"Grendel!" Henry cried, snatching the girls once more and racing in the opposite direction.

"What is a Grendel?" Sabrina begged, doing her best to keep up.

"He killed hundreds of Vikings—and ate most of them. There's a poem about him."

"That thing's in a poem? Ewwww!" Daphne cried.

Puck flew leisurely overhead. "Yawn! I've never been afraid of anything that appeared in a poem. Next time you guys will be trembling over the Cat in the Hat."

"He's no joke, Puck," Henry said as he continued to run. "A warrior named Beowulf chopped off his head once. It still didn't stop him."

"Big deal! Who here hasn't had their head chopped off?"

"This is exactly why I wanted you girls to wait in the mirror. We don't just have your grandmother to deal with—the town is overrun with members of the Scarlet Hand, and unless you have forgotten, they let all the monsters out of the Hall of Wonders, too."

"What are we going to do?" Daphne said. "He's gaining on us."

"Just keep running until I can come up with a plan of attack," Henry said.

"Plan of attack?" Sabrina said. "The plan should be to keep running."

"We can't outrun that thing," Henry said. "All right, Puck, you still have those stink balloons?"

"I never leave home without something disgusting!" Puck reached into the folds of his hoodie. What came out were four more of the disgusting sludge-balloon bombs he had tested on Sabrina.

"Good! You hit him high and I'll take him low."

Sabrina could feel panic squeezing her neck. "Wait! You're going to attack him with some water balloons and your bare hands?"

"And my feet, too," Henry said.

"Are you feeling all right, Dad?" Daphne asked.

"Don't underestimate the weapon that is your own body. If you know what you're doing, you can be very dangerous," Henry said.

"What should we do?" Sabrina said.

"Nothing! You haven't been trained in a fight," Henry said.

"Then train us!" Sabrina said.

"Fine! Lesson one! Watch from the safety of these trees," he demanded as he shoved the girls behind the thick trunk of an ancient maple.

"Dad!" they groaned.

"I'm serious. Don't get involved no matter what. If something bad happens, run for the mirror. All right, fairy, let's do this," their father said, taking off at a sprint toward Grendel. Henry roared like a barbarian berserker.

"Your dad rules," Puck said, circling in the air and mimicking Henry's wail.

"I thought it was stupid to run headfirst into a fight," Sabrina grumbled.

Puck tossed his disgusting bombs at the creature, nailing Grendel in the face. Enraged, the brute snatched at the boy's leg, but Puck was too fast and darted away from his deadly claws again and again. While Puck kept him busy, Henry snuck up until he was standing within arm's length of the monster.

"Lesson number two!" Henry shouted to the girls. "The first thing you do when you are about to fight someone—or something, for that matter—is take them off guard. Screaming like a maniac startles your opponent. The confusion will allow you to observe his weaknesses. While Puck was freaking him out, I was looking for a place to attack. Look at his left knee. See? It's bigger than the right one. It's bulging and red and the skin is pulled tight around it. It means he has an infection, which also means that if I kick it . . ."

Henry delivered a vicious kick with his boot heel. Grendel shrieked and bent over to protect his injury.

"Your grandpa Basil taught us to have careful eyes," Henry continued, circling around the creature until they were nearly face-to-face. "Now, while Grendel is bent over we can get a closer look. Notice his left eye. The pupil is milkier than the right eye, which means he's going blind in it, which also means he can't see me as well when I'm standing on this side of his body. Which also means he can't see this!"

Henry punched Grendel in his left temple. The monster fell to the ground and lay there silently.

"Whoa," Daphne said.

Sabrina was just as surprised. What happened to her super-careful father? Henry was a man who refused to step off the curb to hail a cab. He wouldn't eat hot dogs from the carts in Times Square because he was afraid of food poisoning. He never left the house without antibacterial spray. Who was this . . . man of danger?

"You knocked him out? Awww, man! Who am I supposed to throw the rest of these balloons at?" Puck complained when he landed next to the fallen monster. "It's no fun to pelt someone when they are unconscious."

He threw one of his balloons at Grendel and it exploded on his cheek.

"OK, it's still fun, but not as much fun! If I don't hit someone with the rest of these, they'll go to waste." He turned to Sabrina and grinned.

"Don't even think about it, dog-breath," Sabrina warned.

"Geez, he's big," Henry said as he knelt down to get a closer look at Grendel. "He's gotta be nine feet tall and mostly muscle. Your uncle and I used to peek through the window in his door but this is the closest I've ever gotten to him. Some say his father was a dragon, and his mother . . ."

"What about his mother?" Sabrina asked, unsure if she really wanted an answer.

"Forget it. That will give you nightmares," Henry said, standing upright again. "All right, we need to get him back to the Hall of Wonders. He's too dangerous to be running loose—" But Henry didn't get to finish his sentence. Grendel was up in a flash.

"DAD!" Sabrina screamed. Henry somersaulted out of the way just as the brute's hulking fist shattered the ground where he'd been standing. A wicked backhand followed, but Henry's fast action avoided the blow. The tree behind him was not so lucky. It cracked in half and exploded all over the forest floor in a shower of sawdust.

"Puck!" Henry shouted. "A little help, please."

The fairy blasted the creature with more of his gag bombs

while buzzing around his head. Grendel swatted and roared, nearly blind from the sickly syrup, but still dangerous.

"Girls, get back!" Henry demanded just before Grendel connected a brutal punch to his chest. Sabrina watched as her father fell to the ground and rolled violently into a nearby tree. She raced to his side and cradled his head in her lap. He was unconscious and bleeding from his left ear.

"Is he OK?" Puck cried as he continued his assault.

"He's breathing, but we have to get him into the mirror," Sabrina shouted.

"I've got this covered," Daphne said. She fumbled through the front pocket of her sweatshirt. A second later she was spilling objects onto the ground: bejeweled rings, a pair of red shoes, a few wands, and some odds and ends. "He's messing with the wrong family."

"You brought magic weapons!" Sabrina exclaimed, overjoyed.

"It's not much. The bad guys took all the good stuff."

Sabrina pointed out a ring with a rose decoration cut into its clear crystal. "What's that? Does that kill monsters?"

"That's the Kingmoor Ring," Daphne said. "It stops a nose bleed."

"So all we've got is the magical equivalent of tilting your head back with a wet rag on your face?"

"You won't need any of those trinkets," Puck said as he continued to taunt the monster. "I think he's getting tired!"

With a burst of speed, Grendel landed an uppercut so powerful it sent Puck sailing straight up into the sky and into the clouds.

With Puck in the air and Henry knocked out, it was just the girls and Elvis versus Grendel. The big dog stood between the girls and their opponent, barking and baring his fangs, which only made the hideous creature do the same. It was a momentary distraction, but Sabrina hoped Daphne would take advantage of it.

She turned back to her sister, praying Daphne had found a magic sword or a Sherman tank inside her pockets, but she was sorely disappointed. Daphne waved a long silver wand with a glittering star on its tip. It looked like part of a cheap Halloween costume, but Sabrina knew what it really was—a fairy godmother's wand. She'd seen one do some amazing things, but could it stop this creature? Daphne must have gone crazy.

When Grendel charged them, the little girl flicked her wrist. The monster vanished into a puff of purple smoke and light— then there was a loud thump, followed by a groan.

"Daphne!" Sabrina cried through the smoke. She could barely make out her own hand in front of her face and couldn't see Daphne at all.

"I took care of it," Daphne said as the haze began to dissipate. Daphne stood over the fallen Grendel, her wand in hand and Elvis by her side. Grendel squirmed and struggled to escape a formfitting silver taffeta dress.

"I don't think he likes the dress," Sabrina said as Grendel ripped the gown off his back.

"It doesn't go with his shoes. I'll try another," Daphne said, flicking the wand once more. The silver gown vanished in another puff of smoke and was replaced by a clown outfit, complete with floppy yellow shoes, rainbow fright wig, and bright red nose. Grendel looked down at himself, completely perplexed.

"Can't you put him in a straitjacket or something?" Sabrina cried.

"I'm trying. This isn't as easy as it looks," Daphne said, twirling the wand erratically, then zapping the creature over and over again: tuxedo with tie and tails, conquistador suit, ballerina tutu complete with tights and slippers, Raggedy Andy overalls, and a life-size banana costume complete with necktie. Each abrupt change only caused Grendel's rage to grow, and eventually he snatched the little girl, jerking her off the ground and forcing her to drop her magic wand.

Sabrina jumped to her feet and grabbed the magical weapon

but immediately threw it to the ground. She was hit with the rolling nausea that overtook her every time she touched anything enchanted. If she held the wand much longer, she wasn't sure what would happen. She might lose control of herself.

She was going to have to fight Grendel without magic. But how? What had her father said about the monster's knee? Yes, it was swollen and infected—if only she could give it one of her patented kicks to the shin. Being an orphan had taught her a lot about kicking and punching.

"Just run to the mirror," Daphne begged.

Sabrina was incensed. "Now you're doing it."

"Doing what?" Daphne said as she dangled high above the ground.

"Treating me like a baby! Since when am I the helpless one in this family?"

She wanted to rail at her sister but she realized Grendel was now standing over her, Daphne in his claw, his good eye staring at her with hungry curiosity. Slick saliva as murky as swamp water dripped from his broken, jagged teeth. His breath was like a coal oven and each blast smelled of charcoal and charred meat. When his jaw opened up to swallow her, Sabrina figured she was about to become Grendel's breakfast.

"I hope you choke on me!" she shouted defiantly, then swung a fist that popped the monster in the nose.

And much to Sabrina's surprise, Grendel cried out in agony. She looked down at her hand, unsure of her own strength. Then there was a flash of fur and claws. Something was attacking the monster, but the action was too fast to follow. Sabrina was not responsible for Grendel's pain.

In an effort to protect himself, Grendel dropped Daphne, and the little girl fell into a wet mound of leaves. She staggered over to Sabrina, who had rejoined their unconscious father, and the two watched the fight. They soon realized that they owed their lives to three massive brown bears. But these were no ordinary bears. The biggest wore overalls, another had on a dress, and the littlest one had a beanie cap with a propeller on the top. Sabrina recognized these bears—all three of them.

"Goldilocks," Sabrina gasped as the stunningly pretty woman stepped out from behind the trees and extended a helping hand.

"Let's get your father to safety," Goldi said. Her eyes were sky-blue, her hair seemingly made from gold. She had sun-kissed freckles sprinkled across her nose and cheeks. She and another woman helped Henry to his feet. This second woman had long auburn hair, creamy skin, and eyes the color of a meadow. No wonder they called her Beauty.

"I don't think your bears can take him, Goldi," Beauty said. "Mind if I cut in?"

"Be my guest," Goldilocks said.

Beauty turned to Grendel and started to sing a sweet lullaby, each note soothing the brute like he was a baby on his way to dreamland. As her perfect voice and lyrics filled the air, the fight drained out of Grendel, and he stood before her in a happy daze.

"That's right," Beauty said as she caressed his horrible face. "You know I like a man with a big smile. Can you smile for me?"

Grendel did as he was asked, and then he cooed like a newborn babe. It was nauseating.

"Oh, we've got a real charmer on our hands here." Beauty giggled.

"Can you get him into the Hall of Wonders?" Henry, now conscious, said weakly.

"Right now I could get him to do the cha-cha!"

Henry turned to Goldi. "Thank you. You saved my daughters' lives."

Goldi rolled her eyes. "Don't be silly, Hank."

"It seems I owe you my life, too."

"For like the fifty millionth time," the woman said with a knowing smile. Henry smiled back and Sabrina watched as a lifetime of memories seemed to pass between them. Sadly,

Goldi's eyes hinted at a world of heartache, too. This peculiar woman still loved her father dearly.

Suddenly, three of Puck's disgusting balloon bombs fell from the sky and hit Grendel in the face. He was so enraptured by Beauty he didn't even notice.

"Yes, my weapons have paralyzed him with fear," Puck said as he drifted down from above. "Like I said. The Trickster King has got this under control."

"What are you two doing out here?" Henry asked Beauty and Goldi.

"Looking for you," Beauty explained.

"Us?" Sabrina cried.

"Yes, and we have to hurry," Goldi begged. "We need your help with Jake."

"You know where he is?" Henry asked. "The magic mirrors couldn't find him."

"He's with us," Goldi said, "back at our camp. It has a diversion spell around it. That's probably why they couldn't locate him. But Hank—he's not himself."

"He did just lose Briar," Henry said. "He went through something like this when our father was killed."

"It's more than grief," Goldi said.

"He's losing his mind, Henry," Beauty said bluntly.

Everyone turned to look at her.

"Sorry, but you need to know what to expect," Beauty said. "He's talking to himself. The things he says—it's very troubling stuff."

"Like what?" Henry asked. "What's he talking about?"

Goldi looked pained, as if what she was going to say would injure herself and everyone around her.

"What is it?" Sabrina asked.

"He's talking about murder."

3

 ctober 14 (part 2)

Thought I better update the journal while I'm back in the Hall of Wonders. Dad and Beauty are locking Grendel up in his old room. It's scary to think the Hall used to house hundreds of monsters like him and that they are all running around town now doing who knows what. Dad tried to put a happy face on it by reminding us that now that we have Grendel we have one less freak to worry about. I reminded him that now we were sleeping next door to said freak. He told me to zip it.

I should be grateful that's all he said because he's pretty angry at me and my sister. Note to self: don't get Mom and Dad angry . . . ever. I forgot how they are when they are steamed, and I think I'd rather face Grendel again. The last time I saw them this steamed was when Daphne invited a homeless man to come live with us. She hid him in our closet for six hours before the housecleaner found him.

Both of them say we aren't allowed out of their sight, and they swore if we ever pulled a stunt like that again . . . well, I probably shouldn't write it down in this journal. I'm so embarrassed. I've read a lot of the family journals and I haven't found one entry where someone got grounded for trying to rescue a family member. It seems like everyone treats me like a child. Even Daphne does it now. Am I that worthless?

Not that we're completely to blame for all the stress around here. Goldi's sudden appearance doesn't help. Anytime Blondie shows up Dad looks like he wants to crawl under a rock, and Mom looks like she'd like to toss that rock at Goldilock's head. I can't blame her. Who would want her husband's ex around, mooning over him?

Goldi doesn't make it any easier. She's so nervous the chatter never stops. Daphne thinks she's doing it to fill the awkward moments (of which there are plenty). She also has this annoying habit of adjusting everyone's clothes all the time.

I don't feel right shifting our attention from Granny Relda to Uncle Jake, especially now that we have found her, but Uncle Jake needs us too. I pray he isn't as bad as they say he is, but I have to wonder: If someone I loved was killed, wouldn't I want revenge—especially when it seemed like there would never be any justice? If someone murdered Daphne, wouldn't I want to hunt them down and end them?

Well, on that bright and cheery note, I have to go. They're calling for me. I'll write more when I can. I have a feeling that I'm going to be spending a lot of time with this journal now that I'm grounded.

With the magic mirror strapped securely onto Poppa Bear's back, the rest of the bears, the Grimms, Puck, Canis, and Pinocchio marched through the forest, led by Goldilocks and Beauty.

"Grendel was as ugly as I remember," Beauty said as she kicked a clump of leaves off her high-heeled shoe. Her sweater dress was awfully thin for a chilly hike through the woods, but she never complained. "You have no idea what it was like coming over here on Wilhelm's boat with him. All that grunting and groaning. I was sure at any moment the chains they used to keep him below deck would snap and he'd eat us all whole. Plus, with all those monsters and Jabberwockies running around—ugh. The only way you'll get me on a ship now is if it's a cruise to the Bahamas."

"Why did Wilhelm bring so many of these creepy weirdos to America?" Sabrina asked.

"Wilhelm believed everybody had some goodness in them—even creepy weirdos," Mr. Canis said, as he struggled along with his cane. Henry had begged him to stay inside the mirror with Red and baby Basil, but the old man had flatly refused. "He took a chance on me and I will always be grateful. Look at some of the people that we now call friends—Morgan le Fay, Baba Yaga—"

"Baba Yaga is hardly a friend," Sabrina interrupted.

"The fact that she's not trying to eat us makes her as close to a friend as we may ever get." Henry laughed.

Goldi giggled. "In my book that's personal growth. Henry, do you remember the time we snuck out in the middle of the night and ran into her? We were up on the cliffs and she came along in that creepy house and we . . ." Goldi's voice tapered off when Veronica flashed her an irritated glance.

Sabrina's father deftly changed the subject. "You kids might someday think of Grendel as an ally. You might even decide he's ready to be free from the Hall of Wonders."

"Or the barrier?" Daphne said. "I mean, if they all have the potential for goodness, why not let them out?"

A pause both big and awkward fell on the group, stealing the air until Pinocchio spoke.

"That's an excellent question. How can you say Wilhelm believed in the goodness of Everafters when he locked an entire town inside a cage?"

"He had to do something drastic," Henry said. "Everafters were threatening to invade the next town and no one would listen to reason."

"So I've heard. Still, with his barrier he punished everyone for the crimes of a few, and even more have stumbled into this town, not realizing they would be imprisoned here for eternity. Take me for instance. I wasn't even here when the troubles started for Wilhelm, but like so many others, I'm trapped in this roach motel."

Henry opened his mouth to say something, but Pinocchio cut him off.

"Even your friends can't escape the cruelty of this jailhouse you call a town. Look at Canis, who has clearly reformed. The Wicked Queen has proved herself to be somewhat trustworthy. Why, we're walking with Beauty, who, from what I understand, recently counted herself amongst the Scarlet Hand. The goodness that Wilhelm claimed to believe in is easy to see in their faces, and yet, they find no reward. They will never leave this town . . . or should I say prison. But that's not right, either. In prison the inmates sometimes get time off for good behavior. This place is something far worse."

Sabrina couldn't stand Pinocchio, but she had to admit he had made a powerful argument. There had been many nights since arriving in Ferryport Landing when she had lain awake trying to understand Wilhelm's intentions. On one hand, the barrier kept evil people safely away from an unsuspecting world. On the other, it imprisoned some genuinely wonderful people. Was the barrier fair? Was Wilhelm's magic wall solving problems or causing them in the first place? She looked to her father for an answer and saw he was equally perplexed. She suspected that he too had spent his fair share of nights trying to unravel the puzzle that was Ferryport Landing.

"So where are we going, anyway?" Puck asked as he flew above them. "I've scouted ahead and there's no sign of any camp."

"You wouldn't see it," Beauty explained. "The castle is invisible."

"Um—the what is what?" Sabrina said.

"We've been building a castle near Mount Taurus," Beauty said. "Boarman and Swineheart designed it and the rest of us work night and day getting it ready."

"Ready for what?" Mr. Canis asked.

"War," Beauty said. "Charming's army is going to confront the Scarlet Hand."

"Didn't you already try that?" Pinocchio chuckled dismissively. "You built a fort, trained everyone, and the Hand overran the place and burned it to the ground. Do you want to make the same mistake twice?"

"This is a little different," Goldi said. "Oh, here we are."

Sabrina saw nothing but forest before her.

"Just a sec." Beauty reached into her purse and pulled out a vial of what looked like purple glitter. She unscrewed the cap and poured some of the substance into her hand, then blew it into the air. As the powder drifted through the trees it collided with the rain, and each drop exploded like a tiny firework, illuminating a structure so tall and wide Sabrina's brain struggled to believe her eyes. Eventually, she realized she was standing in front of a wall dozens of stories tall, higher than some of the skyscrapers back home in New York City. Around the impossibly steep walls ran a trench ten feet deep. It was an impressive structure; even more so to Sabrina was the fact that it had been built in only two days.

"How?" Sabrina cried.

Goldi winked at her, then stuck two fingers into her mouth. She blasted a rather unladylike whistle, and a moment later Sabrina could hear the turning of a heavy wheel and the rattling of chains. A giant wooden door in the wall tilted forward to span the trench. The drawbridge hit the earth on the other side with a clang and a thud. Behind the drawbridge was an iron gate.

"We haven't had time to fill the moat yet," Goldi explained as she led the group across the drawbridge. "We're still trying to find alligators to live in it."

"I can help with that," Puck said, floating down from the air. "I know a guy."

Goldi led the group through the stone arch and the gate rose to admit them. Once past it, they saw a castle standing nearly four stories tall, built from thick white stones and framed by two towers that spiraled several stories higher. On each tower were battlements festooned with fluttering purple flags and ominous black cannons.

On either side of the castle were several crude log cabins. The nutty smell of fresh bread wafted from one of them, and horses neighed from another. Throughout the yard Sabrina saw old friends, all pounding hammers and sawing timber. She spotted Puss in Boots, Morgan le Fay, the Scarecrow, even the Pied Piper and his son, Wendell.

"So how many people do you have in this army?" Pinocchio asked.

"Twenty-two," Goldi said.

"Twenty-two! That's preposterous," Pinocchio said, chuckling.

"What does preposterous mean?" Daphne said.

"He's calling it silly," Sabrina said.

Goldi shrugged. "Well, as Gepetto always says, 'We're small, but we're spunky.'"

Suddenly, Pinocchio's sneer slipped off his face. "My papa is here? Is he well? Is he injured?"

"Your father is fine. As you know, he's a very talented carpenter, and along with the pigs and Mordred's magic they've made the place into something livable that we can also defend. I can take you to him."

"Look!" Daphne cried.

Across the courtyard stood Morgan le Fay's son, Mordred. The last time Sabrina had seen the warlock he was engrossed in a very violent video game from the comfort of his mother's couch. It didn't look like he had changed his black T-shirt and pants, but at least he was now doing something productive. A stream of white light emanated from his fingers and enveloped a newly constructed water tower lying on its side in the courtyard. Slowly the tower struggled to right itself, hobbling back and forth. Boarman and Swineheart looked on, wearing hard hats and studying architectural plans.

"Now we see how you got this castle built so quickly," Henry said to Goldi.

"Mordred is really indispensable. Unfortunately, there are some complicated side effects to his magic."

Sabrina watched as the water tower suddenly lunged away from Mordred, stomping up and down and attempting to squash the pigs and the warlock. Mordred shot a couple of fireballs at the ground beneath it and it backed down from its attack.

Goldi shrugged. "Everything he brings to life turns evil and murderous for the last few minutes of the spell. It calms down eventually, but it's a bit unpredictable for a while."

Puck grinned. "I have to party with that guy."

As everyone watched Mordred subdue the evil water tower, Prince Charming and Mr. Seven approached. Sabrina had never been so happy to see them. Charming needed a shave and a bath, but he was still staggeringly handsome, even wearing his trademark scowl. Mr. Seven was as friendly as ever—perhaps even more so. He was as filthy as Charming, with his shirtsleeves rolled up and yellow sawdust all over his clothes and shoes, but his smile looked exceptionally big.

"Hello, Grimms, Canis. Ladies, a word, please!" Charming growled as he turned to face Goldi and Beauty. "I thought we had an agreement. No one leaves the castle without my approval."

Beauty gave him a smile and batted her eyelashes. "We were only gone for a little while."

"Don't try the 'calming the savage beast' nonsense on me, lady," Charming said. "The rules are here to keep everyone safe."

Sabrina rolled her eyes. It seemed as if she wasn't the only one in town sitting at the kids' table.

"We needed Henry. He's the only one who can reach Jake," Goldilocks explained.

Charming threw up his arms in surrender. "Jake is hardly the biggest of our problems, but fine. It's not like I can control the two of you, anyway."

"I'm glad you finally understand," Goldi said.

Beauty nodded. "We were wondering when you were going to catch on."

"Interesting. Some people break the rules and it makes things better," Sabrina muttered within earshot of her father.

Henry flashed her a warning look that said it was much too soon for sarcasm. Sabrina mimicked locking her lips with a key, then tossing it behind her back.

"It's so good to see you too, Billy," Daphne said, wrapping him in a big hug. The prince stood patiently, if uncomfortably, while the little girl clung to him like a monkey. Daphne adored the stuffy, overbearing man, even if the feeling was not mutual.

"Um, yes, let's get you to your uncle," Charming said, pushing her gently aside. He turned and led the group along the castle wall, where there were even more log cabins.

"So you're going to try to fight them again?" Henry asked the prince.

"We don't have much of a choice," Charming said. "Most of the citizens of this town joined the Scarlet Hand either by pressure or force. Those left in this camp are the ones the Hand didn't want. We fight or we die. We could use some help if you're willing to stay."

Henry looked to Veronica. "No. We need to rescue my mother and then I'm taking my family far away from this place."

"So you're leaving us to clean up the mess, Henry?" Charming said. Henry ignored him.

"It's good to see you girls," Mr. Seven said to Sabrina and Daphne with a big, toothy grin. "Lovely day, huh?"

"Mr. Seven, we can always count on your good mood," Sabrina marveled, looking around at the dirty castle and the drizzling rain.

"Of course he's in a good mood," Charming said. "The fool has gone and fallen in love."

"And it's spreading," a voice said from behind them. Sabrina turned and saw Morgan le Fay approaching with a basket of herbs and berries. Morgan was a curvy beauty and quite glamorous, with the kind of face you might see in an old black-and-white movie. Even wearing a hard hat and overalls, she was a stunner. Seven rushed to her side and when the woman knelt down to his height, he planted a kiss on her that made everyone blush.

"Mom, please!" Mordred groaned from the corner, where he'd finally subdued the water tower. "Can you two give it a rest?"

"Sorry, honey," Morgan said. "My darling boyfriend has swept me off my feet. In fact, he popped the question last night. We're getting married!"

"As soon as everything calms down," Seven explained.

Puck flapped up to the happy couple. "Wait a minute! You have to ask someone to marry you? No one told me that! I thought you just hit them with a club and dragged them back to your cave!"

Henry put his arm around Sabrina. "You're officially grounded from ever getting married."

"Thank you," Sabrina whispered sincerely.

Charming grumbled. "All this kissing and hugging is becoming quite tiresome. There is serious work to do here. The west wall needs fortifying. The armory is still not ready. The stables need cleaning. We can't move into the castle until it's complete. And these two are running off at the drop of a hat to stare into each other's eyes!"

"I seem to recall a certain handsome prince doing the same with me last night," Snow White said from the doorway of one of the cabins. It seemed you couldn't throw a rock without hitting some gorgeous princess or exotic enchantress around here, but Snow White was in a class all by herself. Her skin was creamy and flawless. Her hair was as black as night and her lips were full and pink. She wrapped her arms around Charming and planted a kiss on his cheek. He looked as if her touch made him dizzy.

"Snow, I—"

Snow giggled. "I'm just teasing, Casanova."

"Harrumph!" Charming said, though he did flash a hint of a smile. The prince and Snow White had a long, complicated relationship. Hundreds of years ago she left him at the altar. In the centuries since, he married Sleeping Beauty, Cinderella, and Rapunzel. None of those marriages had worked out, and Sabrina suspected the reason was Snow. Even after countless centuries, William Charming could not get her out of his system.

"Come to join the army?" Snow asked the Grimms.

"No," Henry said. "We're here to see Jacob."

Snow White's smile disappeared. "Oh. Henry, maybe you want to leave the girls here with me."

Henry looked to Veronica. "Maybe—"

Sabrina interrupted. "Sure, Dad. That is, if you can trust us out of your sight."

"We do have a tendency to get into shenanigans," Daphne said.

Henry frowned. "No, they'll stay with me."

Daphne shared a knowing wink with Sabrina.

As they continued their walk along the perimeter of the fortress, the group came across Gepetto, who, despite his advanced age, was splitting firewood with an ax. Pinocchio watched him for several moments, silently, as if preparing for a big speech. Finally, he sputtered out, "Papa?" like a little boy. Sabrina realized immediately it wasn't a speech Pinocchio was readying—it was a performance.

"Pinocchio!" Gepetto dropped a handful of wood and rushed to the little boy. He scooped him up in his arms and showered him with kisses. "My son! My son!"

Pinocchio hugged the old man and forced a few tears. "Oh, Papa! I thought . . . Oh, it's too terrible to say."

Sabrina and Daphne looked at each other in bewilderment.

"And the Oscar goes to . . . ," Sabrina said.

"Papa, you have no idea how bad things have been for me," Pinocchio cried. "These horrible people expect me to sleep on the floor and they are incredibly rude! We're living on rice and—"

"I know what you did, son," Gepetto said.

Suddenly, the crocodile tears dried from Pinocchio's face. "Then—then—you have to hear my side of the story," he stammered.

"Your side of the story is that you betrayed a family I consider amongst my dearest friends. You helped to loot and destroy their home, leaving them with nothing. You conspired with their mortal enemy—my mortal enemy. You helped a . . . a monster who tried to steal the body of a little boy and when that failed took Relda Grimm for his puppet. You remember what it was like to be controlled by a master, and yet you allowed it to happen to someone else!"

"Mirror promised to turn me into a man."

"A man! What makes you think you are ready to be a man? Do you think playing chess and reading big books without pictures makes you a man? It takes more than the interests of an adult to make you one. Why, I wouldn't be surprised if the Blue Fairy's spell keeps you as a child until you are ready to grow up. Is that something you've ever considered? Perhaps you are too immature!"

"Papa, please," Pinocchio cried. "You don't understand."

"I understand perfectly. I have failed you as a father, but that is going to change as of this moment. You are going to become a good person. I'm going to make sure of it or I will speak to the Blue Fairy myself and have her turn you back into a puppet!"

"I was a marrion—"

"Your first lesson is to shut your mouth when your father is speaking to you!" Gepetto roared.

"Why, you act like you don't love me anymore, Father." Pinocchio whimpered.

"Oh, I love you, son, more than I can ever say. But right now, I don't like you very much." He picked up the ax and placed it into his son's soft hands.

"What's this for?"

"Chopping wood, of course. You're the one who wants to be a grown-up. Grown-ups have jobs. Get to work," Gepetto said.

Pinocchio turned to the Grimms with a look of desperation on his face.

"Don't look at us," Sabrina said. She and the others all turned their backs on him and walked away.

As Charming led them around one more corner Sabrina felt something whiz past her head, followed by a loud *thunk!* The next second she spotted a knife impaled in the chest of a straw dummy propped on a stake not more than a foot away. The dummy was dressed as the Sheriff of Nottingham, complete with a leather jacket and hat. Another dummy dressed as the Queen of Hearts was nearby. It had another knife buried in its forehead.

"Sabrina!" Uncle Jake cried, racing to her side. "I'm sorry. I did not know . . . Henry, Veronica, what are you all doing here?"

"We came to see you," Henry said. "We're worried about you."

"I suppose they've told you I've lost my mind." Uncle Jake scowled and slumped into an old wooden chair placed near a grave marked by a wooden cross. Despite the freshness of the plot, it was completely covered in gorgeous white roses in full bloom. This was the grave of Sleeping Beauty, also known by her friends as Briar Rose. Surrounding her plot were candles, beads, dried flowers, and photographs of Jake's former love. Seeing them brought on a stampede of memories for Sabrina about the night she died. Why did someone so kind and lovely have to be taken away? Sabrina had prayed for an answer many times, but it had never come.

As she struggled to hold back tears, she became painfully aware of her uncle's current appearance. He was a wreck: exhausted, filthy, gaunt, and angry. His smell was oppressive, like a hot summer night in New York City. Sabrina knew at once that Goldi and Beauty had done the right thing coming to them for help.

A large black crow with a red ribbon tied about its neck fluttered from above and landed on the back of Jake's chair. "No one thinks you're crazy, big guy," the bird said. Normally, Sabrina would have felt queasy. Talking animals made her uncomfortable, but Sabrina recognized this particular bird as the Widow, Queen of the Crows.

"I'm fine!" Jake said as he leaped from the chair. The crow hopped down to the ground. "I have no plans to kill myself, if that is what you are worrying about."

Henry gestured to the knives impaled in Jake's stuffed targets. "It's your other plans that are worrying us."

"That's none of your business," Jake said. He snatched his weapons and shoved them into the pockets of his jacket.

Henry shook his head. "I understand you're hurt—"

"Hurt? I'm a little more than hurt, Hank. I am destroyed. I promised Briar's fairy godmothers I would look after her and now she's gone. Those monsters killed her, Hank. Right in front of my eyes."

"Revenge won't bring her back," Henry said. "It will just hurt you more. It will hurt your soul."

Jake turned to his brother with a look of utter disbelief. "My soul! You've got to be kidding me, Henry. Do you want to see my soul? It's in that hole, right there. It's buried six feet deep!"

He hefted a quill of arrows onto his back and scooped up a bow leaning against the wall. Then without another word he marched in the direction of the drawbridge.

"Where are you going?" Henry called after him.

"It's better that you don't know," Jake shouted back. He activated the drawbridge and was across it and into the woods before anyone thought to stop him. Sabrina could feel panic squeezing her heart. Her uncle was exhausted and obsessed with two incredibly dangerous people. Who knew what might happen if he found them.

"We have to go after him," Veronica said. "He's not thinking clearly."

"The Hand is crawling all over these woods," Charming said. "Bringing you all here was a tremendous risk to begin with. I can't have you stumbling around in the forest drawing attention to us."

"He's my brother!" Henry shouted.

"I'll keep an eye on him," the crow squawked and flapped into the air. "Sometimes he listens to me. I'll do my best to keep him out of trouble."

Once the Widow was gone, Charming activated the machine to raise the drawbridge, but when it was barely halfway up, it came to a jerking stop.

"Boarman! Swineheart! What is wrong with this infernal machine?" he shouted.

The pigs rushed to investigate, inspecting the chains and pulleys, but stepped back and scratched their heads.

"Nothing's broken, boss," Swineheart said. "Push the button again."

Charming did, but just as soon as the mechanisms started, they stopped again.

"Fix this!" Charming huffed. "Keeping this door open makes this castle vulnerable."

A woman's voice rang out from outside the wall. "Where are the Grimms?" There was something otherworldly about the voice, as if it were being artificially amplified. The question was repeated.

"Who is that?" Veronica asked.

"Get your weapons!" Charming shouted to his army. "Someone has found the castle. We can't let them through the gate!"

The castle inhabitants rushed to arm themselves. Sabrina was about to do the same when her father clamped his hand on her shoulder. He had Daphne held with his other hand. "Don't even think about it, girls," he said.

There was a terrible metal straining sound, and then the chains on the drawbridge snapped. The bridge fell forward and slammed into the trench. Henry stepped in front of his family and prepared to fight. Puck landed next to him and drew his wooden sword. Even Mr. Canis had his shaking fists in the air.

Suddenly, a woman stormed through the gate. Her frightening voice did not match her appearance: She wore a pretty black dress, milky pearls, and expensive heels. If Snow was the most beautiful woman in the world, this woman was a close second. It made sense. After all, she was Ms. White's mother—a woman some called Bunny Lancaster, while others knew her by her more well-known name, the Wicked Queen.

"Mother?" Snow said. "How did you find us?"

"There are few things in this world that my eyes cannot see," Bunny snapped.

"Bunny! You broke my drawbridge!" Charming cried.

The witch dismissed him with a wave. "I want everyone to follow me."

Henry stepped forward. "We had some things we wanted to ask you, Bunny."

"No questions! It's time we got to work saving the world," the witch replied.

She stepped over to Poppa Bear, and with the slash of her hand the ropes that held the magic mirror onto his back were magically severed. She eased the big mirror to the ground and leaned it against a cabin wall, then turned to Sabrina and pointed a finger at her. "You! Where are you keeping the other mirrors?"

Sabrina pointed toward the mirror and without a word the queen plunged through its reflection. Sabrina looked at her father, who was still holding her and Daphne tight, but he eased his grip and led them into the mirror as well.

"Hurry, now!" the witch demanded as soon as they broke the surface and entered the Hall of Wonders. Everyone followed them, eager to hear what Bunny was planning. "Which room is it? Time is wasting. Don't you want to save Relda?"

Red rushed down the hall to meet them with baby Basil in her arms. "What's going on?"

Sabrina shrugged. "I don't have a clue." Then she hurried ahead and unlocked the room in which they stored the other mirrors. Sabrina had barely swung the door open when Bunny pushed past her into the room. Once inside, the Wicked Queen looked around, bewildered. "Someone has not been taking care of these mirrors."

"They were like this when we found them," Daphne said.

The queen gazed closely at the shards that were glued to the walls, marveling at the different places they revealed. "Fascinating. These are pieces of other looking glasses."

"The Master used them to spy on us and everyone in town," Sabrina said.

"He could see into any mirror he wanted," Daphne added.

"I know very well what he was doing with them, young ladies," she said, and then walked over to the fifth intact magic mirror, which was empty as always.

"That one's guardian has never appeared to us," Mr. Canis said.

"That's because it doesn't have one. This is the one that resets them all to their factory settings. Ongegn!" Bunny cried, and a scarlet-red handprint appeared in the fifth mirror. There was a loud humming that seemed to shake the very air and then suddenly the broken shards peeled themselves off the walls and floated about in midair. Like bees to nectar, they darted into the correct empty frames and reformed themselves, melting into one another until their surfaces were clean and whole. When the mirrors were completely repaired and looking as good as new, the witch raised her hand above her head. Sabrina watched as it turned bright red, cracking and popping and smoldering like a charcoal briquette.

"Give it a second," Bunny said. "They need to reboot."

After a moment, the red handprints appeared in all the newly mended mirrors and just as quickly faded.

"Mirrors, I require your presence," Bunny said sternly, and in the blink of an eye twenty-four different heads floated in twenty-four silver pools. Many looked as normal as any human being, but other guardians seemed more beastlike. One had a pointy nose as long as a yardstick, and another had eyes and lips as big as a trout. There were faces that were clearly human and a few that seemed as if they came from outer space. One was a huge iguana-like thing and another had the face of a beautiful woman with the antlers of a deer. One had the eyes of a crocodile and a smile to match. Sabrina was happy to see that Reggie, Fanny, Titan, and Donovan were amongst them, but she was especially overjoyed to see a familiar face—Harry, who had been the guardian of Prince Charming's mirror, the Hotel of Wonders.

"Hello, Mother," they said with great respect.

"Please, stop calling me that. Arden, I come seeking a prophecy," Bunny said.

"Ask what you will," the antler-woman said, and her reflection rippled and shimmied. The other mirrors followed suit until each guardian was now barely visible behind their churning silver. Daphne slipped her hand into Sabrina's and squeezed. After a long, unsettling moment, the mirrors stilled and each guardian's eyes glowed with the power of a full moon.

"WE SEE ALL. EVERY DAY THAT HAS PASSED. EVERY DAY TO COME. THERE ARE A MYRIAD OF POSSIBILITIES. MANY PATHS THAT CAN BE TAKEN, MANY POSSIBLE OUTCOMES."

"Mirrors, mirrors, our future is cursed. Tell me how to defeat the First," the queen said.

"YOU CANNOT," they replied as one.

"You are mistaken," the witch said.

"THE FUTURE IS WOVEN LIKE A SPIDER'S WEB,

WITH MILLIONS OF STRANDS LEADING TOWARD THE CONFLICT YOU SEEK. IF YOU CHOOSE THIS QUEST FOR YOURSELF YOU WILL FAIL. IN ALL POSSIBLE FUTURES THE ONE YOU CALL MIRROR WILL DEFEAT YOU. HE WILL DESTROY WILHELM'S BARRIER. HE WILL UNLEASH HIS POWER ON MANKIND. NATIONS WILL KNEEL BEFORE HIM. MOTHER, YOU CANNOT STOP OUR BROTHER."

"Nonsense!" the queen cried. "I created Mirror! I very well should be able to destroy him."

"THE FUTURE SAYS OTHERWISE."

Bunny shook her head. "Then you're saying there is no hope."

"NONE ALONG THIS PATH."

The witch turned to the crowd. "I'm sorry. I was mistaken. My suggestion to you all is to run and hide. I wish you luck."

Sabrina was stunned. The mirrors had to be wrong. She stepped forward so she blocked Bunny's way. "You're just going to give up?"

The Wicked Queen's lip curled. "The mirrors don't lie, child."

"Well, then your mirrors are stupid," Daphne said.

"This is all your fault," Sabrina said. "You made Mirror, then abandoned him. You sold him like he was an old chair, and he wound up with owners that were twisted and cruel. It's no wonder he's gone crazy and taken my grandmother. So, you fix this. You find a way!"

The Wicked Queen's eyes were bright with anger. Sabrina could feel dark magic building in the air around her. Everyone was afraid of this woman, even her own daughter, and it appeared Sabrina was going to find out why.

"Mirrors, the child did not hear what you said," Bunny said through clenched teeth.

"LISTEN TO OUR WORDS. THE QUEEN CAN DO NOTHING TO STOP THE FIRST."

"Fine! Bunny can't do it. But someone else might have a chance," Sabrina argued.

"THE FATE OF THIS WORLD FALLS IN THE HANDS OF THE SISTERS."

"Huh?" the witch said.

"The sisters?" Daphne asked.

"WE SEE MANY WHO WOULD STAND BEFORE THE FIRST: HEROES, WITCHES, FAIRY FOLK. BUT IN ALL THESE OUTCOMES ONLY TWO MEET YOUR GOAL SUCCESSFULLY, AND ONLY TOGETHER. IN ALL THE WORLD AND OTHER REALMS, THERE ARE ONLY TWO WHO CAN STOP MIRROR: SABRINA AND DAPHNE GRIMM."

"What?" Sabrina cried.

"Um, I didn't hear you say my name," Puck said.

Henry and Veronica pushed to the front of the crowd. "This has to be a mistake," Henry said.

"They're just little girls," Veronica added.

"YOUR CHILDREN HOLD THE KEYS TO THE FUTURE. EACH MUST USE HER OWN STRENGTHS, BUT WHEN THE TIME IS AT HAND IT IS THEIR BOND THAT DEFEATS THE FIRST."

"Wait! What strengths?" Sabrina cried.

"DAPHNE CREATES THE COVEN," the mirrors said. "A CRONE, A TEMPTRESS, AN INNOCENT THREE."

"What's a coven?" Daphne asked.

"Shhh!" Bunny snapped.

"SABRINA LEADS THE ARMY INTO BATTLE," the mirrors continued.

"I'm twelve years old!" Sabrina said. "I can't lead an army."

"ACT IN HASTE. THE FIRST IS COMING FOR YOU. BLOOD WILL SPILL. HEARTBREAK WILL COME. BUT THE SISTERS ARE YOUR ONLY HOPE."

"But how do we do it?" Daphne said. "We need details, people!"

"THE STRANDS ARE COMPLEX AND UNEXPLAIN-

ABLE. THE TWO OF YOU WILL SAVE THE WORLD, BUT MANY THINGS WILL HAPPEN OUTSIDE OF YOUR CONTROL TO MAKE IT POSSIBLE. NOTHING WE CAN SHARE WILL LEAD YOU TO SUCCESS. BUILD YOUR COVEN. WAGE YOUR WAR."

Then the mirrors shimmered again and returned to normal, with the guardians in their places. Each looked tired and disoriented, but the faces that concerned Sabrina the most were those of Charming's army. They looked at her and Daphne with fear and shock.

"We're going to save the world," Daphne said, raising her hand to her sister so she could deliver a high five. Sabrina, however, stood dumbfounded, unable to speak.

Puck laughed. "We are so screwed."

4

he commotion in the mirror room made it hard to think. People were shouting and arguing, and the crowd was entirely too close. Sabrina suddenly felt wobbly and short of breath.

"Wait, what?" Sabrina said. Never in her life had she felt so off-kilter. Had she really heard the mirror's prophecy correctly? Was she really essential to saving her grandmother and the world, too? She wanted to shout that they were wrong. She wanted to know if they were joking—or, worse, insane.

And then her father was there, taking her by the arm and pulling her out of the room, out of the loud, hot chaos. Her mother followed with Daphne and Basil in tow, and soon they were through the portal door and marching across the court-yard.

"Head for the train station and get on the next one to Grand

Central," Henry said. "I have to stay and rescue my mother, but I'll meet you there as soon as I can."

"Henry, we should stay together," Veronica said.

"Dad—"

"This isn't up for discussion, Daphne," Henry barked. "I should have sent you away the second I had a chance. I won't make that mistake again."

"But you heard them, Dad. If we don't stop Mirror, he will take over the world. That's like really bad," Daphne said.

"The world will have to worry about itself."

Daphne wouldn't let it go. "Mom, can you—"

"Henry, I think Daphne has a point," Veronica said.

Sabrina only caught snippets of the conversation around her. Her mind was back in the room, watching the Wicked Queen's face as the mirrors predicted the future. Like the others, she'd been shocked, but there was something else in her eyes— acceptance of what the mirrors were saying and even—hope? Sabrina couldn't be sure, but it didn't matter now. None of it mattered. Mirror was going to have his way. Soon, her world would go through another upheaval. She needed to prepare for a life on the run.

They were almost to the drawbridge when the Wicked Queen came charging after them. "You can't leave."

Henry turned on her. "Watch us."

"The girls are the keys to everything, Henry," she said.

"Your mirrors are busted," Henry said.

"I know all there is to know about wanting to save a child from tragedy and danger. But this is their destiny. The Council of Mirrors sees all possibilities and they have led us on our only path. I don't like it any more than you do, but if they don't carry this burden, then we will all suffer. Running is futile, Henry. When Mirror breaks through that barrier, he will unleash massive power on a world that believes magic only exists in children's books. Their guns and bombs will be useless against him. Every person on this planet will suffer at his hand and he will hunt his enemies down one by one. There will be nowhere you can hide, and instead of standing up and fighting when you had the chance, you will doom us all. Do you understand me? Forget the world, Henry. Be practical. Think of your daughters first. The only way to save them is to let them fulfill their destiny."

"No one can know that!" Henry cried.

Bunny snatched his arm before he could step away. "I wouldn't be talking to you if that were true."

Henry pulled away as if the queen's hand were the jaws of a venomous serpent and continued for the gate.

"What about our stuff?" Daphne asked as they stormed past log cabins and half-built ramparts.

"We'll buy new things in New York City," Henry said.

"What is going on?" Red cried as she rushed to catch up with the family.

Suddenly, Puck dropped down from the sky and blocked their way.

"I never thought I'd see the day."

"Ignore him," Henry muttered.

"I guess you folks are chicken," Puck said, spinning on his heels and morphing into a red rooster. He squawked obnoxiously and pecked at Henry's shoes. "Forget saving the world. Are you really going to just give up on the old lady? After all that she's done for you? The cooking, the cleaning, the bedtime stories, how she hosed you down at night."

"She didn't hose us down at night," Sabrina said. "Just you."

"And I'm not giving up. I'm getting my family to safety and then helping Mom," Henry said.

The rooster spun around and Puck returned to normal. "The old lady would never run. Are you sure you're actually related to her? I'd like to see some paperwork."

"I have to protect my family."

"If Sabrina and Daphne leave, no one will be safe," Puck said.

But Henry ignored him and continued to march the family toward the stronghold's iron gate despite the small crowd encircling them.

"You can't just walk away!" Puck shouted.

"What do you want me to do? Let my kids die?"

"Your kids did just fine while you and Veronica were sound asleep," Beauty said.

"Henry, let's just stop and talk about this," Veronica said.

"Now you want to argue with me, too?" he said, turning to face his wife.

Mr. Canis hobbled forward. "They will have all of us at their side."

"I'm sorry, but I can't put my faith in an army of children, talking animals, and the elderly," Henry said. He led his family across the fallen drawbridge and into the woods, leaving the castle and their friends behind. As the girls glanced back, the castle magically disappeared from view.

Henry marched with determination, seemingly undeterred by the lack of a path. The girls and their mother, carrying Basil, did their best to keep up with him. Puck followed from the air.

"Once you get into Grand Central," Henry said, "head for Brooklyn. Dana and Steven will take you in."

"Henry, they probably think we're dead after all the time we've been missing, and what are we supposed to do for money? Do you have any for train tickets?"

Henry sighed but his pace didn't slow. "Yeah, money. I've got ten dollars in my wallet. I'm sure our credit cards have been canceled. Just get on the train. They may kick you off, but not before you're out of the town. Once you're on the other side of the barrier you'll be safe. Call you sister in Australia."

"Henry, I haven't spoken to her in a decade," Veronica said.

"Tell her we'll pay her back whatever she can lend. Our money is still in the bank . . . somewhere."

Veronica threw up her hands in exasperation but still urged the girls forward. Sabrina stared back at Puck from over her shoulder. He looked defeated and confused, and then it hit her. She would never see him again. He was trapped in Ferryport Landing like all the rest of the Everafters. He would never be able to follow her to the city. This was it.

"The train station is a disaster," Puck shouted just before he disappeared from Sabrina's sight. "When we were spying on the old lady, I flew overhead. The Scarlet Hand ripped up the tracks."

Henry stopped. The hesitation prompted Puck to fly into the air, until he landed to block Henry's path once more.

"We'll go to Mom's house and get her car—"

"That heap of junk got crushed when the house was destroyed," Puck said.

"Then we'll walk," Henry snapped.

"Great idea," Puck said. "What with all the monsters running around. But I'm sure they're not all as bad as Grendel. Besides, the rest of the family is trained to fight just like you, right? The baby knows how to throw an uppercut, I'm sure."

Henry threw up his hands and collapsed onto a fallen log.

"Honey?" Veronica asked.

"I just need to think," he said, waving her off. Then he shook his head and glared up at Puck. "I'm disappointed in you."

"Then things are getting back to normal," Puck said.

"I would have thought your puppy-dog crush on my daughter would make you more protective."

Puck's mouth fell open and his ears turned red with embarrassment. Puck, the boy who proudly collected his farts in mason jars, who never cared what anyone thought of him! But her father's accusation seemed to have upended his cocky confidence. He stammered, as if unsure what to say next, but then the boy fairy shook off his awkwardness and grinned mischievously.

"Well, it's a little more than a crush, Henry," Puck said. "I'm going to marry your daughter someday, so it's sort of important to my plans that she save the world."

"OMG," Daphne said, as she bit the palm of her hand.

Veronica's eyes were as big as pie plates.

Henry fell off his log, and if Sabrina had been sitting on one, she would have done the same. She wanted to dig a hole and bury herself in it.

Puck stood over her father and chuckled. "You can't embarrass me, Henry. I'm the Trickster King—true King of Faerie, crown prince of the over-confident, leader of the self-deluded, spiritual hero of all who think too highly of themselves. Now, are you going to listen to reason or do I just have to kidnap your daughters so we can get to work?"

"Do I get a vote in this?" Veronica asked.

Everyone turned to her.

"Yes, Mom has an opinion!" Veronica snapped. "So listen up. We're staying."

"Veronica!" Henry said as he clambered to his feet.

"I want more than anything to get Basil and the girls away from this town," Veronica said. "But what if the mirrors are right? What if the girls are supposed to rescue Relda and make things OK again?"

"The mirrors didn't say the girls would save the world. They said they had a chance," Henry explained.

"Yes, but they were certain that no one else had one. If they don't try, then it can't be done at all. I can't live with that. I haven't raised the girls to turn their backs on others."

Henry looked at his wife for a long time. His face was full of worry and fear.

Daphne nodded. "Mom's right! Grimms don't run. Especially when we're in a prophecy."

"How many prophecies have we been in?" Sabrina growled.

"Just one, but do you think we'll be in any more if we screw up the first one?" Daphne said, turning to walk back to the castle. "We need to go back!"

"Daphne!" Henry shouted.

Daphne turned to face her father. "It's shenanigan time, Dad."

Red, Mr. Canis, and the Wicked Queen were waiting for them in a clearing just outside the invisible castle. The witch said nothing but nodded respectfully to Henry.

"So, what do we have to do?" Henry said.

October 15

Let me tell you what happened yesterday. After Goldi and Beauty saved us from Grendel, they led us to our missing uncle, who is now intent on revenge and may be committing murder as I write this, but then the Wicked Queen showed up, fixed all the broken magic mirrors, then ordered them to make a prophecy that says my sister and I are going to save the world but my dad said "forget that" and tried to squirrel us out of town until we realized we're kind of stuck and have to stay and do the right thing even though all the Everafters looked like they're sure we're going to get everyone killed.

And that was all before dinner.

Today is a new day and I'm hoping it's a little more relaxing. I mean, all I have to do is train and lead an army. I should have that finished before breakfast (insert sarcastic facial expression).

It seems that everywhere I go, people are staring at me, and there's nowhere to hide. Now I know what it's like to be a goldfish. Some of them watch me with curiosity, studying me as if they might uncover some secret strength they have previously overlooked. Others watch as if they're about to see a terrible car accident, helpless to prevent vehicles from piling on top of one another and exploding. Some watch me out of the corners of their eyes while others stare at me directly until I notice, and then they try to act like they were looking at something else. Daphne is oblivious. In some ways I envy her ability to tune out the overwhelming disappointment of Charming's army. But on the other hand, seeing her singing her little songs and making a face out of two fried eggs, a slice of bacon, and a pancake makes me feel as nervous as the others. We are so young.

• • •

Charming sat next to Sabrina and her family as they were eating breakfast in the camp canteen. He did not look happy. Then again, neither did anyone. Most of them ate listlessly, bending their ears to catch every word that came from their conversations.

"How long are you going to lollygag around here this morning?" he hissed.

"What does *lollygag* mean?" Daphne said.

"He's saying we're being lazy," Sabrina explained. "What he means I don't understand."

"Then let me be a little more clear," Charming said. "When do you plan on doing something about the prophecy?"

"Cut the kids a break, William," Goldi said from a nearby table. "It just happened last night."

"Well, you may have slept peacefully, but everyone else in this camp was up all night, worrying that a couple of kids who haven't even hit puberty yet are responsible for their lives. The morale in this place has hit an all-time low. So unless the girls want these folks leaving in droves, I suggest they do whatever it is the mirrors told you to do."

Sabrina frowned. "We're on it," she said.

Charming thanked her with a thick helping of sarcasm and stormed off to supervise work inside the castle.

Canis filled Charming's seat at the table. "A word, Your Majesty," he said in hushed tones to the Wicked Queen.

"Of course."

"I understand that we have a book in our possession that could fix our problems," he said quietly.

Bunny raised her eyes. "You know about the Book of Everafter?"

"Relda shared a number of things with me. I also understand you've had a little experience altering its contents so that the world received the benefits."

Sabrina cocked an eyebrow. She knew exactly what Mr. Canis was talking about. Bunny had used the magical book to completely erase a human being from existence. Could it work on Mirror?

Bunny shook her head. "It's not as simple as putting pen to paper. The story has to be managed and prodded, written and rewritten. The results are unpredictable at best and staggeringly difficult. It took me nearly twenty-five years to make the changes I made."

"But certainly you should try," Canis said.

"Relda Grimm doesn't have twenty-five years," Bunny said.

"What exactly are we supposed to do, then?" Sabrina whispered.

"We do the first thing on the prophecy list," Bunny said. "The Council of Mirrors says Daphne has to build a coven."

"And we will, as soon as I find out what a coven is," Daphne said, shoving an entire link sausage into her already full mouth. Elvis sat nearby, watching with envy.

"It's a group of witches," Sabrina said.

"Three, to be exact," Morgan added as she and Mr. Seven approached the table. "Glinda from Oz, Frau Pfefferkuchenhaus, and I were a coven. I'd be happy to join yours."

Daphne grinned. "You would be my first choice, Morgan, and then you, Ms. Lancaster."

Morgan and the Wicked Queen looked at each other and shrugged.

"OK, but there has to be three. Who's last?" Bunny asked.

"I have a great idea for number three, but . . ."

Sabrina saw a twinkle in her sister's eye that she had seen many times before. Daphne was about to say something that would make Sabrina's life miserable. It might as well have been a neon sign reading TROUBLE AHEAD!

"Why do I think I'm going to hate your choice?" she asked.

Daphne folded a pancake in half and shoved it into her pocket, then grinned at her sister. "I have no idea."

• • •

"Of all the witches in this town, you have to pick the one that wants to eat me," Sabrina complained as she stomped through the woods toward Baba Yaga's hut. Bunny, Daphne, Morgan le Fay, Puck, Elvis, and her father followed closely behind. None of them were thrilled by Daphne's choice. They took turns trying to talk her out of it, but Sabrina's sister insisted that if they wanted to build a coven of super-powerful witches they should ask super-powerful witches to join.

"Can we please try to keep it down," Bunny whispered to Sabrina. "I don't like this idea any better than you do, but we don't need to whine quite so loudly. There are other things in these woods to be afraid of—like the Scarlet Hand."

"Sorry," Sabrina whispered back. "But I'm completely freaked out. I think this is a really bad idea. We can't save the world if we're in Baba Yaga's belly. Why can't we use Mordred?"

"No boys allowed in a coven. It has to be a crone, a temptress, and an innocent. Besides, boys have cooties," Morgan said with a giggle.

"Is that what these things are?" Puck asked as he scratched at his armpits.

"Fine, what about Mallobarb and Buzzflower?" Henry asked. "Briar's fairy godmothers use a lot of magic and they're already living in the castle."

"They're fairy godmothers—not witches," Daphne said. "Duh!"

"Why not Ozma of Oz?" Sabrina begged. "She could be the innocent, Morgan would be the temptress, and Bunny the—"

An angry glance from the queen cut off the end of Sabrina's sentence.

"So how do you plan on getting her to agree?" Sabrina said, quickly changing the subject. "She's not exactly the joining type."

"We're still working on that part of the plan," Daphne said as she scratched behind Elvis's ear. "Aren't we, buddy?"

"Please! Keep your voices down!" Bunny shouted, then closed her eyes and calmly counted to ten. "We don't have to announce to half of Duchess County that we're coming."

"Are you afraid of Baba Yaga, Bunny?" Henry asked.

The witch rolled her eyes and laughed. "Hardly. My power nearly rivals hers."

"Nearly?" Sabrina asked. "'Nearly' is not as good as 'totally rivals' or 'is better than' or 'spits in the face of.'"

The queen scowled and marched to the front of the group. Following her directions, they trudged deeper into the darkest and loneliest part of the Hudson Valley forest. Signs of life became more and more scarce, which meant they were walking in the right direction.

The trees were black and bare and looked more like shadows than living things. The grass grew in thin, gray clumps. The path was knotted with ugly vines, thick as chains, and covered with thorns that jabbed at ankles. Sabrina started to feel that throbbing, woozy sensation she got when she was around magic. She told herself to be strong and pressed onward.

Following a bend in the path, they came upon the old witch's home. It was a ramshackle hut with a sagging roof covered in abandoned birds' nests. The two small windows and the single black door looked suspiciously like a face scanning for intruders. As if in mockery of a normal home, the hut also had a white fence, but instead of pickets, it was constructed from bones—mostly those of large animals, but more than a few looked human. A walkway of bleached skulls led to the front door.

With a grimace, Daphne unhooked the fence latch and swung the bone gate aside. The family followed her into the yard. "Who's going to knock?" she asked.

"It's your coven. You knock," Sabrina said.

Daphne cringed. "I'm scared."

Puck rolled his eyes. "I'll handle this."

"No," Henry said, stepping forward. "I've dealt with her a few times. The secret is to be respectful."

"Yes, remember to say please and thank you when she's chewing on your face," Sabrina muttered.

Henry raised his hand to knock on the door but quickly pulled his hand away.

"It burned me," he said, looking down at his knuckles. Sabrina could see the painful blisters forming on his hand. Henry searched the ground for something to use as a knocker, but the only thing available was a loose skull from the path. He yanked it out of the soil and clunked it against the door. Moments later, it swung open, but there was no one in the doorway.

Puck chuckled. "I hope everyone brought a change of undies, 'cause I think this is just going to get spookier and spookier."

Henry peered into the house and waved the group forward.

The witch's home was just as unsettling as it was the last time Sabrina had visited. Rusty cages big enough to imprison a child were stacked in a corner. Pots of strange, bubbling potions and jars filled with animals, some still living, crowded the floor, along with a bent tray scattered with what looked like fingernails. On the far wall a fireplace raged with an angry flame that flickered to reveal the suffering faces of shattered souls begging for release. A thick book with a cover made from what appeared to be human skin rested on a table. Sabrina wasn't sure if it was all the magic in the room or the fear racing through her veins, but it looked like the book's cover rose and fell as if it were breathing.

"Old Mother!" the Wicked Queen shouted. "We respectfully request an audience."

The flames in the fireplace roared as if fed by gasoline and Daphne leaped into her father's arms.

"Old Mother, this is Bunny Lancaster. I wish to speak with you."

"Maybe she's gone. We should come back," Morgan said, heading for the door.

"She's here," Bunny said, scanning the room.

"Perhaps she is shy," Puck said as he swaggered around the room. "I can be very intimidating to some people."

Henry cringed. "Don't taunt her, Puck."

"You guys have got yourselves worked up over nothing. I mean, really—"

And then, quite suddenly, a figure stepped out of a shadow behind Puck. Baba Yaga had long gray hair that hung on her head like a rotting mop. Her one good eye spun in its socket and her nose was as pointy as a steak knife. Puck screamed like a little girl. Sabrina would have spent months ridiculing him if she hadn't done the exact same thing.

Baba Yaga squinted as she examined each member of the group. When she got to Sabrina, she leaned in close. The air temperature dropped at an alarming rate. Sabrina's teeth chattered and frosty breath escaped her lips.

"The last time I saw you, I told you I'd make a coat of your skin. You are either insane or have the courage of a lion," the old crone said to her.

"Hello, Old Mother. I'm sorry if my girls have been a trouble to you," Henry said. "My mother had her hands full while—"

"I know where you were, Henry Grimm!" Baba Yaga replied. "There is little that happens in this town that I am not aware of."

Baba Yaga crossed the room to a table. She picked up an apron with the words VERMONT IS FOR LOVERS and slipped it over her filthy smock. Then she snatched a knife from the table with one hand and fished a frog out of a jar with another. Sabrina was grateful that the woman's back blocked her view of what came next.

"Then you know why we're here," Bunny said, seemingly unfazed.

Baba Yaga opened a small tin, smelled its contents, then threw it on the floor. She peered into a jewelry box filled with spitting centipedes, fished out a fat one, and then ate it. "I do."

"The fate of the world is at hand," Morgan said.

"Oh, sweet girl, the world isn't in any danger. It's the people who live on it that are going bye-bye."

"Not if you help us," Daphne said.

Baba Yaga cackled and spittle covered her hairy chin. In her amusement she kicked a can of something into the fireplace and it exploded. "Take yourselves and leave while I'm still feeling inclined to let you."

"Old Mother, you must reconsider!" Bunny cried.

Baba Yaga turned and soared across the room with lightning speed until she was within an inch of the Wicked Queen's nose. "You should respect your elders, poison maker. What do I care of this world? The Old Mother will live on. Probably with far fewer interruptions."

The queen stood her ground. "This isn't a request."

Baba Yaga chuckled.

"You dare laugh at me?" the queen cried, her voice like thunder. She stretched out her hand. Resting on her palm was a spinning ball of light and energy.

Baba Yaga had only a moment to register the light before it blasted her across the room and into one of her tables. She lay sprawled on the floor, seemingly dead, before an ancient and unintelligible chant came from her mouth. When it was

complete, hundreds of pointy legs erupted from her body. She flipped over and scurried along the floor like a centipede, eventually scuttling up the wall and onto the ceiling, where she swung from a filthy chandelier.

From there, she leaped onto Bunny's back and the two fell to the floor. The attack sent pots of bizarre potions splattering all over the room. Several monkeys locked in a cage in the far corner shrieked and pounded on the bars of their prison. There was a crash and the floor was immediately covered with creepy-crawlies by the thousands.

"You cannot turn your backs on the rest of us," Bunny shouted. "Billions will die."

"A dog feels no sorrow when his fleas are extinguished!"

"Stop fighting!" Daphne cried.

Bunny shouted an incantation and Baba Yaga went flying across the room again. In return, the old crone waved her hands in the air and her body transformed into twenty flying daggers that sped toward the Wicked Queen with deadly accuracy. Bunny cast a spell and a glowing red shield appeared, knocking the daggers to the ground. They melted into a thick pool, from which Baba Yaga rose.

The old crone reached into the folds of her raggedy dress and brought something out. She held it to her mouth and blew.

Hundreds of hairy spiders leaped from the device onto Bunny, burrowing under her skin. She screamed in agony.

Before anyone could stop her, Daphne pushed between the dueling witches. "Cut it out!"

Baba Yaga sneered at the girl but took a step back. "I have no appetite for this fight. Gather yourselves and go."

"No!" Daphne cried. "Sounds to me like you're afraid."

Baba Yaga's head turned toward the little girl so quickly Sabrina heard the bones rattle inside the witch's neck. "What did you say?"

"You heard me. You're a coward," Daphne said, standing her ground. "You're terrified of going up against Mirror, but you're hiding it under your usual grouchiness. I'm not fooled."

"Daphne, shut up," Morgan pleaded.

"I will kill you and suck on your bones, little one," the witch raged. "I've made soup from children like you who were far less lippy."

Daphne cringed. "Fine. You're going to eat me. That doesn't mean you're not a lousy witch. You like to hide in this creepy house, but how scary could you be if my sister and I keep coming back here? You've lost your touch, Old Mama."

"Daphne, shut up!" Henry cried.

"It's Old Mother," Baba Yaga seethed.

"Whatever! Maybe I made a mistake thinking you were the most powerful witch in town. I guess I'll have to go find Ozma of Oz."

Baba Yaga's anger was so intense her ratty hair stood on end. "Ozma of Oz? That child doesn't have a fraction of my power!"

"Maybe, but she's beating you in bravery," Daphne shouted back.

There was a long, awkward pause and then Baba Yaga started a new chant. The floor beneath their feet began to shake and rock. The walls drew inward as if the group were trapped inside a deflating balloon, and a moldy chandelier crashed to the floor mere inches from where Bunny was picking bugs out of her skin. Sabrina clenched her fist, preparing for a fight, when her father yanked her and Daphne by the arm.

"OK! Everyone outside," Henry cried. Unfortunately, the door was closed tight, and no matter how hard Sabrina pulled, it wouldn't budge. Henry took a turn but got the same result.

"Step aside," Morgan said. Her eyes glowed red and an invisible force as powerful as a hurricane hit the door. It flew off its hinges and sailed into the woods.

Once free, the group, led by Elvis, spilled out through the opening, only to be stopped in their tracks. Standing at the gate were two figures. The first was Granny Relda, or rather, something horrible wearing her skin. Sabrina cried out, seeing her beloved grandmother under the control of such evil.

The second person waiting for them was wearing ancient chain mail armor and heavy boots covered in spikes. His sword was immense, with a golden hilt inset with a ruby that looked like a bloodshot eye. His long hair, the color of blood, hung lifelessly down his back like a waterfall of death.

"Atticus," Sabrina gasped. She had first seen the evil prince inside the Book of Everafter, but out here in the real world, he was flesh and blood and, by the look in his eyes, eager to hurt someone.

Granny was the first to speak. The voice was neither hers nor Mirror's, but a monstrous combination of the two. "I've come to make you an offer."

"You let go of my grandmother first!" Sabrina shouted.

"I wish I could, Starfish, but at the moment I'm sort of stuck," Mirror said. "It's an unfortunate consequence of the monkey wrench you threw into my plans. If you had just let me have Basil, I wouldn't be trapped in this elderly body with all its aches and pains. But here we are. Oh, let me introduce you to my business associate, His Majesty Prince Atticus Charming."

The Wicked Queen stepped forward with her hand twisted into an angry claw. "YOU!!!"

"Well, if it isn't my mother-in-law," Atticus said. "It's been a long time."

"Not long enough," Bunny seethed.

"Where is my wife? With my brother, no doubt," he said as he drew his deadly sword. "No mind. He will not keep her. Locking me away for hundreds of years has not stopped me. Nothing will stop me."

Both the witch and the warrior looked ready to attack, but they were interrupted by Baba Yaga, who charged through the door of her home like an angry bull. She swiveled her head from the Grimms to Mirror and his companion. "Now, what is this?"

"Who is this withered old grape?" Atticus said.

Mirror raised his hand for silence. "Your Majesty, it would serve you well to learn a little respect. This is Baba Yaga, a great and powerful sorceress. You should apologize."

Atticus laughed, but Mirror was not kidding.

"You're serious? OK, fine, I'm sorry, m'lady," he said with an exaggerated bow.

Baba Yaga was having none of it. "So another steps forward to mock the Old Mother. Enough!"

"No! I'll take care of this," the Wicked Queen said. She swung her arm forward as if slashing at Atticus with an invisible sword. A tidal wave of destruction sprung from her hand. The magic leveled trees and threw earth skyward. A cloud of dust and broken stone enveloped everything as far as Sabrina could see. When the debris settled, Atticus and Mirror remained untouched and unharmed.

The queen was shocked. "How?"

Mirror winked. "Now, that would be telling."

This time Morgan unleashed her power. Blasts of lightning and plasma rained down on the two villains, but like before they remained untouched. When Morgan raised her hands for another attack, a blast of fiery flame erupted from Mirror's fingertips. The magic slammed into Morgan, and she flew backward several yards into the wall of Baba Yaga's hut.

"You insult my home, little mirror. It makes me . . . angry," Baba Yaga hissed.

She reached into the folds of her dress and removed three slimy toads. Their slippery legs squirmed in her hands as she held them up to her mouth. "Bright Morning! Dark Night! Red Sun!"

She dropped the animals onto the ground, and before they had a chance to hop away, they began a disturbing transformation. Their skin bubbled and their bodies stretched, legs growing several feet. With each passing second they twisted and changed unnaturally, until three full-grown men, each with the face and webbed hands of a frog, stood in front of Baba Yaga. They were dressed in tunics and armor each reflecting their names—white, black, and red—and they held flaming swords. With their super-strong legs they sprang into combat, slashing and stabbing at Atticus, whose own sword was raised in preparation.

Mirror sighed as if the battle were a mild inconvenience. "Enough of this unpleasantness," he said as if what had just occurred was nothing more than a glass of spilled milk. "We're all friends here, and I've come to make you the offer of a lifetime. I will let you all keep your lives and all you have to do is lower the barrier. Old Mother, I know that it is within your power. After all, it was you and Wilhelm who created it in the first place."

Baba Yaga chuckled.

"What if I said pretty please?"

"You are a curious thing, little mirror," Baba Yaga said as she lurched toward him. She studied Granny Relda's face as if she could see the creature hidden beneath. Sabrina stared as well. What was it that Baba Yaga saw—some weakness? "The mirror that refuses to see that he is broken. Ah, I see. The answer is always in the eyes. Yes, I know how to beat you now. I can see your biggest weakness and how silly it is."

Her laughter was a combination of unnerving hacking and loud croaks, but the sound only unleashed Mirror's rage. He let loose a blast of raw energy that swept across Baba Yaga and swallowed her whole. It was magic so strong it ripped the flesh right off of the old witch's bones like she had stepped into raging hot fire. Within seconds her skeleton was picked clean. It fell to the ground alongside the bones of her fence and pathway.

"NO!" Bunny cried.

Mirror clapped his hands as if to remove the dust of hard work. "Tsk, tsk. What a shame. Now I have to spend the rest of my day searching her house for the spell."

But to everyone's surprise Baba Yaga's skeleton clambered to its feet and stood upright. Sabrina gasped. The muscle, veins, organs, and skin began to grow over the bones, slowly inching across joints and through its rib cage. In no time at all, the old witch was whole again.

Mirror cocked a curious eyebrow. "Now that is a good trick."

"Get into the house!" Baba Yaga shouted, running for the door, and without hesitation everyone scrambled back through the doorway. Henry helped Morgan to her feet, and once inside, the old crone commanded her house to rise.

Sabrina felt the floor heave beneath her. One side of the room tilted steeply and the group slid across the floor, crashing in a pile against the wall. Then the other side of the room was hoisted high and everyone slid the other way.

"I love this house!" Puck crowed.

"I hate this house," Sabrina said. She had seen it move from the outside: it had legs—big, claw-footed things like those from a monstrous chicken.

"House, run!" Baba Yaga cried, and the house took off at a clip. Everyone inside bounced around like they were inside a popcorn machine.

Baba Yaga darted to her window and shouted a few screeching threats out at Mirror and Atticus. Then she reached over her head and a spear made from magic and smoke appeared in her hand. She hurled it out the window, followed by another, and yet another. Bunny took the other window, letting fly long tendrils of lightning from her fingertips. Despite their efforts, a massive explosion rocked the house, knocking everyone off their feet.

"Now do you see what we're up against?" Bunny demanded

"You have my power at a price, poison maker," Baba Yaga said.

"A price?" Morgan cried.

"What is in it for the Old Mother?" Baba Yaga croaked.

Sabrina was incensed. "You get to live in a world that isn't ruled by a maniac."

Baba Yaga laughed. "The world is always ruled by a maniac."

"Fine, Old Mother. You want payment for your services. Name your price," the Wicked Queen said.

"Your eyes."

No one in the house spoke, and for a moment all they could hear were the explosions outside. Had Sabrina heard the old witch correctly? Had Baba Yaga just asked Bunny Lancaster for her eyes? She glanced around the room. On a table nearby was a jar of what she had previously hoped were hard-boiled eggs. Now she realized that had been wishful thinking.

"Her eyes?" Henry repeated.

"A witch's magic is in her eyes," Morgan explained. She looked distressed.

"Every spell I've read, every experience I've lived through, every vision that has ever come to me are held in them. In essence, giving her my eyes is giving her my power," Bunny said.

"That's my deal, Your Majesty. This coven requires a crone—unless you want to dig up Frau Pfefferkuchenhaus's worm-eaten corpse." Baba Yaga cackled.

Another blast slammed into the house, and this time the structure could not stand its ground. It stumbled forward and crashed face-first into the forest floor. Sabrina grabbed her sister's hand just as everyone slid with an orchestra of groans into the windows in a mess of legs and arms. Elvis got the worst of the weight and whimpered at the bottom of the pile.

"Get up, house!" Baba Yaga screeched, and the house obeyed. Unfortunately, its efforts to regain its footing sent the people inside bouncing and tumbling again. It was a miracle that no one was killed, especially when the house rocked back and forth like a prizefighter shaking off an uppercut. It lumbered onward, only to be blasted and fall yet again.

From outside, Mirror called to them. "Is there really any point to the running? What I'm asking for is such a small thing! You'll only suffer by refusing."

"Don't listen," Atticus shouted. "The suffering is my favorite part."

"We have to fight them," Puck said, pulling his sword from his belt.

"That thing out there has access to all arcana. We don't have the magic. We need the power of three if we stand a chance," Bunny Lancaster said.

The house was rocked by a third massive assault. When Sabrina righted herself, she saw Baba Yaga extending her hand to the Wicked Queen.

Morgan gasped. "Bunny, don't do it."

"I have made bigger sacrifices," the queen said as she reached out and took the crone's hand. "Very well, Old Mother. We have a deal."

Baba Yaga smiled a ghastly smile. There was a flash and a rumble and to Sabrina's shock and disbelief it looked as if their hands turned to stone—like the hands of a statue in a sculpture garden. Then the rocky flesh cracked as if filled with red-hot magma. Both witches then extended their hands to Morgan, who joined them. Her hands went through the same eerie change until they all looked toward the ceiling and said, "We are bound by coven."

The electricity in the air made everyone's hair stand on end. The trio faced the open windows and chanted an incantation in an ancient language. A wave of tremendous magic exploded out of their chests and flowed out the window. Sabrina raced to the window just in time to see the magic transform into a massive giant, a hundred feet tall, made of mist and wind. The mist giant attacked Mirror and Atticus, snatching them in its unearthly fists. Atticus fought with his sword and Mirror launched into a barrage of spells, but their efforts could not stop the creature.

"Crone, you've got them occupied for the time being, but we need to get this house out of here," Henry shouted.

Baba Yaga ordered her house to run, and it got back up on its legs and dashed away, leaving the villains far behind them. As they left Mirror and Atticus in the distance, Sabrina watched the two villains—one with a face of evil and one with a face of love. She quietly prayed that the next time they met she would know how to stop them both.

5

ctober 15 (part 2)

So, our attempt to boost the morale around the castle has sort of backfired. Well, not sort of—totally. Mainly because our latest recruit has freaking terrified everyone. Baba Yaga has been walking around eyeing everyone and licking her lips like they were all pieces of fried chicken. The Pied Piper and Wendell barricaded themselves in one of the cabins. Puss in Boots darted underneath a shed and refused to come out. The Scarecrow burst into tears, ruining his face. He had to paint on brand-new eyes and a mouth, which in my opinion makes him no less creepy than Baba Yaga. Bunny is trying to assure everyone that they are safe and that the old witch is a big part of the plan. I'm wondering what this plan is, 'cause I feel like we're wandering in the dark.

Anyway, now that the coven has been built I guess it's my turn to do my part—leading everyone to their deaths. I did a head count of *my "troops" to see what I'm working with, and our grand total is 24 people. We've got two old men, a beauty queen, a little boy with a harmonica, some circus bears, a man made out of hay, a bird, a cat wearing work boots, a feng shui consultant, and now a flesh-hungry witch and her walking house. And these people have the nerve to look at me like I'm going to let them down.*

Bunny says she's going to get me help, but she's asked for something in return. She wants us to keep our mouths shut about Atticus. She says she doesn't want to make things any more complicated, especially with Snow, who already keeps her mother at arm's length. We agreed, but in my opinion Snow has a right to know about the man and more importantly she has a right to know what her mother did to protect him from her. I suppose Bunny is trying to find the right way to explain it all.

Oh, and on a side note, Puck told my dad he was going to marry me.

Worst. Day. Ever.

That night, Sabrina and her sister slept in one of the fortress's cabins with Elvis. They pushed together two cots so they could sleep as they had been doing for years—side by side—and snuggled close to each other to fight off the room's many drafts. Elvis lay at the foot of the bed, eventually making his way between them and then entirely on the pillows. It was a fitful night for Sabrina, filled with terrible nightmares. In each dream, Mirror was strangling her and laughing. She woke several times, breathing hard and grasping at her throat. Daphne lay next to her, her little arms wrapped around the Book of Everafter. Elvis, who was usually as heavy of a sleeper as Daphne, snuggled up with Sabrina and licked her chin, but his attempts at comfort didn't help.

"I heard your shouts," a voice said from the shadows and Mr. Canis stepped forward. "I came to investigate."

Sabrina nodded. "Bad dreams."

"You have my sympathy," the old man said. "I've suffered all my life. I find meditation before bed to be the most effective."

"What are you doing up so late?"

"Trying to be useful," the old man said, then pointed at the Book of Everafter. "This camp is filled with people who are untrustworthy. Perhaps I should take the book for safekeeping."

"I'll talk to Daphne about it in the morning," Sabrina said. "She's convinced she's going to find something in it that will help."

"Very well," Mr. Canis said, and was soon gone.

Sabrina lay still listening to the wind and the forest and the world. Meditation might help, but right now what she needed was some air.

She snatched an extra blanket from under the cots and wrapped it around her like a cloak, then stepped out into the frosty air. The moon hid behind storm clouds that turned its light dull and milky, and a wind brushed through leaves and branches.

She wandered around the grounds wirhout a destination, just content in her aloneness. Eventually, she came across Briar's grave. There, she spotted Uncle Jake sitting in his chair. She was happy he was back and wanted to rush to him and tell him that she loved him and that he wasn't alone in his grief, but she suddenly understood that, like herself, he probably wanted to be alone. She was about to creep away when she heard his voice. At first she thought he was talking to himself, but then she realized he was talking to Briar. Sabrina listened as he talked about what he had seen in the forest that day: the colors of trees, the crunch of his feet under leaves, the signs of animals preparing for winter, and the beauty of the long, red sunset. But mostly he talked about how hard it was not to share those things with her firsthand.

Before Sabrina knew it, she was wiping tears off her cheeks.

"You got something to say, Sabrina?" Jake asked.

Sabrina stepped into the light. "I didn't mean to spy. I couldn't sleep."

Jake smiled. "I like to talk to her," he said as he gestured to the grave. "I like to think she can hear me, wherever she is. I tell her how much I miss her and how I'm going to avenge her."

"Please don't do it," Sabrina said quietly.

"I don't expect any of you to understand. If what I do makes me the bad guy, well, I'll have to live with it, but I can't live with letting it go." He scooped up his bow and arrows. "I only stopped by to say hello to her. I've got to get back to work."

She followed him to the gate and watched as the drawbridge, recently repaired, lowered. Before he crossed the bridge he turned to her. "I heard the news about the prophecy. I'd wish you luck, but these days I'm not sure the world is worth saving."

Sabrina wasn't sure how to respond. Her instinct was to argue and give the man a pep talk, but at the same time she had to admit she often felt the same way. Life seemed to be mostly loss and pain and heartache.

"It's a stupid prophecy," she said. "Two kids are really going to save the world?"

"Save the people you love," Uncle Jake said. "Who cares about the rest of the world?"

And then he was gone, leaving her alone with the murky moon.

• • •

In the morning, Sabrina woke to a knock on her cabin door. When she opened it, she found Charming, Mr. Seven, and Mr. Canis standing in the doorway.

"We need to talk," Charming said. "We've had a deserter."

"Who?"

"Puss in Boots," Mr. Canis said. "He slipped out early this morning."

Daphne sat up in bed and rubbed her eyes. "Why? Is it because of Baba Yaga?"

"We hope," Mr. Seven said, "though there's a chance he could have been a spy."

Sabrina shook her head. "The cat wasn't a spy and it wasn't Baba Yaga. He was afraid Daphne and I were going to screw everything up."

Charming sighed. "He may just be the first. The mood around here is definitely dark. We can't afford to lose more, so you and your sister need to get out of your jammies and get to work."

"And what do you suggest we do?" Sabrina grumbled. "There's only twenty-four people in this army."

"Twenty-three, now," Daphne said.

"We're not talking about the army," Canis said. "Mr. Seven has another idea."

"Our people have been suffering for a long time. It's hard to be afraid all the time, especially when it looks like things just get worse and worse every day. We're going to throw a party," the little man said.

"What do you want us to do—rent a bouncy castle and a cotton candy machine?" Sabrina asked.

"Actually, I was thinking we should have a wedding," Mr. Seven said.

"A wedding?" Sabrina repeated.

"How romantic!" Daphne cried. She jumped up in bed and clapped happily.

Seven smiled. "A surprise wedding. One where the bride doesn't know she's getting married until she walks down the aisle. We need your help."

When Sabrina looked over, Daphne was already biting hard on her palm.

• • •

Sabrina couldn't be sure if the wedding would boost morale, but she was happy with the effect it was having on her. Keeping it a secret tapped into an old familiar feeling: being sneaky. Not so long ago, Sabrina was known as the Queen of the Sneaks. She had earned the title from her year in foster care. She knew how to open a creaky window without making a sound. She knew how to slink across a room without stepping on a loose floorboard.

She knew how to crawl out onto a roof, shimmy down a trellis, and tiptoe past a watchdog without making a peep. Keeping the wedding plans from the eyes and ears of Morgan le Fay reminded her that she wasn't a complete loser. She had skills—occasionally illegal skills, but skills nonetheless—and she was determined to make the most of them.

In the shadows and in whispered conversations she gave everyone a job. Flowers, music, food, and the most important job of all, keeping the bride busy until everything was ready. Since the castle was nearly finished, its rooms also needed to be decorated. Morgan had a simple spell for creating furniture from thin air, and Sabrina knew exactly who to team her up with: Goldilocks. Goldi had an eye for interior design. She also had an obsession with things being just right. Under her direction, Morgan would be busy all day.

And it worked. All the pressure and frustration of the prophecy was pushed aside and the tiny community leaped headfirst into planning and preparation. It was the first time Sabrina had seen everyone smiling since her arrival. She even caught Pinocchio humming the wedding march as he and Gepetto built a platform for the couple to stand upon when they exchanged their vows.

"A wedding under the stars is a lovely idea, Sabrina," Snow said as the two stood back and admired the yard.

"Your boyfriend gave me a lot of the ideas," Sabrina said. "He's quite the romantic."

"I've always thought so," Snow said as she gazed lovingly at Charming, who was working with Nurse Sprat to create some sort of seating chart. "I just hope he saves some for our wedding."

"Has he asked?" Sabrina said.

Snow smiled. "He will. Or I will, if I get tired of waiting. I hope it's half as nice as this one."

Wildflowers lined the path to two beautiful wooden arches interwoven with roses and white lilies. Several rows of chairs, each wrapped in more of the flowers, awaited guests. Mallobarb and Buzzflower hovered overhead on their wide insect wings. They showered the space with magical glitter, making the scene appear otherworldly. It was enough to take Sabrina's breath away. She hoped Morgan would feel the same.

"Well, I better get ready. I didn't exactly pack for a formal engagement," Mr. Seven said, nervously. "I hope my bride doesn't hate my sneakers and blue jeans."

Sabrina looked down at herself and gasped. She was a mess. She couldn't wear her ratty hooded sweatshirt and grungy shoes to a wedding. She rushed into the cabin that housed the magic mirror and darted into the Hall of Wonders. On the floor of her room was a stack of dirty clothes. She sorted through it, desperate to find anything that could be described as an "outfit." All that she had managed to save from Granny's demolished house were three pairs of pants, an oven mitt, a moth-eaten sweater, and eight shoes—none of which matched another. Desperate, she reached for her father's Red Hot Chili Peppers concert shirt from 1990. She slipped it on, then ran into the mirror room to see how she looked. There was a huge green stain on it from one of Puck's pranks. It was ruined.

Sabrina was a card-carrying member of the tomboys club, but this particular injustice stung. It wasn't like she needed a pretty dress or fancy shoes. She just wanted a declaration to the world that things weren't that bad. If she could have her hair done and wash her face and put on a necklace and show up to a wedding during a war, then the battle hadn't beaten them. A simple ribbon in her hair would have done it—evidence that there were still very normal things in this abnormal world, and someday, those normal things would return. But she couldn't win this fight. She couldn't even find a clean T-shirt.

Sabrina wandered over to the Council of Mirrors for some company. "No one has anything nice to wear, honey," Fanny said as she and the other guardians appeared in their mirrors.

"I know. I still want to try," she said.

"For Puck?" Donovan asked, then mimed some exaggerated kissing.

Sabrina frowned. "No! Not for Puck. Who cares what he thinks?"

"Don't tease the girl, Donovan," Arden chided.

Sabrina buried her face in her hands while the mirrors tried to console her. "Everything is a mess."

As she sobbed, she felt a hand in hers and sniffed. "I'm OK, Daphne."

"No you're not," a voice replied, but it wasn't Daphne. It was Red. "None of us are OK."

Red's attempt to comfort her took Sabrina off guard. Of all the people in the Grimm family, Sabrina had been the most indifferent to the little girl. It was hard to forget that Red had tried to hurt her family, even if she had been under the control of an evil force. Sabrina knew it wasn't fair to hold a grudge, but there was a wall around her heart nonetheless.

"Where's Daphne?" she asked.

"She's busy with Morgan's flowers. You know how she bites her palm when she's excited? I thought she was going to chew her hand off when Mr. Seven asked her to be the flower girl." Red took out a brush and went to work untangling Sabrina's blond bird's nest of hair. "She put me on hair duty."

Sabrina forced herself to let the little girl work while she brushed some crusty residue off of her pants.

"You're going to be fine," Red continued. "Of all of us, you'll be fine."

"What makes you think so?" Sabrina said.

"Because you're brave. That's your gift."

"My gift?" Sabrina laughed.

"Yes. Your dad is the one who watches over everyone, your mom is the leader, your sister is the smile-maker, and you— you're the brave one. You just jump in and fight. Mr. Canis says he's never seen you run."

"Mr. Canis hasn't been paying attention. Listen, if anything my gift is being the stupid one. I get into a lot of trouble because of my bravery. Every time I turn around someone has to save my butt."

"You do your fair share of butt-saving too." Red giggled. "We all need saving sometimes."

"Did Mr. Canis say that, too?" Sabrina asked.

"No. I say that," Red said. "Look at Mr. Canis. These days he's feeling old and useless. He doesn't feel like he has a purpose, so I'm saving him."

"How?"

"By making him my father."

"So maybe that's your gift," Sabrina said.

"How do you suppose?"

"You can make even the grouchiest person care about another," Sabrina said. She looked into one of the mirrors and spotted Red's smile.

The little girl set down the brush. "I did the best I could. Not as good as Daphne, but . . ."

"Looking good!" Reggie said when Sabrina studied herself in his reflection.

Red turned to go, but Sabrina took her hand. "Um, want me to comb your hair?" she asked.

Red smiled. "I would love that."

• • •

Sabrina slinked into the courtyard, hoping no one would notice her clothes. She found a seat next to Henry and Veronica. Baby Basil was slumbering in his mother's arms. Veronica studied her son's beautiful face. The only time the little boy would sit still for her was when he was asleep, and Veronica took full advantage of the time to worship her cherub.

"You look uh . . . lovely," Henry said, when Sabrina sat down next to him.

"Nice try, Dad," Sabrina replied. She turned in her seat to check out the other guests. Fanny was right. Most were dressed in the best clothes they had, which turned out to be nothing more than T-shirts and sneakers. Nurse Sprat and Snow White had stolen flowers from their chairs and woven them in their hair. Even Charming had a rose pinned to his shirt. Everyone had done the best they could. Sabrina took a flower from her chair and twirled the stem around her ear. It was better than nothing.

"He's been trained well, honey," Veronica said. "Don't worry about it. We're all a wreck. The bride is wearing farmer's overalls."

"Has she got any clue?" Henry asked.

Sabrina grinned. "Not one."

Puck dropped clumsily out of the sky into the chair next to her.

"Where have you been?"

Puck had a dead skunk in his hand. "Shopping for the happy couple. I didn't check the registry, but I'm sure they don't have one of these."

"You got them roadkill as a wedding present?" Henry asked.

Puck seemed confused. "It's a wedding! Aren't you supposed to send the couple off with things they'll need for their home? Which reminds me, when your daughter and I get married, it's customary in the fairy world for the groom and the father-in-law to challenge each other in a fight to the death. Glad to see

I'll have a worthy contender. It's very disappointing when the bride's dad gets killed right away. It can totally kill the mood of a reception."

"Has anyone seen Uncle Jake today?" Sabrina asked to change the subject.

"I don't think he's in the mood for a wedding," Veronica said.

The Pied Piper and his son stood at the front of the audience with their instruments in hand. They played an up-tempo march and the crowd stood to greet the wedding party. Daphne was the first to appear, and Sabrina's jaw hit the floor. The little girl was dressed in a beautiful silk dress lined with delicate lace. Her shoes were spotless and her hair was clean and flawless. She strolled to the front of the crowd, sprinkling rose petals behind her, and when she got to the platform she reached into her flower basket and removed the star-tipped fairy godmother wand.

"Attention, everyone," Daphne said. "I thought and thought about what kind of gift I could give the happy couple, and I hope you don't mind, but this is what I came up with."

Daphne flicked her wrist and there was a loud *POP!* The air filled with a purple mist. When it lifted, Sabrina looked down at herself. Her jeans and T-shirt were gone, replaced with a soft pink gown and white shoes. Pearls draped her neck, and her face and hands were scrubbed clean and fresh. Sabrina glanced around the courtyard. Everyone was dressed just as beautifully. Even her father's four-day beard was gone.

"Wow!" Puck said.

Sabrina turned to Puck, hoping for a compliment, but the boy fairy was looking down at himself. He was wearing a smart black tuxedo with a black tie. His hair was shiny and combed. There wasn't a single fly buzzing around his head, and he had the pleasant aroma of soap about him. "This suit is going to look great when I roll in those deer droppings I found by the front gate."

Sabrina sighed and told herself she should have known better.

"Enjoy the clothes while they last, 'cause at midnight we all go back to being slobs," Daphne said.

Everyone laughed and broke into applause as Mr. Seven appeared in a blue tuxedo, top hat, and tails. He thanked everyone for coming. He pointed to Sabrina, thanking her for all her hard work, and also thanked Daphne for the fancy suit but, he insisted, the crowd hadn't seen anything yet. He pointed to the back of the courtyard and there was Morgan le Fay. Her dress was the color of vanilla cream, and it was embroidered with seed pearls and tiny crystals. The dress's train spread behind her for several yards and her jet-black hair was woven with little white daisies. She was the most beautiful bride Sabrina had ever seen.

"She's breathtaking," Veronica whispered.

By her side was her son, Mordred, who through the help of magic or his own effort had a perfectly combed head of hair. He grinned nearly as wide as his mother. He led her to the arches, where he placed his mother's hands into Seven's. That was when the Scarecrow approached the couple. He greeted everyone with a broad smile on his burlap face. "Thank you for coming to this most wonderful of events. As the former emperor of Oz, I have the privilege and honor to officiate this ceremony."

The Scarecrow invited the crowd to join him in a prayer for the happy couple. Then Seven and Morgan spoke of their brief but intense love and how fate had finally brought them together. Morgan cried as she promised her life to Seven. Mr. Seven did the same, and when the Scarecrow pronounced them man and wife, Morgan planted the biggest kiss on the little man that Sabrina had ever seen.

Confetti showered down on the newlyweds and music floated over the crowd. There was much cheering and shaking of hands and kissing of the bride.

"You're a lucky man," Gepetto said to the groom.

"I'm the lucky one," Morgan cried, swooping the little man into her arms for another kiss.

And then Charming called for everyone's attention. He had a

glass of champagne in his hand and Sabrina watched as several trays of the bubbly stuff magically floated through the crowd. "Just one more interruption, folks. This morning Mr. Seven came to me and asked me to be the best man at this wedding. For some strange reason he thought a wedding could be planned in one day."

Everyone smiled knowingly.

"He also believed, for some reason, that I enjoy being in front of a crowd."

Everyone roared with laughter.

"Well, let me tell you, this party has been incredibly trouble-some. After all, we're only trying to build a castle, raise an army, and prepare for a war. Mr. Seven and his bride have been a terrible inconvenience."

Suddenly, the laughter was gone. Sabrina was incredulous. Charming had a history of being selfish, but was he really going to grouse during a wedding?

"But that is love, isn't it?" he continued. "It's terribly incon-venient. It sweeps you up and steals your attention and slows down your work. Our labors fall behind, our friends report us missing, and everything comes to a screeching halt! Everything, that is, except what truly matters in this life—true love. We've all been there. We know the feelings. So when we see it in a friend, a dear, dear friend, we throw down our work and we celebrate. We rejoice. We raise a glass. Because when we recognize it in the hearts of friends, it reminds us of how important it is in our own. Mr. Seven, you are and always have been my companion and friend. You have made me a better man, and almost on a daily basis you have reminded me that I too need to celebrate the love in my life."

Everyone turned to Snow. Her face was rosy red and she was grinning wide.

Charming held up his glass. "So, my friends, in this lovely courtyard, let us raise a glass and celebrate the maddening, all-consuming, time-killing, terribly inconvenient magic called love."

The crowd raised their glasses and drank, then burst into rousing applause.

Together, the crowd cleared the chairs away and there was dancing and singing and food. Where the feast came from, Sabrina could hardly guess, but somehow these runaways and refugees had prepared a spread for a hundred people. In the midst of the party Mr. Hamelin found himself a guitar, and his son, Wendell, blew on his harmonica. Sabrina watched Charming whisper something into Snow's ear that made her giggle. She paid for the laugh with a kiss. Henry and Veronica waltzed around the courtyard, holding sleeping Basil between them. Even Red dragged Mr. Canis onto the dance floor for a spin.

Sabrina couldn't help but get swept up in it all. The dread of the last few months and the threat of tomorrow were pushed into a corner of her mind. As she watched the revelers, it dawned on her that the wedding was more than a party for two people coming together as one, but rather, a celebration of life and its possibilities, even in the midst of madness.

"I guess we're supposed to dance," Puck said, suddenly appearing beside her.

"Do you know how to dance?"

Puck rolled his eyes. "I'm royalty. That's all we ever do."

He took her by the hand and taught her an elaborate dance that seemed to be part waltz, part square dance. It was more theatrical than what she thought of as dancing, and it drew way more attention than she wanted, but soon the entire gathering was mimicking their every step. She pushed her embarrassment aside and surrendered to the fun of it. She couldn't even be mad at Puck for not noticing her dress.

As the night marched onward, the crowd began to thin. People drifted off to their cabins and crawled into bed. The new Mr. and Mrs. Seven thanked everyone profusely until they were practically pushed into their honeymoon suite—

the only finished and furnished room in the castle. Veronica carried Basil and Henry carried Daphne, both asleep, back to their beds.

Soon the only people left were Gepetto, Pinocchio, Puck, and Sabrina. Sabrina was too excited from the night's events to go to bed, so she offered to clean up the mess, and the other three joined her—even Pinocchio, though he did do quite a bit of grumbling. As they stacked chairs and picked up trash, Sabrina could still hear the music in her ears, beckoning her to spin in circles. Gepetto decided to leave the flowers where they were as a reminder to everyone of the happy time they had shared, then said good night, promising his son that tomorrow would be another busy day. Pinocchio groaned as he followed his father back to their cabin.

And then Sabrina was enveloped in a glowing light. When it was gone, she looked down and saw that her beautiful dress was no more. She was back to being filthy. Her hair was a mess and she smelled. Puck's fancy suit was gone as well.

"It must be midnight," Sabrina said.

"Thank goodness," Puck said. "I don't enjoy the feeling of being clean."

Sabrina rolled her eyes but didn't move. Instead, she looked up at the moon hanging over the yard.

"So . . . ," Puck said.

"So . . ."

"Nice party," he said. "It reminded me of Sven the Soul Eater's thirteenth wedding. Or was that the fourteenth? It's hard to say. He kept eating his wives. Still, I did think it was strange there wasn't a forest fire. I've never been to a wedding that didn't have some kind of uncontrollable devastation."

Sabrina wished he would just stop talking. He was going to ruin the night with some snarky insult. She just knew it!

"By the way, when I said 'wow,' I was looking at you," Puck said.

Sabrina's face lit up in a grin. Who was this boy? He could drive her crazy with his pranks and taunts, but then, when she least expected, he could be the sweetest and most thoughtful person in the world. He was maddening and impossible to understand, but at that moment he was awfully cute. And she thought she might like to kiss him but couldn't decide. The moment was all too perfect. Asking for more would be pressing her luck, but then again . . .

"Um . . . kind of late, isn't it?" her father said, appearing from the shadows.

"DAD!" Sabrina cried. She could have died from embarrassment.

Puck rolled his eyes. "All right, smell you later," he said. He was in the air instantly, flying off to wherever he slept.

"Get to bed, 'Brina," Henry said as she turned back toward his cabin. "We're going to put an end to this war tomorrow."

Sabrina slipped into her room and found Daphne big-eyed and frantic.

"Have you seen it?" she asked.

"Seen what?"

"The Book of Everafter. It's been stolen!"

6

he morning came all too soon. Sabrina woke her sister and they dressed sleepily. They agreed it was best to keep the missing book a secret. They were pretty sure it had to be somewhere in the castle or its grounds and it would be easier to find it themselves than start an uproar that would lead to a lot of questions about what the book was used for. They divided up the camp so that each of them would have a different section, then stepped out into the bright sunshine.

Before they took a single step, Snow White was marching toward them.

"Are you ready for your training?"

"Huh?"

"Billy thinks it might be wise, in light of the prophecy, that you learn to fight. He also thinks it might be good for everyone to see the two of you out here at the crack of dawn preparing for war. Who better to train you than me? Remember the self-defense class I taught at the community center?"

Sabrina shrugged and turned to her sister, who was still barely awake.

Daphne grumbled. "Without breakfast?"

"We can eat during our first break," Snow said.

"First break implies that there will be more than one, which also implies there will be time between the breaks when we are not breaking," Sabrina said.

"Don't be lazy, girls," Snow said as she handed each girl a long black pole, nearly four feet in length. They were polished and smooth and heavy.

"What's this?"

"It's called a bo-staff and it's very useful in a fight," Snow said.

"It weighs a ton," Sabrina said, trying to swing it over her head only to drop it on the ground. "And it's clumsy."

"That's because your muscles are weak. When you grow stronger, your ability to use it will grow too," Snow said. "Trust me, when I started learning martial arts I had the upper-body strength of a tadpole, but now . . ."

Snow spun the staff at an incredible speed, twirling it around her head like the blades on a helicopter. She passed it from hand to hand, still spinning, then swung it around her back, along her arms as she ducked into a crouch. She stopped her last swing with the staff only inches from Sabrina's nose. "I think that's what your sister would call very punk rock."

"My catchphrases are trademarked, Ms. White," Daphne said with a giggle.

"You're going to teach us to do that?" Sabrina asked.

"I am."

"How is this going to help me stop a madman who is made out of magic?" Sabrina said. "Listen, Ms. White, I appreciate the help, but you've already taught my sister and me plenty of self-defense stuff. I don't need to know how to scare someone off with a big stick."

"I'm not here to teach you to scare someone with a big stick," Snow said, stepping forward. "I'm going to teach you how to hit someone with it. Welcome to the Bad Apples."

That afternoon was the most painful in Sabrina's memory. Though Snow took it easy on her, the staff still slapped against her shoulders, knees, shins, and fingers. It was also heavy and hard to hold, so after a few hours her shoulders were burning like hamburgers on a grill. But what hurt most was how each strike her pole blocked sent a jarring vibration into her hands and up her arms, stopping at her neck. When one attack came, it hurt so much the staff fell out of her hands and bounced on the ground.

As she bent down to retrieve her weapon, she saw that she had an audience. Nearly everyone within the walls of the castle had slipped into the courtyard to watch. Some were smiling at her, almost beaming with pride. Others were merely curious and watched without expression. Pinocchio was smirking at her, but this didn't bother her as much as her mother's and father's anxious expressions. She tried to push their worry out of her mind and focus on her training. If she learned anything that day, it was that Snow knew when you weren't paying attention, and she made you pay for it.

"Well, that was a good first day," Snow said, taking the bo-staffs. "I'll see you back here at five."

Sabrina groaned. "Five!"

But Snow walked away.

"We still need to find the book," Daphne said.

"I need to be taken to a hospital," Sabrina said, wincing at her bruises and strained muscles.

Suddenly, Puck stepped forward with three wooden swords in hand.

"What's this about?" Daphne asked.

"I'm your next teacher. You can call me Mr. Puck," he said,

handing the sisters each a sword. "I'm going to teach you the art of swordsmanship—or in other words, how to totally kill someone with a sharp, pointy thing."

Sabrina's arms were so sore she could barely lift the weapon. Daphne was struggling as well.

"We're too tired," Sabrina said.

"And too beat up," Daphne added.

Puck didn't listen. He launched into an attack and the girls were forced to defend themselves. For ten minutes Sabrina managed to fight him off, but not before he used his wooden sword to smack her in her head, poke her in the belly, and crack her across the shins. It didn't help that the sword, though wooden, felt as if it were cast from iron and attached to barbells. Snow's workout had taken nearly all of her strength. She fell to her knees and surrendered.

"Get up," Puck said as he stood over her.

"Puck, we're tired," Daphne cried.

"Get on your feet," he demanded.

"What are you doing?" Sabrina said as she tried to fill her exhausted lungs. She was surprised by his attitude. She had never seen him so serious—so—so *mean*. Where was the dancing boy from the night before? Where was the Puck who she wanted to kiss?

"I'm teaching you to fight," he said. "Pick up your sword!"

She stared up into his eyes, hoping he could see her hurt, but they were cold.

Sabrina looked to the crowd. They looked back at her like she was a turtle who had flipped over on its back and could not right itself. She could hardly blame them. She wouldn't want her own life put in the hands of children, especially ones as abysmally normal as Daphne and her. She wanted to stomp over to them and shout that she had not chosen this path for herself. She wanted them to know that she wasn't any happier about it than they were. She wanted to scream that it wasn't fair.

"You have this camp's attention," Puck said. "They need to see that you can be pushed and fight back. They want to see that when things get hard you aren't going to lie on the ground and whine. You failed them today." Puck stormed off. "The party and the dancing are over, Grimms. It's time to get serious."

"Who is he to talk about getting serious?" Daphne grumbled as the girls watched him walk away.

Henry and Veronica approached. They helped Sabrina to her feet.

"Girls, this isn't working." Henry sighed. "We don't have time to train you properly. We have to do something else."

"Your father and I have an idea," Veronica said.

• • •

Sabrina asked Red to spread the word that she and her sister wanted to speak to the army, and soon everyone returned to the yard. She stood before them all, painfully nervous. She had no idea how her parents' idea would be received and she wasn't sure she would do a good job convincing everyone to give it a try, but she was relieved that someone—anyone—was taking charge.

"I hope everyone had a good time last night," she said to the crowd, "but now we have to get back to our plans of stopping Mirror. We're a small group—too small to be much of a problem for him. I think I know how to change that. But before I explain, I asked the Widow to fly down to the town and report back on what she saw."

The Widow flapped up onto Mr. Canis's shoulder. "It's a horror show. I can't put it any prettier than that. If you owned a business down there, you might want to go ahead and fill out that insurance claim. The streets are a disaster, almost unrecognizable. And it's overrun with the Hand, who are using it as their own personal playground. I saw two trolls tossing cars around like they were in a snowball fight. There are tons of Everafters looting and destroying things just for the fun of it. All of them have that creepy red hand painted on their chests. And then there's Relda—I mean, Mirror. He . . . she . . . wow, this is confusing. Let's just say the bad guy is camped out in the old police station, and she looks worse than I've ever seen her. He's got members of the Hand running in and out of the place. He's ordering everyone to cause as much chaos as possible. Plus, there's this red-haired lunatic who seems to be Mirror's right-hand man."

"Red-haired lunatic?" Charming asked. "Is this someone new?"

"I've never seen him before, but he's got a sword as big as a boat oar."

Sabrina cringed. The red-haired man had to be Atticus. She looked to the Wicked Queen, who was cringing as well. Apparently, the witch had not yet told her daughter or her daughter's boyfriend anything about their past, or the wicked man who haunted it. Bunny exchanged a knowing look with Sabrina, then cast her eyes to the ground. Sabrina turned to Morgan and then Baba Yaga, who hovered at the back of the crowd. Neither one of them were going to say anything, either. The bonds of the coven were deep.

"How many members of the Hand do you think you saw, Widow?" Sabrina asked.

"Probably close to two thousand."

"Two thousand!" the Pied Piper cried.

"We'll be slaughtered!" Beauty said.

The crowd broke into panicked chatter. Sabrina was sure she

had lost them, but she continued, urged on by her parents' confident smiles. "It does sound like a lot. That's why they're going to be super-surprised when we beat them. And that's where my parents' . . . where my idea comes into play. It couldn't hurt to have a few more people on our side."

"And how do you propose we do that?" Buzzflower demanded.

"We're going to ask them to join us," Sabrina said.

"That's insane! The Hand is full of murderous lunatics," Nurse Sprat said.

Henry waved the argument away like a pesky fly and then stepped over to his daughter. "Yes, that's true, but it's also full of people who are afraid, desperate, and manipulated. I believe that many of the Hand are just people who turned to the Master for the sake of survival. They don't see an alternative. We can provide them a way out. We can take them in, protect them, and in turn, they'll join our fight. I believe most will jump at the chance."

"That's a very big risk," Goldi said.

Henry nudged his daughter and she continued her speech. "We're going to give them a big dose of the truth. The Master lied to them. He told them they would take over the world together, but once he got his chance he turned his back on them and tried to escape the town alone. I'm betting they don't know that, and I think the news will make them pretty angry."

"I don't think you can get them to listen to reason," Swineheart said.

"That's where my mother comes in. My mom can make anyone listen," Sabrina said. "She managed to win the peace with King Oberon and Queen Titania back in the city, and those two were impossible. If there is anyone who can convince members of the Hand that they should join us, it's her."

"Except one thing!" Beauty said. "There are Everafters in the Hand that despise your family; more than a few would like to see you dead. Most won't even consider what your mother says just because she's a Grimm."

"We won't win them all," Veronica said. "But we could win enough to make a difference. And maybe, once they see the rest of their crowd turning away from evil, the real diehards will realize their cause is hopeless."

"It's worth a try," Gepetto said. "It might save a few lives."

"And it might get us a proper army," Mr. Canis said.

Beauty stepped forward. "I'm in. I got wrapped up in the Hand's plans myself, once. I didn't see another choice, but if someone had given me some hope—well, I'm sure I would have seized it. Besides, my husband and daughter are amongst those people, and I'm not ready to give up on them."

Morgan le Fay nodded. "Glinda of Oz was one of my best

friends when we worked for the mayor's office. I know she doesn't want this fight."

"Then it's settled," Henry said. "I think it's wise if we call for a meeting in the town square."

The crowd gasped.

"Didn't you just say the town square is a war zone?" Pinocchio said. "Are you intentionally trying to get us killed? Are you going to suggest we paint targets on our backs too?"

"Hush up, boy," Gepetto demanded.

"We aren't going in unprepared," Henry said. "The Pied Piper will be on crowd control. Baba Yaga, Bunny, Mordred, and Morgan can handle magical attacks, and Buzzflower and Mallobarb can create diversions if we need to escape."

"It's a bold idea. I like it," Charming said. "There are a few people in their crowd we can count on too. Robin Hood and his men as well as King Arthur and his knights have infiltrated the Hand and sent me information about their movements. When the time is right, they will fight for us, but my hopes are it will go well. I'd hate for them to be exposed as spies."

"All those in favor?" Snow asked.

Sabrina glanced at the crowd. Every hand was raised except Pinocchio's and, much to her surprise, Puck's. He was standing in the back of the crowd, arms crossed, and looking at her disapprovingly. Was he still angry about the sword fighting?

"Then it's settled," Canis said. "We should send word immediately that—"

"I'll have no part in your truce," a voice said from the back of the crowd. Sabrina craned her neck and spotted her uncle.

"You cannot trust one of them. Not one," he barked. "You will reach for their hands in friendship and they will stab you dead. This plan is a perfect opportunity for them to find this castle and overrun it. I will not help you."

"Jake, they aren't all like Heart and Nottingham," Veronica said.

"Yes, they are!" he shouted angrily. "Charming, this is your castle, but it's also Briar's grave, and I will kill any member of the Hand that lays one toe in this camp."

"Jake!" Henry said.

"I mean it. Not one step through those gates!" He stormed away.

Sabrina was worried how Jake's outburst would affect the crowd, but it didn't seem to change their minds. The crow was sent out to deliver the message. Tomorrow at noon the Scarlet Hand would be getting a visit from Sabrina Grimm's army.

• • •

Much to the girls' surprise, when they returned to their cabin for the night, Daphne found the Book of Everafter under the bed.

"You had me stressed out about nothing!" Sabrina said.

"I swear it wasn't under there this morning," Daphne said, hoisting the book up and eyeing it as if it were responsible for its own disappearance.

Sabrina crawled into bed and pulled the covers over her head. She was too tired for mysteries, especially mysteries that weren't mysteries at all. "I think the only thing missing is a pair of glasses on your nose."

She fell asleep without hearing Daphne's reply. It had been a long day.

Sabrina woke up late at night to the sound of arguing. She sat up in bed and strained her ears. She recognized the voices ringing through the yard. Her father and her uncle were in the midst of a terrible fight.

Sabrina's curiosity got the best of her. She crept to the site of Briar's grave, where she knew they'd be. She hid behind a stack of chopped wood so she could listen without being seen.

"Jake, this is as good a plan as any," her father said. "You can't stand in the way. The girls' lives are in jeopardy."

"And whose fault is that?" Jake said. "Sending them into that hornet's nest tomorrow is as good as aiming the arrows right at them."

"Not everyone in the Scarlet Hand is bad," Henry said. "It's not fair to paint them all with the same brush. I know you're hurting and I know you're angry. I would be too, but you are slipping off the deep end, Jake. This is not what Briar would want for you."

"Don't tell me what Briar would have wanted for me!" Jake shouted.

"You have to find a way to get ahold of this anger."

"Oh, trust me. I have a plan to deal with my anger."

There was a long silence.

"What you're planning could blow up in your face," Henry said. "It could make things worse."

"How could things get worse?"

"If you kill Nottingham and Heart right now, you will destroy any chance of the Hand turning against the Master. They already can't trust us, and now you're going to be a murderer. It will be like throwing a match on a stack of dynamite. People will get hurt. Jake, my wife and kids will be in the line of fire," Henry said.

"Consider yourself warned," Uncle Jake said dismissively.

And that's when Henry punched his brother. Jake fell to the

ground and lay there in the dust. Sabrina gasped, and hoped neither of them could hear. She had never seen her father so fierce and confrontational. So many people had told her that her dad was an impulsive and emotional kid, but she had never witnessed it. Here before her eyes was the Henry Grimm of so many stories.

"Since when do you talk with your fists, Henry?" Uncle Jake said.

"My girls adore you and you would put their lives in danger for your stupid revenge? Well, I won't let it happen, Jake. I will not let them be hurt just because you are heartbroken. I'm sorry she's gone, Jake. We're all sorry, and you have a right to want revenge. But you don't have a right to have it, and if you try I will hit you again. Stand up and find out if I don't mean it," Henry threatened.

"I'm fine where I am," Jake said.

"What's going on?" Goldi said as she rushed forward. Somehow she had not seen Sabrina.

"We're fine," Henry said as he calmed himself. He extended a hand, but Jake refused the offer.

"You weren't there, Hank! They sent a dragon after her and it swatted her away like she was nothing. You didn't hear the sound! You didn't see her eyes!"

Henry sighed and kneeled next to his brother.

"I had a ring, Hank!" Jake continued.

Goldi knelt down beside them, but Sabrina's father shook her off. "Goldi, this is family business. You should go."

Goldi looked surprised. "But—"

"The three of us were a long time ago," he barked.

Goldi fought her tears and rushed toward her cabin.

When she was gone, Henry turned back to his brother. "Jake, I have a lot on my plate. My son doesn't know me. My girls are on the front line. Our mother is in big trouble. Our family needs to stick together. When all this is over, we can talk about Nottingham and Heart. We'll get justice for Briar."

Jake got to his feet. "There is no justice until those two are in the ground!"

"Grimms don't murder people."

Jake frowned.

"Grimms *don't* murder people!" Henry repeated.

Henry tried to hug his brother, but Jake shook him off. He sank back into his chair and looked out over Briar's grave. Henry watched him for a long moment until finally heading back toward his own cabin. Sabrina kept watching her uncle. He leaped from his chair, furious and raging, and punched the castle wall, splitting his knuckles so that blood dripped down his arm.

He stared at the wound for a long time, as if it might hold some answers, but then he slumped against the wall and slid down to the ground. He buried his head in his hands and wept with abandon. Sabrina wanted to reach out to him—to find a way to take his heartbreak away—but she also knew that her uncle needed to cry. She slinked back to her cabin, where her sister and Elvis were sound asleep. She sat on the edge of the bed and cried for Jake.

October 18

Uncle Jake is gone again. Red said she saw him walk across the drawbridge and into the woods. He had his bow and a quill full of arrows strapped to his back, and his pockets were full of daggers. Apparently, his argument with Dad did not change his mind. He's determined to have his revenge.

Dad and Canis want to go after him, but Charming convinced them to give it up. He says Uncle Jake is on his own path now and we would only be delaying the inevitable.

It's a problem we didn't need today. There are a million things to worry about. We're walking into an angry mob that wants everyone in my family dead. Even though it would ruin the plan, I'm kinda hoping that no one bothers to show up for the meeting. I would breathe a big sigh of relief if we found ourselves alone in the middle of the town square.

On a side note, Puck, who was bordering on being sweet just two days ago, has turned into a sour sack of socks. He's not speaking to me or Daphne. If I wasn't so tired I'd sit on his chest and demand an explanation. Boys are moody and stupid.

If someone were to ask Sabrina to list her virtues, patience would not be one of them. Waiting made her grouchy. She remembered one Christmas in particular. While waiting to sit on Santa's lap she took a gander at the long line of kids in front of her. She was sure their lists were filled with silly wastes of time, but hers was something St. Nick would want to get started on right away. So she had to act. When her father's grip on her hand loosened for a moment, she darted to the front of the line, stiff-armed an elf, and hopped into Santa's lap. She shoved her wish list into his white-gloved hand just before security guards yanked her away. Her parents were horrified and dragged her from the store, but Sabrina didn't care. Such an important list couldn't wait.

So waiting for the Widow to return was painful. What made it worse was that there was no one to talk to. Her mother and father were too busy writing Veronica's speech for the Scarlet Hand, and her sister was giving Elvis a much-needed bath, though it looked more like Elvis was giving the little girl a bath.

To take her mind off the wait, Sabrina tried to busy herself with chores. She collected her family's dirty clothes and scrubbed them in a bucket of water. There wasn't any detergent available, but she hoped the socks, jeans, and T-shirts might lose some of their peculiar funk if she drowned them a few times.

After she hung them up to dry, she offered to help Pinocchio build a compost pile his father insisted he finish. But ten minutes later his constant whining and declarations that he was "too smart for menial labor" forced her to leave him to his task.

She took Basil beneath a shade tree and the two counted the rusty orange-colored leaves left in the skinny branches. She fed the horses, then fed the chickens. She watched Boarman milk a cow. She helped Mallobarb and Buzzflower hang a tapestry, then wandered through the castle to explore the rooms, which would hopefully be living spaces for the new soldiers. None of her efforts distracted her for long. Eventually, she threw up her hands and marched off to see the magic mirrors. Maybe they had some news.

She found them all waiting in their frames when she entered. Reggie, Titan, Fanny, Donovan, and Harry were all smiling, but the rest eyed her warily.

"How was the wedding?" Fanny asked. "What did the bride wear?"

"Was there any dancing?" Donovan said. "I was hoping someone would ask me to play some records. I have the most extensive collection of disco and funk in the known universe. Half of my collection is from bands that are purely imaginary."

"Who caught the bouquet?" Titan roared.

"Everything was lovely," Sabrina said. "It was like a fairy tale, but it's all over now and drama has returned to Castle Charming."

She explained her family's plan, what her mother would do, and what they hoped to gain.

"So it sounds like they're finally taking you seriously," Reggie said.

Sabrina nodded, but she wasn't sure. It seemed that ever since the mirrors had made their prophecy, everyone was bossing the girls around more. She had offered her parents a few ideas about the speech earlier that afternoon, but they had all been dismissed. At the time she was OK letting her mom and dad make all the plans. After all, what did she know about any of this? But now, with the mirrors reminding her of her earlier complaints, she felt a little silly. "I guess they are."

"So what can we do for you?" Harry asked.

"This meeting is scary. Everyone I know might die, including me. I think I need a reminder of why I'm doing it. Can you show me Granny?"

The mirrors' reflections became milky vapors until they coalesced into a lone figure wearing a filthy white dress—Granny Relda. Her long gray hair was a tangled briar, sticking out in all directions. Her eyes were smoldering black coals and her face, once kind and amused, was convulsing with bloodthirsty rage. Sabrina watched the old woman with increasing horror. Granny's head cocked to the side as if she were peering back at Sabrina, and then she laughed. It was a low, foul, otherworldly sound, filled with violence and frenzy.

"Stop!" Sabrina cried, tears in her eyes. "I can't see this!"

"We're sorry, honey," Fanny said as she and the other guardians returned.

Titan roared fiercely. "I hate to see you so, girl. I swear on my life that the First will pay for his crimes. We'll find a way to punish him and rescue your grandmother."

Sabrina prayed silently that Titan was right.

"Hey! The black chicken is back," Puck said. He had crept into the room without her knowing.

"She's a crow," Sabrina said, wiping the tears from her cheeks.

"Whatever," Puck said. For a moment his face had softened as he watched her cry, but now it was angry and determined again. He stomped out of the room, shouting behind him, "It's time to go!"

"He's grouchy," Fanny said.

Sabrina sighed. "Yeah, well, whatever's bothering him is going to have to wait until I get killed."

She said good-bye and hurried out to find the Widow surrounded by a crowd, all eager to hear how their invitation had been received. As Sabrina drew closer, she saw there were several unfamiliar birds with the crow.

"I invited everyone I could find that didn't try to kill me, which wasn't too many," the exhausted crow squawked to the gathered crowd. "And I managed to recruit a few along the way. Allow me to introduce to you our new aerial spy network: the Silver Pigeon, the Gold Pigeon, the Clockwork Owl, the canary, the duck here is named Lenchen, and the big one with all the plumes is a firebird. Don't know his name yet, but the others say he is reliable."

The Firebird squawked in agreement.

"Did you see my husband and daughter? Did you invite them?" Beauty asked.

The Widow nodded her tiny head and hopped from the ground onto a tree stump. "I did. Now, whether they come or not is anyone's guess. I told Beast not to bring any weapons. Then he fired a crossbow at me. Real special guy you got there, Beauty."

"He's not really a bad person. He's just caught up with the wrong people," Beauty said.

"Beast would be a great recruit," Charming said as he handed a piece of paper to the Scarecrow. "I've made a wish list of some Everafters that would be very useful: the Ice Queen, the Frog Prince, Glinda, the Spider, and Big Hans are just a few. If any one of them shows a hint of coming our way, we need to help make it happen."

"We better get started if we want to make it to the town square on time," Goldilocks said. The previous night's encounter with Henry still seemed to be bothering her. She seemed self-conscious and wouldn't look directly at Sabrina's father.

Mr. Canis agreed. "We should get there early. I don't want to walk through a hostile crowd."

Veronica planted a kiss on Basil's face and turned to give him to Red, who happily agreed to stay behind and look after him. "Be good, little man."

"Give your mommy a hug and say bye-bye," Red told the toddler.

Basil turned and looked up at Veronica apprehensively. Then he wrapped his arms around her leg.

"Bye-bye," he said.

Veronica glowed like she had a string of Christmas lights inside of her.

The group filed out into the woods for what Charming

predicted would be a good two-hour hike. Unfortunately, the ground was a soupy mess from all the rain they'd been getting, and it slowed them down considerably. Someone suggested they all step into Baba Yaga's house for an easier trip, but only Puck thought that was a good idea. It was also unusually chilly, made even colder by the sun-blocking trees. Still, the army marched onward.

Mr. Canis hobbled forward to walk alongside the Grimms. "I don't like this plan," he growled. "We'll be out in the open and vulnerable to all those thugs."

"We've got some of the most powerful witches and fairies in town on our side, Mr. Canis," Sabrina said, "as well as the Hamelins and Beauty. Plus, for brute strength we've got the Three Bears, and Charming is no slouch."

"I can deliver a pretty mean kick to the shins too," Daphne bragged.

"I think you're all entirely too overconfident," Canis growled.

"Don't worry, we've got Puck, who has a variety of, um . . . unique talents," Sabrina said.

Puck stomped forward, interrupting the conversation. "Exactly what am I supposed to do?"

"You're keeping an eye on the girls," Henry explained.

Puck groaned. "I have been in the middle of a hundred wars,

many of which I started myself. Why waste my sword on your rugrats? Can't we just lock them in a playpen until it's over?"

"A playpen?" Sabrina said.

"Yeah, like babies," Puck said, then he stomped to the back of the line.

"He's moody," Morgan said.

"I think it's something in the air," Goldi grumbled.

Finally, the group reached the edge of the downtown business district. The Widow's description of the destruction of the town didn't do it justice. Streetlamp poles had been uprooted and were leaning against trucks, broken electrical wires popped and snapped on the ground like striking cobras, huge slabs of concrete were completely missing from sidewalks and streets, and there was an overpowering smell of burning metal. Worse, as Mr. Canis had feared, the army was late for the meeting. A sea of the Scarlet Hand waited for them at the gazebo. Sabrina and the others had to walk through the hostile crowd to get to the stage. She fully expected a magical attack or the feeling of a blade in her back. Many of the attendees were notorious troublemakers. Beast was there with his daughter, Natalie; as was Mayor Heart, Sheriff Nottingham, Glinda, the Three Blind Mice; Ms. Muffet and her husband, the Spider, as well as their creepy spider-boy, Toby; the White Rabbit, and a large contingent of ogres, imps, trolls, goblins, orcs, leprechauns, and brownies. A beautiful but very pale woman in a long white dress stood out from the crowd. The ground beneath her was a sheet of ice. Worse still were the faces in the crowd that Granny Relda once called friends: Mowgli, Baloo, Jack Pumpkinhead, Tik-Tok, Ozma, Hansel and Gretel, Old King Cole, Little John, and Mother Hubbard, each with a bright red handprint painted on their chests. If there was a silver lining, it was that Mirror and Atticus were nowhere to be seen.

Mayor Heart and Sheriff Nottingham roughly shoved their way to the front of the crowd. Nottingham wore black leather pants and a matching overcoat. Heart was in a ball gown decorated with hearts and lace. Her face was as white as her powder wig, which stood in stark contrast to her bold, garish makeup. Whoever told her that swamp green and bright red would look good on her face was not the queen's friend.

"Say what you've come to say!" Heart barked through her trusty electronic megaphone. "Your bird said it was important and it better be. If you waste our time, I can't guarantee this crowd will not rise up and attack you."

The crowd cheered and laughed. Many shook swords and knobby clubs in the air.

Henry gave Veronica the thumbs-up, and she stepped to the

front of the stage, fully vulnerable to the crowd. Sabrina could feel the panic rising in her throat as she imagined the endless number of attacks that could strike her mother down. They had put themselves at the mercy of a group of villains that wanted to see them dead. What were they thinking?

"May I have your attention?" Veronica said.

The crowd ignored her, so she asked again, with similar results.

Finally, Heart blasted an angry "PIPE DOWN!" which quelled the crowd. "Let her talk! It's the least we can do. She'll be dead by nightfall."

The crowd's second roar of approval infuriated Canis. He clenched his fists and looked ready to attack anyone who might approach, but the mob was not intimidated as they once might have been. For once, Sabrina missed the Big Bad Wolf.

Unfazed, her mother looked out on the crowd. "Thank you for coming. I know that by standing here with us you are putting yourselves at risk, so I won't waste your time. My name is Veronica Grimm. I am not known to many of you. My time in this town was short, but I developed a deep, personal relationship with the Everafters in Manhattan. I was considered an asset to the people of Faerie and to the late King Oberon, who turned to me for counsel. I can be of help to you, as well."

"Can you bring down the barrier?" Chicken Little squawked from the front of the crowd.

Veronica shook her head.

The audience booed loudly. A few bottles were flung at the stage and shattered at Veronica's feet. Pieces flew at Morgan, but Mr. Seven swatted them away. Mordred's hands glowed green and several people in the front of the crowd cried out in fear, so Henry begged him to stop. Mordred reluctantly did what he was asked.

"Don't worry, Grimm. When the crowd gets ugly. I'll be here to save your butt," Puck said to Sabrina. "Like always."

"What's the matter with you? You've been a crybaby for days," Sabrina snapped.

"I'm just bored with saving your life. If you think I'm going to do this after we get married, you can forget it."

"First, we are not getting married, ever. Second, if you're so put out, feel free to stop. I don't need your help."

"Yes, you do!"

"No, I don't!"

"Trust me, you do."

"Trust me, I'm fine. Find something else to do with your precious time. That nose of yours isn't going to pick itself."

"I would love nothing more than to give my nose the attention it deserves, but if I did, you'd be dead within minutes," Puck said. His head suddenly morphed into that of a lion and he roared angrily.

Sabrina roared back, though it lacked the ferocity. It sounded ridiculous, but what was worse was the realization that the entire crowd was watching her and Puck. She had never been so embarrassed. Puck had an almost magical ability to get her to make a fool of herself. He could always find something that she was sensitive about, sometimes something she didn't even know bothered her, and then poke at it until it made her crazy.

"Ahem," Veronica said, then turned her attention back to the crowd. "We have come here with an invitation. Join our cause."

There was a moment of silence and then an uproarious laugh so loud it hurt Sabrina's ears.

Veronica waited patiently until they calmed. "We know there are those among you who have been pressured through violence or threats to join the Hand. We know that you aren't sure where you can turn. We have a place where you can be safe. You don't have to live in fear any longer!"

More bottles came crashing onto the little stage until Mordred had to step forward and cast a shield to protect the group.

"The Master has turned his back on you," Veronica shouted over the bedlam.

"Who are you to question the Master?" Heart barked into her megaphone.

"Because he is a liar," a voice said, and the crowd grew deathly quiet. Sabrina turned and saw her uncle Jake climbing the steps to the gazebo. She looked to her father for an explanation, but he seemed just as confused.

"Watch your tongue, Grimm, or my blade will remove it," Nottingham raged.

"Two years ago, your savior kidnapped my brother and his wife, then cast a sleeping spell on them. Veronica was pregnant, and while they slept a baby grew inside her. Once that baby was born, the Master stole him for a sick and perverted purpose. He wanted to put his spirit inside the child. Now, why would he do that?"

"If you must know, he wanted to escape the barrier in the body of a human being," Heart snapped.

Jake smiled sympathetically. "How would that help you?"

Heart stammered as if the question had never crossed her mind.

"Once he was on the other side, he could find a way to lower this magical cage your family built!" Nottingham howled.

"Once he's on the other side? Nottingham, you're a smart man. How could he turn it off from the outside?" Jake said to the crowd. "There's no magic button on the other side. If he can't lower it on this side, he can't lower it on the other. He was playing you all for fools. He's not going to set you free. He's going to betray you the same way he did my family."

"He told me himself he had no plans of freeing you," Sabrina said. "You would be too much competition for power."

"You lie!" Nottingham growled. "The Master will free us all, and together we will wipe out your foul, inferior race. This world will belong to Everafters, as it was intended."

"I know you don't all believe that," Jake said, scanning the crowd. "I can see it in your faces. You know that what is happening here is wrong, but you're too afraid to stand up to this mob. You can stop. I am extending the olive branch myself. Join us."

Sabrina was flabbergasted. What happened to her uncle's broken heart and anger? Where was his hostility and promises of revenge? Even Heart was speechless.

Nottingham took the opportunity to speak. "Don't listen to this liar. He wants to keep us in this cage like dogs! We can't know the Master's plan, but he deserves our loyalty for opening our eyes to the truth! For too long our destiny has not been our own, and there is no one to blame but this family who now stands here begging us not to kill them. They know they cannot beat us this time, so they come arrogantly waving the white flag for truce. Well, they should be waving it in surrender."

"The Master said he was all-powerful," the White Rabbit cried. "He said if we helped him with his plans, he would free us. But we are still trapped here."

Nottingham seethed. "Then perhaps he needs some more help! The spell that keeps us here says that when the last Grimm dies the barrier falls. If we kill them now, we'll be free."

The crowd grew louder and more excited.

"Except that killing us won't get you what you want at all, you moron," Jake said. "The Master is inside my mother's body. He thought he could just walk out of town but it hasn't happened. He can't escape any more than you can—in fact, he's making it worse on you because now he's a Grimm too. Even if you were to kill everyone in my family, there would still be one Grimm alive—and who here is going to kill your all-powerful savior?"

The crowd grew silent.

"Now you're getting it," Jake continued. "The Master can't get his freedom and he can't give it to you, either. There's only one person in the world who will give you your freedom. Me!"

"You?" the Frog Prince cried.

"Fifteen years ago I tried to do my brother a favor by letting his then-girlfriend out of this town. I snuck into Baba Yaga's house, found Wilhelm's spell in one of her books, and stole it. Then I turned the magic off long enough for her to leave."

"It's true," Goldilocks said as she stepped forward. "He let me out. I lived outside of the town for fifteen years before I came back to help save Henry and his wife."

Jake reached into his pants pocket and took out a well-worn piece of paper. He unfolded it gently and held it up so everyone could see it. "Turn your back on the Master, help us save my mother, and I will free you. This is the spell to lower the barrier."

"Jake, what are you doing?" Mr. Canis said. "You'll ruin everything."

"What do you mean?" Sabrina asked the old man, but he brushed her off in frustration.

Nottingham took the megaphone and was ready to hurl more insults, but Heart snatched it back. "Sheriff, let him talk," the queen said.

Sabrina looked out on the crowd. The angry faces were fading. People were considering Jake's offer.

"We will join you," said voices from below. The Three Blind Mice pushed forward, their canes clicking on the ground as they walked. As they climbed the stairs, a number of threats were hurled at them.

"Traitors!"

"You will pay for betraying the Master."

"You have signed your own death warrants!"

"Wonderful!" Veronica cried, ignoring their anger. "Who else?"

"Can you protect me?" a lion said, though he was bigger than any lion Sabrina had ever seen in the Bronx Zoo. This one was as tall as a horse and wore a shiny gold medal with the word COURAGE around his neck.

"Ab . . . abso-solutely," Sabrina sputtered before the gigantic beast.

"Then I'll come with you," the lion replied as he leaped onto the stage.

"Good to have you, old friend," the Scarecrow said.

Sabrina shook her head in disbelief. Had her father been right? Would the Everafters do the right thing if presented with the opportunity?

"Please, James," Beauty said to her husband, who stood defiantly within the crowd with his overgrown daughter, Natalie, at his side. "Bring our daughter and come up here and join us."

Beast shook his head and Natalie looked at her mother with disgust. Poor Beauty's face fell.

Several goblins and a troll pushed through the crowd on their way to the stage before Nottingham stopped them.

"You fools! This is the Grimm family," Nottingham said. "They can't be trusted."

For a moment, Mayor Heart looked as if she was ready to take Jake's extended hand, but Nottingham pushed past her. He had his dagger in hand and murder in his eyes. "I'll put a stop to these lies for good!"

Charming pulled his own sword and waved it in Nottingham's face. The sheriff stumbled backward, fearful of the prince's deadly blade.

"My quarrel is with them!" Nottingham shouted.

"Then your quarrel is with all of us," Charming said. "This man extends his hand in peace and you move to slice it open? You disgust me."

"I will kill you, Charming," Nottingham seethed.

"Is there courage in those words, Sheriff? Perhaps you should prove it."

"If it's courage you seek, little brother, I have it in spades," said a strange, deep voice.

"Who said that?" Charming asked, scanning the crowd. Sabrina did the same and spotted the mane of greasy red hair moving through the mob.

"Atticus," Sabrina gasped. She turned to Bunny, who stepped in front of her daughter. Mr. Seven joined her.

"Don't you remember me, brother?" Atticus cried. "You destroyed my family and stole my rightful seat at our father's side. But your most wicked of crimes was stealing my wife while I have been away."

"I am not your brother, and I have never stolen any woman," Charming said.

Atticus leaped onto the gazebo. He stared at Charming for a long time, his face contorted with amused hatred. For the first time, Sabrina could see the resemblance between the two men. They had the same eyes and jawlines. Their cheekbones were identical, as were their lips, but while all of Charming's features combined to make him handsome, Atticus's features were twisted and rough, making a person want to look away in disgust. Charming stared back, mouth agape, at the strange man. Atticus reached for his sword but then seemed to think better of it. Instead, he turned to the crowd. "The Master has sent me with a message, people. He is disappointed in you and wants you to know that being here, speaking to your jailors, is treachery. Turn away from the Grimms or blood will spill."

"Who in the blue blazes are you?" Charming asked.

"Who am I?" Atticus said, then snatched Snow White by the wrist and pulled her close to him. "Surely you remember me, my dearest. Surely you remember your husband?"

"Let go of me," she said. "You've lost your mind."

Charming grabbed Atticus's hand and pulled it away from his love. "Don't touch her."

Atticus laughed, then with a burst of ferocity, he slugged Charming in the nose. The prince fell backward, blood spraying across his face. Atticus drew his long silver sword and hovered over the fallen man, looking to attack, but Snow stepped between the two men.

"You've made a mistake. This man is not your brother," she said, but Atticus slapped her and she fell to the ground next to Charming.

"You filthy harlot!" he bellowed at her. "You do not argue with me. You are my property!"

"That's enough!" Mr. Seven said.

"No, it's not enough. Not enough at all," Atticus said, and with all the effort one might make to cut a pat of butter for some toast, he stabbed Mr. Seven in the belly. The sword slid through him and out his back. Then with an irritated jerk, Atticus pulled his weapon free.

"Nooo!" Morgan le Fay cried. As Mr. Seven fell to the ground, she raised her hands above her head. A ball of vicious red energy formed in between them.

"Morgan, no! Save the magic for Seven! Get him out of here," Henry barked, taking control. He raced forward and clocked Atticus in the face. The villain staggered, but only temporarily. His sword was in the air sailing toward Henry's head when a blast of white energy slammed into Atticus. Sabrina turned to find the source.

"I told you once I would kill you if you touched my daughter again," the Wicked Queen said. Her hands were growing red with ancient arcana. She loosed the power on Atticus and it sent him flying through the crowd, knocking people aside as if he were a runaway truck.

Sabrina rushed to Morgan's side. The poor woman hovered over her husband, sobbing. Sabrina forced Morgan to look into her face. "Find Nurse Sprat!"

Morgan looked bewildered.

"Nurse Sprat can help him," Sabrina said. Morgan nodded and went to find the nurse.

Goldi and the Three Bears rushed forward. "What should we do?"

"Crowd control," Sabrina said. "Find Beauty and try to calm down this mob before anyone else gets hurt."

Goldi crawled onto Poppa Bear's back and they charged into the madness.

"Puck!" Sabrina cried. "Get Canis and the rest of my family to safety."

"Fine, but just so you know, you're not the boss of me."

"What should we do?" a voice said. Sabrina turned and found the Frog Prince, his wife, and their daughter, Bella—all members of the Scarlet Hand and bitter enemies of the Grimms. At first Sabrina stumbled back, but then realized they were sincere.

"You're joining us?" Sabrina asked.

The Frog Prince nodded. "If you'll have us."

"Fine! Help anyone who is in danger of being trampled by this crowd."

Bella and her father sprang into the air and leaped around the crowd, hoisting people off their feet and planting them safely on the outskirts of the melee. Sabrina had no idea that a person could jump so high, but she reminded herself that father and daughter were part amphibian. Now she knew why Charming put them on his wish list.

When she turned to see if there was anyone else in need of help, she saw Nottingham hovering over her with his twisted knife and even more twisted smile. Mayor Heart stood by his side, watching the action with bright eyes.

"One Grimm down, six to go," he hissed as he thrust the blade at Sabrina.

"Not today, you psycho," Uncle Jake said, punching the villain in the belly and then kneeing him in the face. Nottingham fell over, gasping for air. His dagger slipped from his grasp and Uncle Jake snatched it up. He stood over the struggling villain, his hand squeezing the dagger's handle until his knuckles were white. For a moment, the dark, tragic expression he had worn for many days returned. Sabrina was sure he was going to kill Nottingham. Then, with a flick of his hand, he threw the blade to the ground.

"The offer still stands, Ms. Heart," he said, extending his hand to the former queen. "The Master is no friend of yours. I'm not asking you to do the right thing. Just do the right thing for you."

Heart eyed him with curiosity but did not take his hand. Instead, she snapped up her megaphone and dashed back into the mob.

An explosion shook the gazebo, nearly knocking everyone to the ground. The Wicked Queen's battle with Atticus had escalated. Bunny blasted him repeatedly, and he slammed into the mob like he had been fired from a cannon. He flew past Sabrina and smashed into the gazebo behind her, tilting it off its foundation. But within moments he was on his feet, chuckling as if he were being attacked by a child.

"Bad news, Your Majesty. That book of fairy tales you tried to bury me in was full of magical weapons. I managed to acquire a few in the last four hundred years. Take this suit of armor I wear—enchanted by Merlin himself. As long as I wear it, no human can kill me. Now put away your card tricks. The Master has need of me, and I'd like to kill my traitorous brother while I have some free time."

The Wicked Queen floated over the crowd. The whites of her eyes were swallowed by blackness and tiny bolts of lightning buzzed around her body. "Card tricks? You don't get a name like the Wicked Queen doing card tricks."

She blasted him with a green rocket that sent him slamming into the ground once more. Still, Atticus recovered quickly.

"Woman!" he said. "If you could kill, me you would have done it long ago, instead of locking me in that book."

"Mother, what is he talking about?" Snow asked.

"Not now, honey, the grown-ups are talking," Bunny said.

The queen stretched out her arms. She shouted "Gladius!" and a flaming sword appeared in her hands. She struck at Atticus. He smirked and then launched into a savage and unrestrained attack. He slashed with his blade, forcing the floating witch farther and farther back. Bunny retaliated, her sword clanging against Atticus's blade. Each strike sent red-hot sparks flying in all directions.

"I need a sword!" Charming said. His own was lost in the fighting.

"Coming right up," Daphne said, and slipped her hand into her pocket. She took out the fairy godmother wand once more, and with a flick of her wrist Charming was in a full suit of armor with a sword in hand.

"I don't need the armor!" Charming groused, pulling off the helmet and tossing it aside.

"Sorry, it goes with the outfit," Daphne said.

Charming charged into the fight, slashing at Atticus.

"So the baby brother dares to pick up his sword?" Atticus said. "How you can defend your actions is beyond belief. The arrogance!"

Swords flew.

One flashed past Sabrina's head and she felt it slice off a chunk of her hair. A second later she and Daphne were whisked into the sky. Puck had saved their lives again.

"I rest my case!" Puck said.

"Fine. I sometimes need your help," Sabrina said.

"Sometimes?"

"Don't push it, bug face," Sabrina said. "There's my mom and dad. Put us down there."

Once they were on the ground, Henry and Veronica pulled them into their arms. Veronica's face was wet with tears and seeing her daughters sent a fresh flood down her cheeks. "Let's get out of here now, kids."

"But what about Charming and Ms. Lancaster?" Sabrina said, turning back to watch more of the brutal fighting.

"They can handle themselves," Henry said.

Goldilocks rushed to the family. "Come quick. It's Mr. Seven."

Henry, Veronica, Sabrina, and Daphne followed the woman through the mob. A crowd was gathered in an alley near the old bicycle shop. Mr. Seven lay in the center, Nurse Sprat hovering over him. He looked pale and tired. A bandage was wrapped around his belly, but a red stain was spreading through it. Morgan le Fay sat on the ground next to him, holding his hand. Seven leaned up with some pain and kissed his wife. "I love you, Morgan."

The witch held on to his hand and would not let go. "I love you too! But everything is going to be fine. We'll just postpone the honeymoon."

"Tell Mordred I want him to look after you," he said.

"You're going to look after me, darling. That's your job," she said.

Sabrina couldn't stop staring at the blood. There was so much.

"I tried everything I can," Nurse Sprat said. "Nothing is helping."

Snow White rounded the corner. The beautiful teacher knelt beside Seven. "Take care of Charming, Snow," the little man said. "He needs you."

"I will," Snow said through tears.

The queen and Charming joined the group moments later, exhausted from their fight. Snow jumped to her feet and wrapped her arms around her boyfriend.

"We managed to fight him off," Bunny said, "but he'll be back. We should get our friend here back to your castle."

Nurse Sprat shook her head.

Charming stepped forward and knelt down next to his companion. "Nonsense! If you think dying gives you an excuse to tell me what you really think of me, you can save it, Seven. You're going to recover and it will be very awkward later."

"William Charming, you are my friend," the little man said.

Charming's face turned red. He fought back tears with as much force as he must have used to fight back dragons.

"It has been my pleasure to look after you," Seven continued.

"Is that what you've been doing?" Charming said with a chuckle.

Sabrina watched Seven lock eyes with the queen. "I've done everything I could to protect him from the truth, Your Majesty," Mr. Seven said. "But it seems it has come nonetheless."

"What are you talking about?" the prince said.

The queen sighed and leaned over Mr. Seven. "You have done your job well. You were the right choice," the queen said.

"I appreciate your saying so, Bunny," Seven said, then looked at his wife. "You are the most beautiful thing I have ever seen, Morgan. And I have been alive a long, long time. I'll be waiting for you."

And for the last time in his life a grin spread across his face. And then he was gone.

Those gathered wept for their friend. Morgan shrieked and Mordred did his best to comfort her. Charming took his friend's hand and quietly prayed. And Sabrina and Daphne cried until there were no more tears to spare.

When Snow could finally speak, she stepped over to her mother and seized her hand. "You are going to tell me the truth."

The queen nodded. "Yes, I am."

7

ctober 18 (part 2)

We buried Mr. Seven by candlelight next to Briar Rose's grave. Morgan sobbed and her son struggled to keep her on her feet. Their love was short but intense and I feel very bad for her. It doesn't help that the decorations from the wedding are still hanging on everything. No one has the heart to take them down.

Everyone said a few words about Mr. Seven, even Daphne, who cried and cried. Everyone, that is, except Uncle Jake. The little man's death seemed to open a fresh wound inside him. He stood in the back of the crowd, more upset than ever.

Charming spoke of his old friend. I wish I had a digital recorder so I could play it back and listen again, but I'll write down what I remember. He said, "Seven was a giant of patience and consideration. He was as quick with a smile as he was with a caring ear. He took *care of me for many years and I am admittedly a difficult man to handle. He was my friend, my counsel, and at times my brother. I hardly imagine I could have become a man without him. Good-bye, old friend."*

When it was all over, the Wicked Queen took one of the white roses from Briar's plot and planted it on Seven's grave. As happened when they buried Briar, it sprouted hundreds of flowers, which bloomed in the moonlight.

Everyone is miserable, but more than that they are afraid. No one ever thinks that a friend will die, especially at the hands of someone like Atticus. Bunny has promised her daughter and the prince answers about Atticus, and she's asked Daphne, Puck, and me to help since we had a run-in with him in the Book of Everafter. I wonder how they will take it.

"He's your brother," Bunny said to the prince.

"That's impossible!" Charming said. "I'm an only child."

"Because that's how I wanted you to be," she replied.

Sabrina watched the confusion on Charming's face. He stood up and paced around the log cabin. Snow stood back in confused paralysis.

Bunny continued. "Just listen, please. What I'm going to tell you is complicated and you need to pay attention. This is the story of your life, William—the story of your real life. A long time ago, your parents, King Thorne and Queen Catherine, had two children—"

Charming jumped forward. "Wait—"

"Shut up!" Bunny snapped. "The youngest was you, and the firstborn was a boy named Atticus, and he was the heir to your father's throne. Your father arranged a marriage between his kingdom and my own. It was a very common practice at the time and helped grow wealth and power. Snow was our princess."

"But I grew up in a village," Snow argued.

Bunny sighed impatiently. "What I didn't know when I consented to this marriage was that Atticus was cruel and vicious. Royalty must often find themselves in loveless marriages, but Atticus was different. I soon learned he was known for killing stable hands and torturing kitchen maids, but when he turned his rage on my daughter, I got involved. William, I went to your father and begged him to stop your brother, but he refused to see the wickedness in his child. While he dithered like a fool, Atticus abused Snow in unspeakable ways. So I took matters into my own hands. I went to the Book of Everafter."

"The book of what?" Charming said. Both he and Snow looked at the witch like she had lost her mind. "What is this bedtime story you are spinning, Bunny?"

Sabrina could tell the witch was losing patience with their interruptions. "The Book of Everafter is a magical collection of stories that was stored in the Hall of Wonders," Sabrina explained. "Every fairy tale from Little Red Riding Hood to, well, the two of you is written in its pages."

"We were inside it," Daphne said, hefting the big book into Charming's lap. "It was kooky."

"Inside it?" Charming said. He cracked it open and flipped through the pages.

"She said it was magic," Puck said.

"Yes, a person can go into the stories if they want to—"

"And they can change them," Bunny finished for Sabrina. "The nature of the book allows you to change the story the way you wish it would have happened. And if the change sticks—if the Editor doesn't change it back—it becomes history, and the changes affect the real people those stories are based upon. It even changes how the world remembers the story. In order to save my daughter, I changed her story."

"What does that have to do with us and that lunatic who killed Seven?" Charming asked.

"The world knows Snow's story as Snow White and the Seven Dwarfs, but the original tale was called The Murderous Blood Prince."

Snow gasped. "I assume that didn't have a happy ending."

"How did you fix it, Bunny?" Charming asked. His voice was stern and furious.

"I erased Atticus from the story—entirely."

"Well, *erased* isn't the right word," Sabrina said. "More like edited."

"Yes, that's right. I rewrote him—or at least I tried. I went through his story and tried to write events that would destroy the evil in him and make him a hero instead, but nothing I did worked. I wrote a mentor into the story that he could learn great things from, but he slit the man's throat. I gave him a loving fairy godmother who looked after him, and he pulled her wings off and threw her into a fire. Nothing I did could change the darkness inside him and nothing I did stopped him from murdering my daughter, so I did what writers call a page-one rewrite. I got rid of the original story and started over."

"Well, if you got rid of him, then who was that man out there?" Charming demanded.

"Billy, please calm down," Snow said.

"I will not calm down. My best friend was just murdered and your mother has something to do with it. Haven't you brought enough pain on us, Bunny? First the poisoned apples and now this!"

"I deserve some of your condemnation, but I ask you to just let me finish before you throw any more insults at me."

Charming snarled and roughly sank back into his chair.

"So I started my daughter's story all over again, but even that was difficult. What happened to Snow with Atticus was so intense that echoes of it invaded the new story. I tried a variety of approaches. I wrote a version with your sister, Rose, where you spent the entire story dancing on flowers. I gave you a kingdom made of starlight. I even tried to make it simple and have you be a maiden on a sea voyage. But each change I made still ended in tragedy. No matter what I did, the book would not allow it to work. Each time, something horrible and unexpected would happen to you. It was as if the book were demanding that you experience pain. And then I realized what you needed was a defender—someone to rescue you from these problems—so I took Atticus's brother, William, and made him into a proper suitor for my daughter."

"Made me?" Charming said.

"Yes. I had to edit you, as well. You weren't what anyone would call princely at the time," Bunny said.

Charming looked at her incredulously.

"Actually, you were a bit of a playboy, and you had a tendency to spend too much money and drink a little too much wine, but you had a good heart. You were someone I could work with. So with a few simple words, I wrote you into the story and made you into a dashing hero on a white horse. I wrote you so that you were regal and dignified, romantic and strong. I turned you into the perfect man for my daughter, and yet that was still not enough. Tragedy happened again and again and again until I figured out what the problem was—Atticus was still in the story—no more than a hint, an echo—but he was there, hovering in the margins, subtly influencing the outcome.

"And the answer came to me as clear as day. The story demanded a villain. It wanted something to replace Atticus. I don't pretend to understand how it works. I just know that's what it needed. But I needed a villain I could control—someone who wasn't bent on killing my daughter—so I did what any mother who loved her child would do to save her life. I wrote myself into the book as the Wicked Queen. As the story's dark enchantress, I could manage the tragedy and control the pain. And it worked! The book was satisfied—even when my inventions were ridiculous. I mean, what kind of witch gets upset because her daughter is better looking? And that ridiculous poisoned apple—ha! Putting you to sleep so that you could be woken by a handsome prince and live happily ever after—*how diabolical*! But it didn't matter. The story had its villain, its dashing hero, and a main character that experienced tragedy, and I thought the horror of Atticus Charming was behind us."

"Except you lost your daughter," Snow said. "I have hated you for hundreds of years."

Bunny nodded. "A small price to pay to keep you safe."

Snow's eyes were distant, as if she were looking back over the course of her entire life. She reached out and took her mother's hand.

Charming, however, was clearly not ready for a family reunion. "What am I?" he whispered.

"I'm not sure what you're asking," Bunny said.

"I'm not real. I'm your creation. You twisted me into whatever suited your needs. Nothing that I am is me. I'm—I'm . . . I'm a fairy tale!"

"Billy, that's not true," Snow said.

"And how does Seven play into this?" Charming demanded.

"For some reason, the dwarfs knew the world had changed. They confronted me and demanded that I change it back. Mr. Seven was the only one who saw my point of view. He realized what I had done was for the better. It created a terrible rift between him and the others, but he stood his ground. He agreed to look after you and Snow and make sure our secret remained that way. He was also there to keep an eye out for Atticus, in case he found a way to return. And lastly, he was there to keep you on the path of being a good person, especially when my daughter refused to marry you. I was worried how you might react when life got in the way of the qualities I wanted you to have."

"Do I even love your daughter?" Charming said. "Or is that one of your inventions?"

"William—"

"It explains an awful lot, woman! Why I couldn't get over Snow after hundreds of years apart, my failed marriages, my obsession with rebuilding a kingdom for us to live in. I made this castle because of that desire. Tell me if it's real or not!"

Bunny looked to the floor. "I can't say whether it's real or not, William. All I can say is it's what I wanted."

Charming got up from his chair and stormed out of the cabin.

"Billy!" Snow chased after him, and Sabrina and Daphne followed. They watched him stomp across the courtyard toward the front gate. "Where are you going?"

"I don't know," he said. He turned to look at the castle he had built. There was disgust in his eyes.

"You can't leave," Sabrina said. "These people need you. You're their leader."

"They'll find another!"

"And what about me?" Snow said.

While the drawbridge lowered, Charming turned to her. "Your mother invented me to be the perfect man for you, Snow. She made me love you. She made me heroic. She made me up. I can't trust my feelings for you. I can't trust why I'm here. I don't know who I am."

"You're William Charming!" Snow said.

"And who is he?"

"He's the man I love!" she said.

"You're in love with a person who doesn't exist. In a town full of people who aren't supposed to be real, I'm the one that's a fantasy." Charming walked through the iron gate and across the bridge. Everyone followed him, but he was soon swallowed by the forest and vanished.

Snow raced to the edge of the woods and begged him to return, but he was gone.

• • •

The cold misty dampness returned with the morning. The gray sky hung low and felt binding, like an outgrown jacket. It was the kind of weather that made bones ache, and it was the absolute wrong weather for a group of people suffering from death and insecurity.

The Pied Piper slouched on a bench sipping from a mug of

coffee. Nurse Sprat was too tired to say good morning. Everyone moved slowly, as if each step were painful. Even Daphne looked puffy-eyed and tired, and she could usually sleep through anything.

If there was any good news, it was that Mordred and the Pigs had finished the castle, and aside from a few evil doors that slammed in people's faces, it was ready for everyone to move in. Finding rooms to fit everyone's tastes kept people busy and their minds off of Seven's death and Charming's departure, but as soon as everyone had gathered in the castle's dining hall, the sour mood returned.

Gepetto stood. "I've decided to dismantle the cabins," he announced to the crowd. "This is a big castle, and we're going to need wood to keep it warm, especially since cold weather is coming. Right after breakfast we can get started."

"We can't stay here, Gepetto," the Pied Piper said. "We need to find a place to hide."

"Hide?" the Three Blind Mice cried.

"You said we would be safe here if we joined you," the Frog Prince said.

"And you would have been if there were a few hundred more of you," the Scarecrow said. "Our plan didn't work. We don't have the numbers to go up against Mirror or that Atticus lunatic."

"Even Charming has left, and he's the most stubborn man I've ever met," Nurse Sprat said. "This was his plan—this whole army—and now he's gone. Now we're being led by a couple of little girls."

Mallobarb agreed. "Maybe Charming has the right idea. Maybe we should just get lost."

"He'll come back," Goldi said.

"And what if he doesn't?" the Cowardly Lion growled. "I took a big risk turning my back on the Hand. When they find us, they will be especially hard on those who betrayed the Master."

Puck kicked Sabrina's leg under the table. "Say something," he muttered under his breath.

Sabrina shrugged. "What am I going to say?"

"They need a pep talk," he shot back. "You're their leader."

"I think they're right."

Puck slammed his hand down on the tabletop and it rattled as if it had been struck with a sledgehammer. Everyone turned their attention to him as he leaped from his chair. "It doesn't matter if he comes back. We don't need him. Most of you were there when the mirrors spoke. Sabrina and Daphne are going to fix this, so stop your bellyaching."

The crowd rolled their eyes and muttered amongst themselves. Puck looked ready to continue his speech, until they heard a commotion from outside the wall. Everyone raced outside as the drawbridge descended and a crowd of Everafters marched into the courtyard, led by Uncle Jake.

"More Scarlet Hand members have joined the cause," Uncle Jake crowed. "It seems as if the plan is working."

But Sabrina and the others were hardly excited by the new recruits. Jake had brought Cinderella and her husband Tom, both quite elderly, as well as their three mice servants. Behind them was Chicken Little, a potbellied robot from Oz named Tik-Tok, a gigantic caterpillar, and the Cheshire Cat from Wonderland, followed by the incredibly thin Ichabod Crane, Rapunzel, fewer than a dozen Munchkins—all well on in years—the Old Woman Who Lived in a Shoe, and a hundred dirty-faced, shoeless children. As the drawbridge began to close, Rip Van Winkle hobbled in on his cane, nearly tripping over his beard. Sabrina's heart sank. Looking at them, she felt the pressure of the prophecy even more.

"We need to prepare for war. Who's with me?" Puck continued, but no one responded. They were just as disheartened as Sabrina.

"This army gets more and more pathetic by the second," Pinocchio grumbled.

While the new recruits were welcomed, Puck pulled Sabrina and Daphne aside.

"It's time to tell everyone your plan," Puck said.

"We don't have a plan," Sabrina said.

"Duh! But they don't need to know that. Just fake it until you make it! That's what I do. Most of the time I have no idea what I'm doing, but if I told everyone, they wouldn't put their faith in me."

"Actually, we are all pretty sure you never know what you're doing," Daphne said.

"Listen, these people need heroes, and whether it makes any sense or not, you're it," Puck preached. "As a ruthless villain I have had my fair share of run-ins with do-gooders and I've noticed a thing or two about them. They aren't confused or unsure of themselves. You have to be confident. If someone asks you a question, answer them—even if you don't know what you are talking about! The secret is to sound sure! If they say, 'Hey, losers, is the moon made out of cheese?' The two of you say, 'It is! I've been there! I ate part of the Sea of Tranquillity and it was delicious.'"

"So being a hero is being a good liar?" Daphne said.

Puck nodded. "Now you're getting it!"

"I'm not going to lie. Let one of the grown-ups speak," Sabrina said. "They don't want to hear from us."

Puck looked angry enough to pull out his own hair. "I can't

believe you. You know what? I'm seriously reconsidering marrying you." His wings popped out of his back and he was in the air and gone before Sabrina could once again inform him that they were never getting married.

Gepetto joined Pinocchio near Sabrina. "We should prepare some rooms for them, son."

Pinocchio rolled his eyes. "Papa, now that the army is growing, maybe we can assign them my chores. Many of them can split wood and heat water for washing."

"Everyone works," the old man said, looking at his son with disappointment. "That's what being a grown-up is about. You want to become a man, correct?"

"But are there not many different types of work?" Pinocchio argued, his words getting shriller with each passing second. "Should those with a genius-level intellect dig ditches alongside the ancient and feeble-minded? I should be working on things that take advantage of my learning and world experience. Mr. Canis is really quite useless in the fight. He could make beds and—"

Gepetto snatched his son by one of his ears and dragged him toward the castle.

Unfortunately, Mr. Canis and Red had heard every insulting word.

"Come along, little one," Mr. Canis said to the little girl with a sigh of surrender. "There are beds to make."

Red slipped her hand into his. He looked down at it but did not pull away. Together they wandered toward the castle.

• • •

As the day passed, more recruits trickled in to join the cause. Among the most welcome were Robin Hood and his band of Merry Men, which included Will Scarlet, Little John, and Friar Tuck. King Arthur and his knights soon followed, with news that the Scarlet Hand was suffering from a wave of paranoia. Both the Merry Men and the knights were concerned that they would soon be exposed as spies. Making a break for the castle seemed to be the best strategy.

As the recruits were initiated into the camp and given rooms in the castle, the Scarecrow came to find Sabrina and Daphne. "Ready for your next class?"

Sabrina groaned. "You're not going to teach us how to fight, are you?"

The Scarecrow shook his head. "Not at all. I'm going to teach you military strategy. You may not know this, but I was once the emperor of Oz. I had to defend the city from attacks."

"How did that go?" Daphne asked.

"I was overthrown by an army of little girls with knitting

needles," the Scarecrow admitted. "But right now, I'm the best you've got."

They went into the Hall of Wonders and then into the mirror room. Inside, the guardians were waiting.

"All right, girls, take a seat. I've got to give you ten thousand years of war in an afternoon," the Scarecrow said. He turned to the mirrors and smiled. "I'm going to give you guys a little bit of a mental workout."

Sabrina and Daphne listened as the straw man used the mirrors to illustrate important military campaigns throughout the history of the world. Each mirror became an audiovisual display, showing portraits of battlefields and grand paintings of military leaders.

Sabrina learned of Gustavus Adolphus's brilliant invasion of Northern Germany in 1630 and how his combination of artillery, soldiers, and horses became the template for most modern war strategies. He even turned Sweden into one of the most powerful nations in the world. The Scarecrow talked about Caesar's invasion of Gaul in 58 BC, which was the first domino to fall in Rome's conquest of the globe. A painting of Genghis Khan appeared in the mirrors as the Scarecrow lectured about the Mongol Invasion of China in 1218. Sabrina learned the strategies of leaders like Alexander the Great, Frederick the Great, Hannibal, and Napoleon.

Then the Scarecrow discussed how small groups of soldiers had managed to defeat huge armies. He pointed out that three hundred Spartans beat back thousands during the Battle of Thermopylae in 480 BC by bottlenecking the army into a small space. He showed how Custer's army was brought down at the Battle of the Little Bighorn by a small number of Indians who drove them into a canyon. He finished his lecture for the night with the American Revolutionary War, in which the military fought off a much bigger invading force by using the terrain to their advantage. By the time he was finished Sabrina's head was so filled with facts she thought her brain was at war with itself.

"Any questions?" the Scarecrow asked.

Just then, the door flew open and a group of men pushed their way inside. The first was King Arthur, followed by Sir Galahad, then Sir Lancelot, Sir Kay, Sir Gawain, and a dozen other sirs. Then Robin Hood, Little John, and Will Scarlet made their way in. They argued noisily as they jockeyed to be at the front of the parade.

"We were told that there is war planning going on in here," King Arthur said.

"Not at all," the Scarecrow said, but he was ignored.

"We demand to participate!" Robin Hood shouted.

Henry pushed his way into the crowded room. "What is this about?" Henry demanded.

"You have placed the fate of this army in the hands of little girls!" Sir Lancelot roared. "Now we're told they're in this room plotting strategy."

"It's madness!" Little John said.

"What can children know about planning a battle?" Sir Kay asked.

"Send them away and we'll take over," King Arthur said.

The guardians of the mirrors appeared. Arden, the beauty with deer antlers, shook her head. "These little girls will save the world, gentlemen. It is prophecy."

King Arthur's face turned beet red. "This is no game, witch! We know what the Master is capable of, and no mere child is going to lead the charge against him and his Hand."

"Arthur, you're not needed in here," Henry said.

"Your family is filled with insolent whelps," Arthur said. "You all believe you know better. You all think you're so wise. Well, look around you, Henry. How are your big ideas working out for you now?"

Henry stepped up to Arthur until they were nearly nose to nose. "I said go."

"Dad, let them stay," Sabrina said. "Let them all stay. He's right. We don't know what we're doing. If anyone in the camp has experience in combat, I need to know about it. I think Arthur and Robin and their men could be a big help."

"Then there is an ounce of sense in this family after all," Arthur said, then turned to the mirrors. "I need to see maps of the town!"

His request magically materialized.

"Whatever you were planning on doing, forget it. It's obvious what you should do. We need to attack in the very center of town with something big and shocking. When the rest of Hand's goons hear about it, they will come running. When they do, we'll be ready for them. We'll surround the town, cram them all into a small space, and pick them off one by one. Henry, take your girls. Robin and our men will let you know when the details of the plan are ready to be announced."

Sabrina, Daphne, and Henry left the Scarecrow behind and stepped into the Hall of Wonders. Outside the door they found Pinocchio sitting with his back to the wall.

"They're crazy," Pinocchio said. "Their plan is pure drivel. I've heard better plans for going to the bathroom."

"And you can do better?" Sabrina said.

"Of course I can," Pinocchio said. "Anyone who has ever read a book of military history can tell you it's better to stay hidden and in small groups. You should surprise them and capture them one by one. It's very similar to the strategy of General Marion during the American Revolutionary War. They called him the Swamp Fox because his soldiers attacked from within the swamps of South Carolina, then sank back—"

"And we should trust that you have our best interests at heart because . . . ?" Sabrina said.

Pinocchio's face turned red, but instead of lashing out he got to his feet. "Well, I tried," he said, then walked toward the portal.

Sabrina felt a little guilty for her attitude, but at the same time, could she really trust Pinocchio? His past was a distraction she didn't need. Besides, Arthur and Robin Hood were leaders. They knew better than a couple of little kids. Just having them in discussing the plan gave her a sense of security. No, she was right. The army needed the smartest people devising the best plans.

She and her sister went back to their room in the castle to wait. The discussion went through the night and into the morning, but Sabrina was too anxious to sleep. Instead, she paced the room while Elvis watched from beneath a blanket on the bed he shared with Daphne. The Scarecrow came to them in the morning and led them back to the mirror room, where they were told that Robin Hood's plan was considered the best of several approaches. She didn't understand most of it, but she didn't have to. She had no physical role in the actual battle. All she had to do was put her stamp of approval on it and the men would take care of the rest.

After breakfast she gathered her army and announced that on that very night they would engage the Scarlet Hand in the middle of the town square. Then she turned over the conversation to King Arthur, who explained the plan in finer detail. Sabrina marveled at his command of the crowd. Like Charming, he had a natural charisma that made people want to follow him. She saw the same thing in Robin Hood and felt herself lucky to have two experienced people helping her with her destiny.

When Arthur finished, Sabrina asked everyone to get as much rest as they could, but that at dinnertime they should meet in the yard with whatever weapons they had. She watched the crowd disperse—some faces filled with eagerness, and others with dread. And then there was only Puck, who stood staring at her, arms crossed, with a face full of disgust.

"What?"

Puck rolled his eyes. "Would you let me know exactly when it's my time to come and rescue you from this fight so that I can be ready?"

Sabrina threw her hands up in the air. "What is it with you?"

Puck's wings popped out of his backs and fluttered like a hummingbird's. "Never mind," he said, lifting off the ground.

Sabrina was tired of Puck's attitude. She wanted an explanation. She jumped in the air just as he was about to fly away and snatched him by the pant leg.

"Let me go, bubble head," he demanded.

"Not until you tell me why you're so moody," she said.

Puck tried to shake her off, but he couldn't. "Let me go!"

"Not a chance, bug boy," Sabrina said, and then she was rocketing into the sky, hanging on with all her might. "Puck! Put us down!"

"You had your chance, loser," the boy said as they sailed over the castle and out into the woods, skimming the tops of trees.

"Puck! I was up all night. I'm too tired to hold on," Sabrina cried. Her arms felt like rubber bands stretching to the point of snapping. She looked down. Too far. She would never survive the fall.

"Wah! Wah! Wah!!!! Help me! Save me!" Puck mocked.

"Puck, please put me down," Sabrina said. Her lack of sleep and the surge of panic was causing black spots to appear in front of her eyes.

"Poor Donkeyface can never do anything for herself," Puck said.

And then her aching fingers gave way and she fell. The air whipped through her hair and she saw the tops of trees pass her, and then a limb smashed into her leg. She opened her mouth to cry out, but the wind stole the sound. She was sure the next thing that slammed into her would be the ground, but then something had her—something warm and soft and strong. She looked up just as Puck set her on the ground. He looked angry.

"Don't you ever do that again!"

"I told you I was too tired to hold on," Sabrina said.

"Well—then—stop being too tired to hold on," Puck said.

"What's wrong with you?"

"I could ask you the very same question," Puck said. "In fact, I will. What's wrong with you?"

Sabrina sighed. She didn't have the energy to fight with Puck. She needed to get to bed. "Puck, just tell me. I'm exhausted."

"What's wrong is how you just gave up," Puck said.

"Huh?"

"Every time I think you're going to stop being pathetic you just throw in the towel and surrender," he said.

"Sorry to be such a disappointment," she replied as she dusted herself off. She looked around the woods, unsure of where she was or which direction to walk.

"Ever since you came crawling into my life you have done

nothing but complain about your lack of control! 'No one listens to me. No one pays attention. Everyone treats me like a child. Boo-hoo-hoo!' Well, of course they treat you like a kid, because every time you get a chance to grow up, you choke."

"Look who's talking!"

"I'm a trickster! I'm supposed to act like a child. It's in my blood! You, on the other hand, don't want to grow up because you enjoy having everyone look after you."

Sabrina wasn't too tired to be angry. She picked a direction and stomped away from the boy fairy without a word. He followed close behind.

"Look at what's happened since you came to town. You've come face-to-face with every kind of monster there is and—"

"And I've lived to tell the tale!" she shouted.

"Because someone else had to save you, Sabrina. It's been me, or Canis, or your grandmother, or your uncle. But now, when you've got the chance to actually take control, you hand it over to those nutters Arthur and Hood!"

"I know you can't possibly understand this with that tiny pea brain of yours, but we're in the middle of a war and I need help from people who know what they're doing. I can't run around using your 'fake it until you make it' approach. People will die."

Puck leaped over her and landed in her path. "I'm sorry, but you were at the whole mirrors speaking prophecy thing, right? They said that you would lead this army. Not the king. Not the thief. You! Hey, I don't like it any better than you do, but the mirrors see the future and they say you're the star of this show."

"I don't know what I'm doing!" Sabrina said.

"When it comes to saving the world, no one knows what they're doing," Puck said. "But they don't pass it off onto someone else when it's their responsibility. The old lady is out there in those woods, and you are going to place her life in the hands of people who don't care about her? Sabrina, it is supposed to be you. If it wasn't, the mirrors would have said so."

Sabrina pushed past him and kept on walking toward where she thought the castle must be. "Well, I know one thing I don't need help doing. Telling you to go jump in the river."

"The old lady would expect more from you!" he shouted after her.

ctober 20

So the army leaves for the first attack tonight. The plan is fairly simple. The soldiers are going to encircle the town. When they're in place, Robin Hood will command Baba Yaga's chicken house to run toward town square. The noise and shock of seeing that house will get the attention of the Master's thugs, who will run to it, and as they do, my army will surround and capture them. My father has demanded that no lives are taken. I'm just hoping that's possible. Everyone who is taken prisoner will be tied up with the help of Mallobarb and Buzzflower and then brought back here to be locked in the Hall of Wonders.

Mr. Canis was preparing to go until Robin Hood told him to stay behind. He's not happy. I just don't know what to tell him. I know he wants to help, but I don't want him to get killed, either. Red and Wendell are sticking around as well.

As I write this I'm sitting in the courtyard watching the prepara-tions. I'm super-worried about this plan. Pinocchio's words still ring in my ears, as do Puck's. I don't know what to do and because I don't know, I think that putting the decision in more experienced hands is the right thing to do. My family and I are going to watch it unfold in the mirror room. I just hope that all these people—who have become my friends—return here when the battle is over.

Baba Yaga's house arrived in the town square as planned, and as predicted, word spread fast. The Hand raced to confront it, shelling it with rocks, sticks, clubs, and magic. Sabrina and her family cheered as they watched through the mirrors. They saw Baba Yaga and the Wicked Queen sweep away dozens with the magical assaults, they saw Robin Hood's men rain arrows down from atop buildings, they saw the Pied Piper and Beauty lull beasties away from the fight and watched Goldi command her bears to stomp through approaching villains. Even Puck transformed into an African elephant and used his pearly tusks to swat aside anyone foolish enough to charge him. For a brief moment it appeared that Arthur and Robin's plan was going to work, but then a flood of red-handprinted Everafters swept into Main Street like a deadly tsunami, destroying everything in its path. There were too many trolls and goblins and ghouls. There were too many knights and princes and witches. There must have been nearly three thousand members of Mirror's army, and when her own feeble forces attacked, they were quickly overrun. Within minutes Sabrina's entire army had scattered with members of the Hand chasing them down.

And people died. Sir Kay was struck with a hammer wielded by an enormous piglike creature wearing studded armor. Mallobarb was brought down by an arrow. Tik-Tok was chased through the streets until his key unwound. He fell over and a mob stomped and smashed him until there was nothing left but springs and sprockets.

Veronica took Daphne, Basil, Red, and Wendell out of the room. Mr. Canis stood trembling as he watched the nightmare unfold. He placed a reassuring hand on Sabrina's shoulder as if to tell her it wasn't her fault, but she shook it off. This *was* her fault.

"I should prepare the infirmary for injuries," Nurse Sprat said, then shuffled out of the room. Gepetto offered his help and followed her through the door. Henry gave Sabrina a hug and told her he should probably help as well. Even Mr. Canis drifted away. That left Sabrina alone with her uncle Jake and Pinocchio.

"They intimidated you," Pinocchio said. "They knew you

were unsure of what to do, and they took advantage of you. You can't let them steamroll you again."

"Again?" Sabrina said. "There won't be an 'again.' You saw what happened. We can't win this."

"Maybe not, but I'll tell you one thing," the little boy said on his way to the door. "You're not going to do it marching into town."

Sabrina turned to her uncle. "Any advice?"

"I wish I had some for you, 'Brina. This was a disaster, and I think we can forget about any more new recruits now. I have to find another way to get—" Uncle Jake stopped himself.

"What are you trying to do?" Sabrina asked, suspicious of Jake's sudden silence.

Uncle Jake shook his head. "I'm just tired. I should go help prepare."

When he was gone, Sabrina watched the chaos for a while longer. In the crowd she saw Chicken Little talking with a troll. She could have spit. He was a traitor. He must have warned the Hand about the attack.

The images of town in the mirrors dissolved and the guardians within reappeared. They watched her with pitying eyes, even the more unfriendly ones.

"Why?"

The mirrors lifted their eyes to her. "Excuse me?" the fish-faced guardian gurgled. His name was Namoren, and the inside of his mirror was an undersea kingdom.

"Why am I the only one who can lead this army?" she asked.

"It's impossible to explain," Namoren said.

"There are so many variables," Donovan said.

"Did you know this would happen?" Sabrina said. "Did you know people would die?"

"Child, you are trying to save the world. Of course some will die," Titan said.

Sabrina fell to her knees and sobbed. "Why didn't you tell me?"

"Oh, Sabrina, we're sorry, but that is forbidden," Harry said from within his Hotel of Wonders. "We can only tell you the future, not how you get there."

Sabrina leaped up and lunged at Harry. "You have to tell me what to do!" The guardian disappeared.

She ran to Namoren and shook his frame. "You have to give me something to work with!"

She pounded on Arden's frame. "People are dying. What do I do?"

"What you have always done," Reggie said.

And then the faces faded and she saw something she did

not expect: herself. Each of the twenty-four mirrors showed different moments in her life. In one mirror, she was helping Daphne out of the second-floor bedroom window of Granny's house and leaping to the ground. In another, she was locking Mrs. Robinson in the closet so that they could escape her foster home. She saw herself racing through subterranean tunnels hunting for her family with nothing but a shovel and a broken arm. She saw herself accidentally kill a giant. She saw herself snatching on to Oz's hot-air balloon as it dragged her off the observation deck of the Empire State Building. She saw herself helping everyone break Mr. Canis out of the town jail, destroying the bank with the Horn of the North Wind, fooling the Headless Horseman with his own head, sneaking past Ichabod Crane as they tried to free Jack the Giant Killer, kicking Mr. Hamstead in the shins, then escaping into a cornfield, and shoving Puck into a swimming pool. She even saw herself tiptoeing past Ms. Smirt's office at the orphanage.

"Why are you showing me this?" Sabrina demanded.

"THIS IS THE GIRL THAT SAVES THE WORLD," the mirrors answered as one. "SABRINA GRIMM, QUEEN OF THE —"

"Sneaks," she said, finishing their sentence. "You're saying this is what makes me special? Being sneaky is what will help me save my grandmother and stop Mirror?"

The faces returned and Sabrina locked eyes with Reggie, who was smiling from ear to ear. "We're not allowed to say, but if I was a betting man, I'd put my money on 'yes.'"

"In your life you've mastered the great art of deception—the ability to pull the wool over anyone's eyes," Titan added. "Yours is the ability to make a person regret taking you for granted: the ability to do the unexpected—to take your opponents by surprise. You've used it a million times to keep your sister safe. That is the gift that sets you apart from others."

Sabrina wiped hot tears on her shirt and blinked at the mirrors.

"And your heart," Fanny said. "You don't let a lot of people visit it, but once they are inside, you love them with all that you are. Those two things are what will win this war and rescue your grandmother."

"It's time to get your mojo back, sister," Donovan said.

• • •

When the wounded were taken care of, Sabrina brought shovels to Robin Hood and King Arthur. They attempted to bury the fallen near Seven's and Briar's graves, but she told them it was better to bury them outside the castle walls. They argued, but she promised them it would make sense in time. When they continued, she turned her back and walked away. She wasn't going to let them bully her any longer. So as the sun's orange glow lit the horizon, Sabrina's army said good-bye to the brave and fallen: Mallobarb, Tik-Tok, Sir Kay, Sir Gawain, the Silver Pigeon, and Will Scarlet. When they left the grave sites and assembled in the castle yard, Sabrina called for their attention. She had spent hours planning what she would say, but when she saw their exhausted faces, she hesitated. What Sabrina was about to tell them might push them over the edge. But she knew she was right.

"When the mirrors told us that I would lead you, I admit I was afraid. I haven't fought in any wars, so I put my faith in the hands of a few well-meaning people. They wanted me to throw a party to cheer you up, then reach out to the Scarlet Hand for help, then train for battle in front of you, then attack at the heart of our enemies. Those people were wrong. But I don't blame them. They were doing what they thought was right. Unfortunately, the prophecy is not about them. It's about my sister and me. I shouldn't have tried to put that responsibility on others. Last night happened because of me—my doubts and fears. It's ironic, because ever since my sister and I showed up in this town, I've complained that no one takes me seriously."

"I can vouch for that," Daphne said.

"Now that you are listening, it's scary. I mean, I'm still just a kid. So I had to ask myself, what's so special about me and Daphne? What do we do that is so different from the brains, muscles, and magic that you all have?

"Well, once upon a time, before any of you met the sisters Grimm, we had a reputation as very successful juvenile delinquents. We were good at moving quietly, good at running and hiding, and good with keys and locks. We were good at getting each other out of tough situations and very good at tricking people into doing things we wanted them to do."

"What my sister is saying is, it's time for shenanigans," Daphne said.

The Cowardly Lion growled. "What do you have in mind?"

"Pack your things. Pack everything you can carry. We're abandoning the castle," Sabrina said.

"Abandoning the castle? That's crazy," the Widow said. "This is the only safe place we have."

"Not anymore. If the Hand isn't on their way, they soon will be, and they will find this castle because we have a traitor in our midst," Sabrina said, turning to Chicken Little.

The hen stepped forward and Sabrina bent over to face her eye to eye. "You are the traitor."

"What?" the chicken squawked.

"You told your old friends in the Hand what we were planning," she said.

Uncle Jake snatched her by the neck and lifted her off the ground. "What you did cost us some dear friends."

"I had to!" the bird cried. "They forced me."

And then Uncle Jake tossed Chicken Little through the iron gates, where she landed with a thud on the drawbridge. She dusted herself off and walked indignantly back into the woods.

The crowd broke into worried chatter, but Sabrina called for their attention. "We have to prepare to go. We leave for the forest as soon as possible."

"And what are we going to do in the woods?" Goldilocks asked.

Sabrina smiled. "We're going to lay traps, build cages, and create every obstacle we can to make the Hand's lives miserable. We'll attack in small groups, capturing one or two of them at a time; then we'll slink back into the trees and disappear."

Pinocchio nodded respectfully.

"But there are thousands of them," Little John said. "We'll never catch them all."

"There won't be thousands of them soon," Sabrina said. "Where are the birds?"

"On patrol," the Scarecrow said.

"When they get back, I want them to deliver a message, and Scarecrow, I want you to write it," Sabrina said.

"I'd be honored. What would you like it to say?"

"It's a final offer to the rest of the Hand to join us. Let them know this is the final time we will reach out, and after this there won't be a third chance."

"Do you think any of them will listen?" Beauty asked. She was obviously still holding out hope for her husband and daughter.

"If they don't, they're going to regret it."

Henry eyed Sabrina curiously. "What are you two planning?"

"We're going to save the world," Daphne crowed.

As the hours slipped away, the small, tired army packed. Sabrina instructed everyone to keep weapons both magical and normal on their bodies, no matter how cumbersome. Carrying food was also encouraged.

Sabrina sat with her sister and watched as the army limped off to bed. It had been a long day, and tomorrow promised to be even harder.

"Can you get your coven to pull it off?"

Daphne rolled her eyes. "Daphne's Fabulous Ladies of Magic can do anything. I just need to get the spell from Uncle Jake. Apparently, you have to hold it in your hand to make it work."

"We can't screw this up," Sabrina said.

"You worry too much," Daphne said. "My girls got the right stuff. They put the pow in powerful."

• • •

That night Sabrina waited up for hours for the Widow to return from delivering her message. The more time that passed, the more nervous she got. At around midnight, Henry drifted out of the castle and joined her at a picnic table in the yard.

"Responsibility is hard," her father said.

Sabrina nodded. "I don't know how you do it. You must go out of your mind worrying about us."

Henry nodded. "That's probably the best way to describe it. There are times I've been so angry I wanted to pull my hair out, and other times so scared I've had to go somewhere and cry."

"We haven't made it easy."

Henry laughed. "That's the understatement of the year."

"I'll do better," Sabrina said.

"You're doing fine. Just do me a favor and every once in a while remind yourself that your mother and father love you."

Sabrina nodded. "You do the same. Oh, here she comes."

The Widow flapped into the courtyard and landed on the picnic table. "Well, I spread the word, but it doesn't look good. Most of them laughed. They like to remind me that they are winning the war."

"What did you say?" Henry asked.

"I reminded them that they're fighting the Grimms. That gave them something to think about. Unfortunately, I don't think we're going to get too many takers this round. They're pretty confident. Want to tell me what you plan to do?"

"Not yet, Your Majesty, but soon," Sabrina said. "Why don't you go and get some rest. Tomorrow is going to be a busy day."

The Widow hopped off the table and wobbled toward the castle, only to stop for a moment to look back at Sabrina. "Hey, kid. We're all behind you."

Just then, Daphne raced toward Sabrina eyeing her father warily.

"Uh, Sabrina, I need to talk to you," the little girl said.

"About?"

"It's . . . um . . . about our messy room," Daphne said.

"Huh? Daphne, this is important stuff we're doing. If our room is a mess, then just clean it up."

Daphne yanked her out of her seat. "No, this is a huge mess. Sorry, Dad. Sabrina's a slob and I'm sick of it."

The little girl dragged her halfway across the yard before Sabrina could get her to stop.

"What is this about?" she said.

Daphne frowned. "Someone got into our room again. They

threw everything everywhere. The bed is broken and our stuff is everywhere. But that's not the worst part. Whoever did it took the Book of Everafter again!"

"This is the strangest crime spree I've ever seen. Whoever is taking the book brings it back, then steals it again. Who would do that?"

"Maybe they aren't stealing it. Maybe they are borrowing it," Daphne mused.

"But why?"

• • •

In the morning, Sabrina took a bath knowing it might be the last one she would get for a long time. She washed her hair and face, brushed her teeth, and flossed. She dressed in a set of clean clothes and pulled on her sneakers.

When she stepped out of the castle, she found the rest of her family helping the Everafters load the last of the carts. As their belongings rolled through the gate of the fortress, Buzzflower hovered overhead, zapping them with a purple dust from her wand. It would cloak them in the same magic that hid the castle, allowing them to travel through the woods undetected.

"There's too much stuff," Robin Hood complained. "We need to travel light."

"We aren't bringing this with us," Sabrina said. "We're hiding it. When the birds did their flyover, they found a cave near the base of the mountain. It's well hidden and deep enough to keep everyone's things safe. We're sending all the young children and elderly there until this is over. We're going to keep our magic mirror there too."

Daphne approached. "There's no sign of the book," she whispered.

"Keep looking."

Daphne raced away.

Snow White approached. "I just don't understand the plan."

"It's better that you don't," Sabrina replied. "Just keep your bo-staff ready."

"Are you going to blow this place up?" Mr. Boarman asked. "Seems like a waste."

"Just remind everyone that when they hear the signal, it's time to go. They will only have five minutes to exit, and if they don't, they're in for a world of trouble."

Red and Canis rushed forward. "What can we do?"

"Go with the kids," Sabrina said, though before she finished she could already feel Canis's disappointment. "Listen, I know you're used to being in the action, but I need someone I can trust to keep things calm. I will never ask you to babysit again. I promise."

Canis sighed, and his backpack fell from his shoulder. A glass jar rolled out onto the ground. Inside it a terrible black shape snapped and scratched. Sabrina felt sweat form on her brow as she eyed it. The Big Bad Wolf was in that jar. Canis scooped it up and put it back in his bag. Then he turned to Red. "Gather the little ones, child, and any animals that are slow-moving."

Red smiled and ran off to complete her task.

"You're good for her," Sabrina said. "You're like the father she never had. It would be sad for her to lose you."

The old man lowered his eyes and hobbled off after Red, picking his way carefully with his cane.

By mid-afternoon, the birds reported that the supplies and children were safe in the woods. The army was checking the castle one last time for any useful weapons or supplies. Most of the cabins had been torn down for firewood, so it was easy work. Sabrina poked her head into the blacksmith tent and found a hammer that might be helpful, so she shoved it into her belt loop. The kitchen was empty, as was the medical tent. Her people had done an excellent job. She took a quick peek at the cemetery and found her uncle and Morgan standing over the graves of the ones they loved.

Morgan noticed Sabrina standing behind her. "I see the

necessity of this and I support your plan, but . . . it's more than I can . . . It's just so wrong," she said.

"I'm sorry," Sabrina said. "I knew you two would suffer the most from what we're going to do."

"I feel like I'm abandoning her," Jake whispered as if he were afraid Briar Rose might hear.

He leaned down and took a rose off of his love's grave and slid it into one of his shirt pockets. He closed his eyes tight, as if preparing to jump out of a plane. "OK, I'm ready. Let's do this before I change my mind."

Sabrina took his hand. "I couldn't do this without you. I think she would be proud."

"Just be careful," he said. "If that piece of paper lands in the wrong hands, things are going to go from terrible to nightmarish in Ferryport Landing."

Uncle Jake and Morgan headed for the castle yard and Sabrina followed. As they turned the corner, she took a look back at the little graveyard and remembered those who lay there. She said a quiet prayer for their eternal peace, then ran to the yard where her army was gathered. Many of them had never held a sword or a bow in their hands before. More than a few had never been in a fistfight, but they were the bravest people she had ever met.

"Your mother and Basil are safe," Henry said as she approached.

Relieved, Sabrina turned to the assembled crowd. "Thank you all for being so patient. I know you're all a little freaked out because I've kept what we're doing a secret, but you can't be sneaky if everyone knows what you're up to. So let me explain. We're going to lure the Hand into this castle—as many as we can. You're going to fight until you hear the signal. Then you're going to run! Get out of the castle. We'll meet at the gathering site, and that's when our war will really begin. I wish you all luck. Daphne, are the witches ready?"

"They are," Daphne said.

"All right, Buzzflower, drop the cloaking spell," Sabrina said.

"Are you sure about this?" the fairy godmother asked.

Sabrina nodded, and Buzzflower waved her wand into the air. Suddenly, the sky went from blue to sparkly purple. Tiny crystals drifted down from above like snow and blanketed the ground, then vanished.

"Here we go," Henry said.

Sabrina took her sister's hand. "Any luck with the book?"

Daphne shook her head. "We can't leave it here."

"I'm not worried about that. I'm sure whoever took it has got it with them," Sabrina said, scanning her army and feeling sad to know one of them was a thief. "Don't worry. It's too important to leave behind."

Then she turned to the crowd.

"Open the gates," Sabrina ordered.

"Wait? Really?" the Frog Prince croaked.

"Yep," Sabrina said.

"Have you lost your mind?" the Cheshire Cat cried.

"She knows what she's doing!" Snow White said. "Now stop with the blubbering and get ready. They'll be here any second."

And Snow was right. Sabrina could already feel the rumbling of feet and the clanking of swords. The first attackers rushed through the door and were met by Arthur and Robin Hood's men. Steel crashed against steel, shield slammed against shield, and a mighty roar filled the air. While they fought, Henry, Uncle Jake, Sabrina, and Daphne crouched beneath a hay cart and prepared for the next part of the plan.

The next onslaught from the Hand came courtesy of the Ice Queen, standing in the open gate. The temperature of the air dropped wildly, prickling Sabrina's skin. The Ice Queen waved her hand at a few of Arthur's knights and they were immediately encased in solid blocks of ice. Luckily, Mordred cast a spell to warm them rapidly. They were soggy, but at least they were alive.

The third wave of attackers was a motley crew of monsters in all shapes and sizes. They swung clubs and hammers with vicious intent. Two of King Arthur's knights were killed within moments, and dozens more creatures piled through the doorway every second.

"Widow, how many more are coming?" Sabrina shouted.

The Widow flew up into the air and circled the battle. A moment later she returned. If a bird could look worried, the Widow was troubled. "At least a thousand, with more on the way."

Puck was in the middle of the action, and Sabrina kept a close eye on him. The boy was arrogant—too confident in his abilities. He fought like war was play, and though he slashed and poked and leaped about, his opponents meant to kill him. She cringed to watch him, but she reminded herself that Puck had been alive nearly four thousand years. He knew how to take care of himself.

Her attention was torn away as another massive wave of fighters stormed into the castle. In this group, there were wizards and witches and mechanical men. They roared as they raced across the drawbridge like they had already won the battle. Sabrina couldn't help but smile. It was exactly what she wanted them to think. *Keep coming*, she thought to herself. *Every last one of you.*

Magical animals followed. Sabrina saw the Swan Brothers and Hans My Hedgehog. Shere Khan and the Ugly Duckling. Large bearlike creatures with the faces of cats leaped into the fighting with merciless ferocity.

And finally a sixth wave stormed into the yard. Strange Everafters she had never seen before. There was a woman who carried her head in her hands, a cat who appeared to be made of glass, a girl made from patchwork quilts, a giant serpent, a stampede of intelligent horses, and a fleet of forks that leaped about, stabbing at anyone close enough to feel their tines.

It was time for the signal. She turned to Daphne, and the little girl nodded.

"Retreat!" Sabrina shouted.

"Sabrina, what are you up to?" Henry asked.

"You don't want to know yet, Hank," Jake said.

Sabrina grabbed her father and her sister by the hands and they darted from their hiding place and raced for the drawbridge. Uncle Jake led the way, delivering punches to anyone that got too close. Bunny, Morgan, and Baba Yaga followed, unleashing spells that hit the charging army like a tidal wave. The Old Mother's house brought up the rear, charging through the crowd and sending bodies flying in all directions.

They ran past the Cowardly Lion, who was mauling a troll.

"Time to go," Sabrina said.

The lion leaped off his victim and followed them. Along the

way, Boarman, Swineheart, and the Pied Piper joined them. Goldilocks and her bears were next, trailed by Rapunzel and the Scarecrow, shedding his straw.

And then Uncle Jake came to an abrupt stop. On the ground in front of him lay Mayor Heart, injured. He looked down at her, initially in disgust, but then reached down and helped her to her feet.

"I won't—I won't go quietly," Heart stammered.

"You're not a prisoner, but I suggest you come with us. We're your only hope," Jake said.

"Jacob, what are you up to?" Henry said. "She can't be trusted!"

Jake ignored him and turned back to Heart. "It's your last chance. Are you coming, Your Majesty?"

"Absolutely not!"

"Come with me or I will turn the lion on you."

The Cowardly Lion roared and Heart shrieked. She nodded to Jake, and then joined those escaping into the woods. They charged through the iron gate and across the drawbridge.

Once outside, Daphne took a folded piece of yellowing paper from her pocket. "Wilhelm's barrier spell," Daphne said, marveling at the ancient paper.

"Let's get this started," Sabrina said.

Daphne signaled the coven, shoving Uncle Jake's spell into Morgan's hands. "OK, girls, as we discussed, Morgan does the reading, Bunny handles the stones, and Baba puts on the light show."

More of Sabrina's fighters darted across the bridge. Robin Hood and Little John helped Friar Tuck, who had a deep gash on his leg.

The Cheshire Cat was next across the drawbridge. "I think they got the Scarecrow. I can't be sure but—"

The Scarecrow was the next out the door. The Frog Prince followed with his wife and daughter in tow.

"My husband won't listen!" Beauty cried as she raced into the woods. Tears were streaming down her face. "I begged him."

"I'm sorry!" Sabrina said.

More and more members of Sabrina's army came through until nearly their whole group had escaped. When they saw Sabrina's ragtag group retreat, the Hand roared from behind the castle walls. As Sabrina had hoped, their enemies wanted to demoralize her army by celebrating their conquest of the castle. Little did the Hand know the castle was a gift.

"Close the gates," Henry shouted. "We're all here!"

"Wait! Where's Puck?" Sabrina asked. Panicked, she searched the crowd, desperate for a sight of his filthy green hoodie or his unruly mop of hair, but he wasn't there. She searched the sky, but he wasn't there, either. She ran for the gates.

"Sabrina, no!" Henry cried after her.

"I can't leave him," she shouted. "Daphne, don't you stop that spell!"

"I'm going with you!" Beauty shouted, and chased behind the girl.

The two found themselves in the midst of a celebration, and so they were able to slip by unnoticed. They pushed through the rowdy crowd, weaving in and out of monsters, until they found Puck. He was still fighting and completely outmatched. His opponent, a disgusting-looking creature with a pig snout and huge tusks, had his foot on the boy and would not let go.

"Oh, hey ugly," Puck said when he saw Sabrina. "Sorry, I'm a little busy."

"Is this yours?" the creature snorted.

"Yes," Sabrina said.

"Then fight me for him," he grunted.

Sabrina looked up into his face. He stood several feet above her, but as she was trembling she noticed the creature's leaky pale eyeball. He was going blind on his right side. What had her father said? Look for weaknesses?

"Fine, piggy, let's fight!"

The creature swung at her, but she darted to his right, where he couldn't see her. She noticed a nasty red wound on his rib cage, fresh and bleeding. She leaped and kicked the spot, and the monster bellowed in pain. None of the other villains noticed the fight, as they were too busy ransacking what was left of the castle. When the creature bent over, Sabrina noticed the green ooze coming from his furry ear. It was infected, and she did as she was trained. She punched it as hard as she could, and the monster fell over, shrieking and sobbing. As he did so, he set Puck loose.

"You saved my life," Puck said, standing. "Well, that's a change of pace."

"Fly us out of here," she commanded. "Wait, where's Beauty?"

Sabrina once again scanned the crowd but for only a moment, as she was soon airborne. Puck had her by the waist and the two were flying skyward, narrowly dodging the spears and arrows flung at them from below.

"Do you see her?" Sabrina said. "We can't leave her."

"There!" Puck shouted, pointing toward the castle gate. Beauty and the Beast were arguing and Beast had his wife's arm clenched tight in his hairy claw. She was sobbing.

"How could you turn your back on us?" the Beast said.

"Please come with me! I'm begging you! The Master lied to you. He lied to all of us."

Sabrina frowned but knew she had to do something. "Set us down, Puck."

"Um, isn't your sister about to—"

"Just do it."

When they hit the ground, Sabrina stepped between Beauty and the Beast.

"Listen, pal, she loves you. Despite your stupid furry face and the fangs and the crappy attitude and the fact that you might be evil, she loves you and she's trying to save you. Since you're not listening, I'm going to lay this out for you. You have thirty seconds to decide."

Stunned, the Beast could do nothing but listen.

"We didn't lose this castle. We gave it away. And now, Baba Yaga, the Wicked Queen, and Morgan are outside reproducing the magic spell that put a barrier on this little town. Except we're putting the barrier over this fortress, locking up as many of the Hand as we can. So you can stay if you want, but if you think it stunk to be trapped in a little town before, wait until you face eternity in a castle infested with trolls, goblins, witches, and monsters—and no indoor plumbing."

The Beast reeled.

"Twenty seconds," Sabrina said.

"Please, James," Beauty begged.

Suddenly, Mr. Canis appeared near the drawbridge. "Sabrina! You have to get out of there now!"

"You're supposed to be with the children," Sabrina said, startled not only by his presence but by the panic in his voice.

The Beast turned toward his cohorts. "It's a trap! Everyone, out of the castle, now!"

"Puck! Get Sabrina out of there!" Canis shouted.

Before Sabrina could say anything, Puck had her and Beauty in his arms and they were flying over the wall. They landed with the waiting army.

"Cast the spell now!" Mr. Canis shouted. "They know the plan."

"What are you doing?" Robin Hood demanded.

"We're putting the Hand in time-out," Daphne said, and Morgan began to read from the magic spell. The words were ancient and not in English, but Morgan handled them with ease. Bunny Lancaster tossed a handful of stones into the air and they stayed suspended before her eyes. She moved them around, as if working some elaborate puzzle only she could understand, switching their places, tilting them, and flipping them over. Baba Yaga raised her hands and squatted down like an angry monkey. She shrieked and bellowed as if demanding the spell to work. All the while, members of the Hand spilled out of the gates.

The Beast was first, then the Swan Brothers, Shere Khan, and the entire nation of Lilliputians. The glass cat, Bungle, and Humpty Dumpty were next, followed by a couple of trolls and goblins. Then Mowgli, Baloo, and Jack Pumpkinhead.

The sky began to lighten, and above the castle Sabrina could see the beginnings of a concrete dome. It looked as if it were being assembled, stone by stone, by an invisible workforce. The faster Morgan read, and the more the Wicked Queen adjusted her rocks, the faster the dome materialized. Nearly a dozen more members of the Hand were able to escape, but soon the last rock was in place. There was a loud booming noise much like the echo of a heavy door shutting and then the stones were gone.

The next person to cross the drawbridge was the Ice Queen, but she tumbled backward halfway across. She stood up and placed a hand out, pushing, but it was clear there was something blocking her way. The Ice Queen raged and blasted it with hail, but her magic had no effect whatsoever.

"What have you done?" the glass cat asked.

"I think they call this winning a battle," Henry said, beaming with pride at his daughters.

Nottingham was one of those who had escaped. He pushed

through the crowd and confronted the mayor. "What are you doing with these traitors?"

"They saved me," Heart said. She seemed confused and disoriented.

"Saved you?" Nottingham bellowed.

Uncle Jake stood between them. "Relax, Sheriff, the lady is injured."

"You have betrayed me!" Nottingham shouted at her.

"I have not!" the queen roared back. She hardly needed her megaphone. "The Grimms saved my life against my will!"

"What kind of fool do you take me for?" Nottingham said. He reached into his long leather jacket and removed his deadly dagger.

"So, what do we do with them?" Arthur said, raising his sword to Nottingham's chin.

That quickly silenced the argument.

"We let them go," Sabrina said, turning to the Beast. "Get lost and tell Mirror that two little girls beat his big old army."

The Beast turned to his wife, defeated. When she didn't say anything, he slinked into the woods with his daughter. The other escaped members of the Hand followed him, with Nottingham bringing up the rear. Just before he disappeared into the trees, he turned and flashed an angry look at the Queen of Hearts, who glared indignantly back.

"Oh, no! Mom!" Mordred cried, rushing to the barrier.

Sabrina searched for what had gotten the warlock so upset. Inside the barrier, trapped with the Hand, was Morgan. Despite the chaos around her she smiled softly.

"We'll get you out!" Mordred cried. "Don't worry. I'll make the other witches break the spell."

"I couldn't leave Seven," Morgan said. "I couldn't bear to think he was in here with them, all alone."

Uncle Jake's shoulders slumped and he stared at the ground.

"Mom, you can't stay in there. That castle is filled with maniacs," Mordred said.

"Honey, I'm a pretty powerful witch. I'll have no trouble getting everyone in line. Don't worry about me."

Mordred looked at Sabrina, then back at his mother, and then stepped through the barrier to join her.

"Mordred, they need you!" Morgan cried.

"I'm not leaving my mother," he said, and then turned back to the others. "I'm sorry. You've got all the magic you'll need."

Sabrina nodded. "Take care of your mother. Is there anything we can get you?"

Mordred nodded. "I need my video games."

Sabrina laughed. "As soon as we get a chance, I'll deliver them myself."

"We should go. Your mother and the others will be worried," Henry said.

Daphne said her good-byes as well and the victorious army headed into the woods. Sabrina took one last look at the castle before it disappeared from view.

9

After reuniting with Veronica and the children, the army marched single-file toward Mount Taurus. Soon, they came upon a site the Widow had found that looked perfect for the next part of Sabrina's plan. She let the crowd know they could stop.

While everyone went to work setting up a campsite, Mayor Heart slumped against a tree, her feet straight out in front of her. Uncle Jake knelt beside her and offered her his water canteen. She drank greedily until the canteen was empty.

"He tried to kill me," she wheezed, bordering on hyperventilation. "Nottingham tried to kill me."

"I'm not surprised," Uncle Jake said. "He's a violent man with a dark past. You're lucky I was there."

The queen looked up into his face and her eyes narrowed.

"And exactly why did you help me? You should have left me to die after the unfortunate incident with that woman."

Sabrina was enraged. *That woman!!* Briar's death wasn't an unfortunate incident! Heart and Nottingham killed her in cold blood. How could Uncle Jake tolerate Heart now? Where was his fire for revenge that only days ago had threatened to drive him insane? It made no sense to her that her uncle was now showing kindness to a woman he once wanted dead.

"I couldn't leave you," he said. "That's not what Briar would do."

The queen's face softened and she let down her guard. "Well, I suppose I should thank you."

"That's not necessary. But there is one thing that would make me very happy," Jake replied as he reached into his jacket. He withdrew a dagger. Sabrina suddenly panicked. He was going to kill her! But then Jake placed the knife in the queen's hand. "Stay alive. I don't think we've seen the last of the sheriff. When he shows his face again, I hope to be there to protect you, but if I'm not, you may have to use this."

The queen looked down and appraised the blade. Sabrina thought she must have had more than a few experiences with deadly weapons.

"I'd hate for you to die before I let you out," he whispered.

Heart stared at him in utter shock. Then her face parted in a smile filled with yellow teeth.

Sabrina set her pack on the ground and scanned the clearing. It was high on a hill, which was ideal. She and Daphne had once had a foster father whose backyard had a similar steep incline, and the girls tormented him for hours with well-aimed acorns and rocks.

"It's a good hill—gives us a great view of the surrounding forest," Pinocchio said as he stood nearby, also studying the camp. "At least for the night. We'll have to find a new one in the morning and every morning until we got the job done."

"We?"

Pinocchio nodded. It was the first time she had ever heard him express a sentiment that wasn't selfish.

"Your father should be proud," Sabrina said, even though the words sounded funny in her head.

"I'd appreciate it if you'd tell him that," Pinocchio said. "I'm fairly certain he thinks I'm a spoiled brat."

He drifted away as she studied their new camp. It was then she noticed out of the corner of her eye that Mr. Canis was hovering nearby. She turned to him, uncertain of what to say. She knew she was supposed to yell at him. That's what you did when you were in charge and someone didn't follow your rules. But she never wanted the responsibility, and it seemed even worse if she had to yell at people she cared about. How was she supposed to scold an old man who was just trying to feel valuable especially when, deep down, she knew she had only sent him to look after the children so that she wouldn't have to worry about him in the battle?

"I had my reasons," he said as if he could read her mind.

"And I had my reasons," she replied. "I know you don't want to babysit. I know you want to be in the middle of the fight, but—"

"I couldn't let you get trapped inside the castle with the Hand," he said.

"Mr. Canis, the spell was for Everafters. I wouldn't have gotten stuck in there with those lunatics. I'm human. I know that no one wants a couple of kids running the war, but—"

Canis interrupted. "It won't happen again."

She wasn't sure she believed him, but she was relieved she didn't have to argue with him. She thanked him and watched as the old man hobbled off to join the others.

• • •

Once everyone had rested briefly, Sabrina gathered her army around her. As she looked at them she realized that the worry and fear in their faces was gone. In fact, they were looking at her with a newfound respect. She was no longer at the kids' table—for better or worse.

"We got lucky at the castle," she said. "We managed to trap a majority of the Hand in our little cage, but we can't rely on luck anymore. There are still a couple hundred goons left in these woods, and they are looking for us. When they find us, we have to be prepared."

"What do you have in mind?" Snow asked.

"My sister and I faced a lot of weirdos before you met us, and we always managed to put them in their place. To do that we've had to plan ahead with some things they would never expect. That's why I'm putting all my faith in the king of the unexpected, Puck."

The crowd let out a collective groan.

"This forest needs the Trickster King treatment."

"Oh yeah?" Puck said as he pushed through the crowd.

"I want to make the Hand crazy. Think of these woods as your own little playground. Do you have some ideas for shenanigans?" Sabrina asked.

Puck smiled. "Major shenanigans."

"Are you sure about this?" the Widow asked. "He's not known for caring exactly who gets pranked. Who's to say we all won't wind up in some pit full of syrup and fire ants or something else just as bad?"

"Listen, I know he's immature, mischievous, and frustrating, but that's exactly why he's the man for the job. He's going to booby-trap every inch of these woods and we're going to help bring his twisted visions to life. Mr. Boarman and Mr. Swineheart will work on designing his traps. Gepetto and Pinocchio will help build the intricate parts. Unfortunately, the rest of us have the worst jobs. We have to collect the ingredients he wants, and from my experience, some of that stuff is going to turn stomachs."

Puck laughed. "It's going to turn more than stomachs. Some of the stuff I want will scar you for life!"

The community went to work on Puck's plans. It took the rest of the day and well into the evening for them to build some of the wild ideas that came from his fertile imagination, including spring-loaded catapults, cannons that shot all sorts of muck and filth, cages that dropped from above, and trip wires that set off explosions. He wanted ditches dug and filled with angry badgers. He wanted logs hoisted high into trees, tied to ropes that swung them down to pulverize approaching villains. He worked magic spells that turned ordinary shrubs into poisonous plants that would cover a person with itchy sores. The Pied Piper and his son,

Wendell, used their musical instruments to lure a furry army of deer, rabbits, possums, squirrels, and chipmunks to do whatever Puck wanted. But what got him most excited was his hope that Bunny could open a new door to his enchanted bedroom.

"When the old lady's house imploded, the door to my room was destroyed," he explained. "But the room still exists somewhere and it's got all the special supplies I need. Plus, I sort of miss my chimpanzee army."

The Wicked Queen promised that she would do her best.

By the time the moon was directly overhead, the boy fairy's demented trips and traps were scattered throughout the woods. Everyone was exhausted and more than a few people were deeply troubled by some of the chores Puck had asked them to do. Rapunzel was particularly upset by having to collect ten pounds of skunk droppings. But, when all was said and done, Sabrina could sense that the army felt as if things were really changing. Even the Cowardly Lion admitted that it seemed they had a chance of beating Mirror.

That night Sabrina lay in her sleeping bag beneath a tree, with her sister cuddling beside her. Puck rested on a tree branch above them, looking out on the woods and fingering the wooden flute he kept with him at all times. The moon illuminated his proud grin.

"You should get some sleep," Sabrina said.

Puck shook his head. "I'm too excited. It feels like Christmas Eve—like I'm going to wake up and find something big under the tree."

"Except it might be something really big," Sabrina said.

"I'm hoping for a troll," Puck said. "Go to sleep, stinker. I'll let you know if we catch anything."

"Puck, you're an awesome villain," Sabrina said.

"Grimm, you say the sweetest things," he said.

Sabrina sat there for a long time, contemplating what had just happened, when she heard someone crying. She climbed out of her sleeping bag and followed the sound into the woods, where she found Snow weeping next to a tree. When she spotted Sabrina, she grimaced.

"I didn't want anyone to see me," she blubbered.

"Worried about the prince?"

Snow nodded.

"Want to see if we can find him?" Sabrina asked.

A smile broke out over the lovely teacher's tear-stained face. "Can we?"

Hand in hand, they crept into the camp where the magic mirror had been propped against a tree. Elvis lay on the ground in front of it, acting as guard dog. He opened a sleepy eye when the two women entered the reflection but did nothing to stop them. As soon as Sabrina and Snow were inside the Hall of Wonders, they rushed to the mirror room, where Snow quickly recited a poem to activate the guardians. "Mirrors, mirrors hanging there, where's my prince with the awesome hair."

The mirrors let out a combined chuckle and their faces faded. In each appeared an image of Charming sitting on the edge of a cliff looking out on the Hudson River. Sabrina had never seen him look so depressed. She wouldn't have believed he was capable of such sadness.

"Where do you think he is?" Sabrina asked.

"Not far," Snow said. "It's called Douglass's Peak. I used to go there when I wanted to be alone. I wonder how he knew."

"He had a magic mirror too," Harry said as his face reappeared in his frame. "He spent a lot of time checking in on you. Not in a creepy way. He just wanted to make sure you were safe."

"I wish I could talk to him," Snow said. "I love him. I want to help him with this."

"We might get caught in one of Puck's traps," Sabrina said.

"Your parents would kill me." Snow sighed.

"Then let's make sure they don't find out."

• • •

"It was love at first sight for us—at least, that's what we always thought," Snow said as they stomped through the heavy brush. "He swept me away. I agreed to marry him after knowing him only two weeks, but when it was time to walk down the aisle, well, something wouldn't let me. Back then I thought I was just headstrong and unsure of who I was, but now I know it was Atticus. His 'echo,' as my mom calls it, was still there and it made me feel like a damsel in distress all the time. I wanted to stand on my own and Billy is the kind of guy who—well, I didn't want him to save me. I wanted to see if I could do it on my own.

"But he never gave up on me. His feelings survived three marriages. And now he thinks those feelings are inventions."

"Invention or not, four hundred years is a long time to be in love with the same person," Sabrina said. "It has to be real."

"Last week I would have been sure you were right." Snow said. "I just hope he thinks so too."

They walked on until they found Charming sitting on the edge of a rocky cliff, just where the mirrors said he would be.

"What if he won't talk to me?" Snow whispered.

"Wait here," Sabrina said, then walked over and sat down next to him. He looked at her but said nothing, and for a long time she did the same. She wasn't exactly sure what to say. What kind of pep talk do you give someone who just found out he's not real, that his memories are inventions, that he's a figment of someone's imagination walking around in clothes? Daphne would know what to say. She always knew how to make a person smile, and she seemed to have a positive effect on Charming. The only effect Sabrina had on him was to make his face curl up as if he had just smelled a carton of spoiled milk.

"Nice view, huh?" she said, gazing out at the river. The water was calm and the moon had painted everything a soft blue. On the far banks of the river was a little restaurant with a dock and beyond that a couple of houses. Sabrina wondered if those people had any clue what was happening across the water. "You know, we never get a chance to just sit and talk."

"What do you want?" Charming grunted.

"Nothing."

"Then go away."

"Hey, I'm just enjoying the scenery. It's a free country," she said, settling down more comfortably and taking off her shoes to let the cool air slip through her socks.

"You're not going to leave, are you?" Charming asked.

"Nope. Now, normally, I would run to the other side of town to avoid having a conversation about feelings, but I'm trying to turn over a new leaf. Think of me as a pal you can share things with. I'll start. I'm running your army and it's scary. I don't really know what I'm doing. I'm afraid I'm going to get everyone killed. You should come back. OK, now your turn."

Charming sighed in surrender. "Is she with you?"

"Snow? Yes. She's very worried about you. We all are."

Charming glanced over his shoulder to take a peek at Snow. "I should go. I don't want to talk to her."

"Listen, William, I know this stinks. But here's the thing—it's not like the Wicked Queen turned you into a weirdo. She made you pretty awesome. You're brave and smart and strong. You're too good-looking for your own good. I wish someone would remake me, sometimes."

"But those things aren't real, Sabrina. I'm not brave because I have some inner strength. I'm not smart because of experience. I'm not strong from hard work. These gifts aren't things I've earned. They don't belong to me. All my dreams and aspirations are hardwired into me. Wanting to build that stupid castle, rebuild my kingdom, everything—it has consumed me for hundreds of years and for what? It's not even what I really want!"

"How can you be sure?"

"That's just it! I can't be sure, and it's maddening. There is nothing about me that I can be certain about—not even Snow. Especially not Snow."

"You think you don't love her?"

"Oh, I love her all right. With everything that's in me. But is that an invention? How can I know it's real? Maybe it's just part of the story Bunny created for me. I met Snow five hundred years ago, and for five hundreds years I have carried a torch for her, and now to think it's just part of my character, well . . . that's earth-shaking."

Sabrina nodded. "Seems to me that if you feel it, then it's real."

"Billy?"

Sabrina turned to see Snow approaching them. Charming climbed to his feet and Snow rushed to him, wrapping her arms around his neck and showering his cheeks with kisses.

"Billy, we can work this out. I know it's terrible but . . . it took so long for us to find our way back to each other. We can't lose that again," Snow said.

Charming pulled away. His face twisted with confusion and pain. "I don't know if I love you, Snow."

"You—what?" Snow cried as if the prince had suddenly begun speaking in another language.

"I'm sorry. I can't be with you," the prince said.

And then in a flash, the dumbstruck look vanished, and Snow lost her temper. Her cheeks turned fire-engine red and her mouth puckered into a pout. "William Charming, I will not have it!" she demanded.

Charming took a step back, and even Sabrina was alarmed by her tone.

"I know that life has thrown you a curveball—"

"It's a bit more than a curveball," Charming said, then turned and walked into the woods, vanishing within its dark interior.

"Billy!"

"I'm sorry," Sabrina whispered.

Snow turned to look out at the milky river. Her anger faded. "I think I've lost him this time."

"Don't worry. The man can't stop thinking about you. You left him at the altar and he still cares."

"I don't know this time. This is different," Snow said, her whole body trembling. "This is big."

• • •

Sabrina managed to get a few hours of sleep before being woken by shouts and hollers. As soon as she opened her eyes, she realized everyone was rushing from the campground into the woods.

"What's going on?" Daphne said as she rubbed the sleep from her eyes.

"I think we've caught our first mouse," Henry said, appearing before them with Basil in his arms. "Why don't you go take a look? Junior and I will prep a room in the mirror."

Sabrina helped her sister to her feet, and the two rushed after the rest of the army. It wasn't long before they found what was drawing everyone's attention. Jack Pumpkinhead was dangling upside down, held in the air by a vine wrapped around his feet. His giant pumpkin noggin was as red as the handprint painted on his shirt.

"Let me down, traitors," he demanded.

"Welcome to our forest, Jack," Sabrina said. "And congratulations, you're the first person to get caught in one of our traps."

"When I get down from here, I swear you'll pay," the man shouted.

"I never get tired of hearing empty threats. Cut this walking pumpkin pie down," Sabrina said.

"Wait! It's not finished," Puck said, and a moment later a dozen chimpanzees plopped down from the limbs. Each wore a soldier's helmet and held fat Wiffle ball bats, which they used to smack their captive. Jack groaned while the chimps giggled like little maniacs.

"So I guess Bunny found a way to get into his bedroom," Sabrina said to her sister.

"Yep. For better or worse," Daphne said.

Over the course of the day, the Master's thugs suffered at the diabolical hands of the Trickster King. Hansel fell into a pit filled with honey (and to no one's surprise, fire ants). His sister, Gretel, surrendered after being chased through the woods by a pack of zombie chipmunks. Bo Peep was hoisted skyward by enormous helium balloons that were quickly popped by tiny arrows. She fell onto a carefully placed hornet's nest. A couple of goblins found themselves caught in the hungry jaws of giant Venus flytraps that magically sprang from the ground. A towering troll stomped through the woods only to be clobbered in the head by a huge log that swung down from the trees. It seemed that every ten minutes or so the quiet of the forest was interrupted by surprised cries and painful bellows and then Puck's gleeful giggles.

By evening, thirty of the Hand's thugs were locked tight in the Hall of Wonders, and it was time to move on to a new camp. Sabrina examined a map of the forest with the help of the mirrors and found another great site for hiding. Traveling by night, the army made their way there just before midnight and set up camp.

The next day started much like the day before. The Patchwork Girl was the first victim. Sabrina had never met her, but the Scarecrow, who had once been very much in love with her, informed everyone that she was made entirely of old pieces of blankets. Unfortunately for her, she was caught when she walked through a trip wire that doused her with gallons of sewage. Sabrina was sure the smell would never come out.

"I wonder if you can dry-clean a person," Goldilocks said through her pinched nose.

The day brought more prisoners, many caught with the help of a thousand little pixies Puck affectionately referred to as his minions: Ms. Muffet and her husband, the Spider, Big Hans and Little Hans, Babe the Big Blue Ox, Jack and Jill, Solomon Grundie, and a blue dragon all got the worst of their little stings and relentless pursuits. Once again, by nightfall, the ragtag army had captured another thirty-five members of the Hand, but their most important prisoner—Beast—was completely entwined in what looked like a giant spiderweb made from bubblegum. It had clumped into his hair, making it painful to move.

"Where's my daughter?" Beauty said coolly.

"Our daughter is safe," Beast said. "You don't have to worry."

"Don't tell me what I have to worry about, James. You don't get to do that anymore."

"They've turned you against me!" he roared.

"No, it's you who walked out on me when you decided to do the wrong thing. You can do what you want, but you won't do it with our daughter," Beauty said.

"You'll never find her," Beast said.

"You're wrong about that," Sabrina said. "The mirrors will show us."

The Beast growled "Beauty, why won't you be reasonable? These people you have befriended have brought us nothing but misery. What happened to the woman who would do anything for our freedom?"

"That woman realized that she was also someone's mother," Beauty said. "One of us has to teach her right from wrong."

The Beast snarled. "So you're finished with me, then?"

"I will never be finished with you, James. I'm always going to love you, but right now you don't deserve me."

Beauty walked with Beast as he was taken into the Hall of Mirrors and locked inside his room. She herself turned the key, then looked through the barred window at her husband. "Figure out how to be the man I loved," she said to him.

In the morning, they set up a new camp and found another twenty-five prisoners to lock safely away. These villains suffered through animal bites, toxic waste, angry bruises, and a few de-pantsings. In between runs to check on traps, Sabrina and Daphne went to the mirror room to give the guardians an update.

"At this rate we'll have every bad guy under lock and key in no time at all," Daphne told the mirrors.

"You should be very proud of yourselves," the strange beaver guardian commended. His name was Shi'arsted. Sabrina was slowly learning everyone's names during her daily visits to check the maps for new campsites.

"Thank you," Sabrina said. "Unfortunately, our two biggest targets are still out there."

"I don't think you'll see Atticus and the First in these woods," Titan said. "They are too smart to fight you on your turf. You're going to have to go to them."

Sabrina nodded, feeling deflated. "I know. I can feel that battle coming at me like a train. I want to get off the tracks, but I can't. We just don't have a clue what to do when it happens. I was hoping you might have some ideas."

"Between Atticus and the First, your best bet is the First. He is locked inside the feeble body of an old woman. If you kill her, you kill him," one of the mirrors said.

"Shut your mouth!" Fanny cried. "That old woman is the kids' grandmother."

"I'm only speaking logically," the mirror said defensively.

"As long as Atticus wears his armor he's going to be unstoppable. No mortal man can kill him. You've got to find a way to get it off of him," Titan said.

Suddenly, the mirrors began to shake, and the guardian's

reflections turned into rough seas. A terrible electrical storm sparked out of each one, which made Sabrina take a step back—but the mirrors surrounded her.

"What's happening?" Daphne cried.

"Run!" Harry cried.

"He's coming, Sabrina!" Fanny warned.

And then, every face vanished, replaced by the mocking horror of Granny Relda and the monster that controlled her. Her wild face and eyes stared at the girls with a smile both dark and diabolical.

"Hello, Daphne, Sabrina," Mirror said.

"What are you doing here?" Daphne said.

"Funny little side effect of once being a mirror is that if I exert enough energy, I can overhear everything you say."

"You've heard what we've been planning all along," Sabrina said.

"Since the start."

Daphne gasped, and Sabrina's hands shook with anger. "Then why did you let your thugs get trapped? Why didn't you warn them about the traps out here in the woods?"

Mirror chuckled. "Well, one, they were starting to get in the way. Two, more than a few of them are pretty smelly. I could get them to burn the town to the ground, but a little body wash was

out of the question. And three, I don't need them any longer to get what I want. It's just me versus two little girls."

Sabrina was shocked.

"Yeah, I heard the prophecy too," he continued. "Wish it didn't have to be like that, Starfish. I . . . well, I have a soft spot for you girls."

"If you care so much, why don't you leave our grandmother's body," Daphne said.

"Trust me," Mirror said. "I wish I could. She's old and tired. It's exhausting being in such a feeble person. But all this trouble can go away in an instant. Just give me the spell that lowers the barrier. I know you have it. If you do, I promise I'll surrender this body and then you can have your dear granny back—sound fair?"

"I can't let you out, Mirror," Sabrina said, mustering every bit of bravado she could.

"That's how it's going to be? That makes me sad." Mirror frowned. "Well, Starfish, you've forced my hand. If you won't give me the spell, I'm going to have to make you give it to me."

Then the surface of each mirror began to bubble and churn. Lightning exploded out of the silver surfaces like before, but this time much more violently. Sabrina grabbed Daphne's hand and backed away, but a bolt of energy blasted near her feet, knocking both girls to the floor. As Sabrina tried to stand she saw long, jagged cracks splintering through the reflections. Soon they multiplied, intertwining like the crayon drawings of a toddler. And then all twenty-four of the guardians reappeared, their faces caught in frozen fear as they joined together in a chorus of pain.

"Don't give up, girls. The First can be defeated," Donovan shouted.

They exploded. The broken shards of mirror ricocheted across the room. Sabrina shielded Daphne with her body while also trying to cover her face as best she could. But the pieces still ripped into her arms and legs and back. Each one felt like a tiny razor slicing across her skin followed by the sting of a red-hot brand.

When it was over, she got to her feet and helped Daphne up. Though her sister was sobbing, she appeared uninjured. However, drops of blood fell from Sabrina's body and rained down onto the silver shards beneath her feet. There was one large chunk sticking out of her arm, and when she tried to pull it out, it melted and seeped into her skin.

Daphne hugged her tightly. Sabrina trembled until she could no longer hold back her tears. And she stood, crying and bleeding, and doing her best not to give in to the ease of losing her mind. She shook herself, then she and Daphne raced out of the room and through the portal, plowing through the woods as screams filled the air. But where was her army?

"Sabrina, your arm!" Daphne said, staring at the bleeding line.

"Forget it. We've got to find Mom and Dad," Sabrina said. "Uncle Jake! Mom! Dad!" No one answered. Where was her family? Were they wounded? She started to panic. "Puck!" There was an odd tightening in her chest, and her skin broke out in a sweat. She used to get the same out-of-control feeling when she was around magic, but she forced herself to concentrate. Her army needed her.

She and Daphne ran through the camp, which was deserted and on fire. Footprints led them up a hill and down a steep embankment, but still they found no signs of life. In the distance she could hear more screaming, and when she looked to the ground—blood! They followed its trail through a patch of trees until they were face-to-face with Atticus. Next to him were two enormous trolls, standing nearly eight feet tall and packed tight with muscles. They were terrifying creatures, but not nearly as fearsome as Atticus's smile.

"So you are the little ones causing all the trouble," Atticus said. He raised his sword and slashed at them. They managed to leap out of the way just in time, but Sabrina stumbled on a stone and fell. While she scampered to her feet, Atticus stalked her. "You know, whatever that is in your grandmother isn't happy. You should hear it screaming and shouting. It even rambles on when the body is asleep."

"Sorry for the inconvenience, but it wasn't my idea for Mirror to steal my grandmother's body."

Atticus laughed, then turned to the trolls. "Get to work, boys. We don't have all day."

The trolls grunted and lumbered into the woods, sending a flock of frightened crows flying into the sky.

Facing Atticus without his monsters didn't make Sabrina feel any less confident. She found a long branch and scooped it up, remembering what Snow had taught her about the bo-staff. This one was similar in weight and length. She spun it around with all her strength, then hit Atticus in the side of the head.

He fell over cursing and shouting threats, then staggered onto his knees, and Sabrina hit him over the back of the neck.

"I thought this suit of armor made him indefensible," Sabrina said.

"Maybe that only counts for parts that the suit covers," Daphne said.

Sabrina brought the branch high over her head and aimed it at the villain's skull for a second blow, but as it came down he caught it in his hand. Wrenching it from her grasp, he leaped to his feet and with a ferocity and anger she did not expect, he kicked her hard in the belly. She slammed back against a tree, and was pinned there by the heel of his boot.

"Let her go," Daphne said. Sabrina turned her head to see the little girl standing next to the tree. Elvis stood by her side, growling.

Atticus laughed. "Shoo, fly."

Daphne reached into her pocket and took out the fairy godmother wand. She shook it in her hand and with a flick, sent a blast of magic at the man. Both she and Atticus were enveloped in purple smoke.

"What are you doing?" Sabrina shouted to her sister.

"Changing his outfit. If we get him out of that armor, we can beat him," Daphne cried through the fog, but when it drifted away, Atticus was still wearing his magical armor. He looked down and laughed.

"Child, you amuse me. After I gut your sister, you will be next and for a laugh I will make it quick," he said.

"Hmmm, I suppose I need to go with plan B," Daphne said.

Elvis leaped forward and chomped down on Atticus's groin, where he had no armor to protect him. He fell over into the leaves, moaning. While he lay there, Daphne snatched Sabrina's hand and they, along with Elvis, ran.

Once beyond the clearing, they darted into the woods shouting for their mother and father, but they heard nothing in response. Eventually, they stumbled upon Puck, who looked as panicked as they had ever seen him.

Puck raced into the clearing. "Come quick! It's Gepetto."

The girls followed him into the woods. They found Pinocchio leaning over his father. The old man wasn't breathing. He had a ragged wound on his chest, probably created by Atticus's sword. His face was calm and his eyes closed. Pinocchio held his hand and wept.

"Papa?" he cried, as if the old man were merely sleeping. "Papa, please be OK."

But he wasn't.

10

 ctober 23

It seems as if every time I open this journal I have to write down another death. I hate these pages. I hate this pen. This is not supposed to be a record of the people who have died because of me. I want to throw this book into the woods, maybe bury it deep in the ground where no one will ever find it, but I don't have time to feel sorry for myself. I have to help dig graves.

The Frog Princess (who I'm told was really named Sharlene), Sir Lancelot, Friar Tuck, and Gepetto were all killed fighting Atticus and his trolls. Poor Pinocchio. He blames himself. He says he was the one who opened the Book of Everafter and set Atticus free. Uncle Jake has tried to console him, but hasn't had much luck.

Sadly, we have another tragedy on our hands. Atticus has taken Snow White. Apparently murder wasn't enough for him. Bunny is *beside herself with worry. She wants to race after him, but Baba Yaga has reminded her that she doesn't have the power to stop him. With Morgan trapped in the old castle, the coven is broken and only the super-charged power of the three kept them alive the last time they encountered Mirror and the blood prince.*

We left their graves in the woods and moved our camp in case Atticus or Mirror returns. We have to keep moving and I need to share less with the others about where we are going. I've asked everyone to destroy any mirror they might be carrying. I can't take the risk that he might be able to see us through them, and the mirror room is locked and off limits.

And then there's me. Something is happening. I'm sick. But sick isn't the right word exactly. I feel weird. When the mirrors exploded, a little piece flew into my arm, and I haven't felt myself since. It started out with dizziness and feeling tired, but now, well, I feel like I'm dying. My eyes are blurry and my head is pounding. I just want to lie down, but I know I can't. Everyone is counting on me.

Sabrina stood before her army, their faces fresh with grief. She tried to stand strong. She knew that she could not let them see how terrible she felt.

"I didn't know this until very recently, but Mirror has been watching us through the Council of Mirrors. He could see us making our war plans from the beginning. The only reason we were able to trap the Hand inside Charming's castle is because the Master let us."

"So he can see us?" Goldilocks asked.

Sabrina shook her head. "Not anymore. The mirrors have been destroyed."

Some of the crowd gasped.

"And we have to deal with him, but first we have to deal with Atticus. He took Snow."

"He tore through us, Sabrina," the Frog Prince said. "Nothing we did stopped him. He's a monster."

Mr. Canis stepped forward. In his hand was the glass jar that trapped the Big Bad Wolf. "Perhaps it's time we had our own monster."

"Absolutely not!" Henry cried. "You are not letting that thing loose again. Canis, you spent hundreds of years trying to get rid of it and now you want to subject yourself to the misery again?"

"I don't want to, Henry. It's just what must be done."

"Having the Wolf running loose is no better than having Atticus," Mayor Heart said. She looked as if she might faint just thinking about the dire possibilities.

"I do have a certain level of control over him," Canis said.

"Which you lost," Mr. Swineheart squealed. In his anxiety, he transformed into his true form as a pig, snorting through his round nose.

"Then you will have to find a way to stop him," Canis said impatiently. "There is always the horn of the North Wind."

"It disappeared when the Hall was looted," Daphne said.

"Then perhaps Beauty can help," he argued.

"I could try," she said. "Though it isn't easy singing to someone who is running around tearing people to shreds."

"I don't like it," the Pied Piper said. "Someone will get hurt."

"This is not your decision to make!" Canis bellowed. Everyone stood agape at his boiling anger. "I know you've all found it perfectly convenient to have me babysitting and watching your belongings, but I am not and never have been a person who stands aside and lets others do what I must do myself. My dearest friend Relda Grimm needs help. The only way to get to her is to take Atticus out of the picture. I'm not here to ask any of you for permission. I'm telling you what I'm going to do!"

Red broke into tears and ran from the camp.

"She needs you, Canis," Veronica said. "She's already been abandoned so many times. Are you going to abandon her too?"

"I'll go and speak with her," he said, scooping up his jar and cane. Sabrina watched him, bent over and struggling, as he disappeared into the trees.

"Sooo," Puck said. "That's going to be interesting."

"He wants to feel necessary," Goldi said.

"He's going to get someone killed," Beauty argued.

"Isn't there someone else who should be here?" Cinderella asked. "Where's William?"

Without warning, Sabrina felt something slice through her thoughts like a knife. She doubled over. The sensation was hot and painful, but along with it came a clear vision of the prince. He was curled on a dirty mattress inside the former mayor's mansion. But how could she see him like this? Was she just imagining things? It made no sense. She staggered and would have fallen if her mother had not been there to catch her.

"Sabrina, are you OK?" Veronica asked.

Sabrina shook off the vision. She nodded. "Just a little tired. We'll go to Charming and convince him to help us," she said. "But listen, if we manage to get lucky and stop Atticus, there will be no more obstacles between us and Mirror. I want to be honest with you all. I don't know what will happen. Our army is savaged, our coven is broken, and Mirror wants the spell that turns off the barrier. I have no idea what he's going to do to get it, but it's not going to be fun. I just know he can't have it. If you've thought about bailing on us, you should do it now so we know what we're working with."

Beauty stepped forward. "I have known your family a long time, and my rage at being trapped in this town has caused me to do things I regret. But there was always something that I respected about your family—your infernal principles! Wilhelm taught his children to stand for something, to look after our community and protect us, even when we didn't want it. Douglas taught Sterling, and Sterling taught Spaulding, and Spaulding taught Josef, and so on and so on. Well, you can imagine how that integrity made us crazy. Now I marvel at it. I envy it. I will do anything to emulate it, so my daughter will know what it is to be a good person. I will die to protect you."

"I will lay my life down for you," the Wicked Queen said.

"You can count on me and my son," the Pied Piper said.

"You have the birds," the Widow crowed.

"You have my men," Robin Hood said.

"And mine," King Arthur shouted.

"It was never a question," Goldi said. The roars of three fierce brown bears echoed her promise.

"I will fight," Pinocchio said through his tears. "I will fight."

All present made the promise, though Mayor Heart did so reluctantly. At the end of the chorus of cheers, the only person who hadn't spoken up was Puck. The crowd looked at him for his answer.

"Well, duh!" Puck said.

• • •

Sabrina, Puck, and the Wicked Queen marched out to find Charming. Bunny claimed she would force William to come back to the army if he wouldn't listen to reason. The group hiked toward the old mayor's mansion. The others were perplexed as to how Sabrina knew where to find the prince. She couldn't explain, but she was beginning to believe that whatever gave her the visions was also making her sick. She was both fevered and chilled and had to stop several times to shake off dizzy spells and nausea. She was having a difficult time concentrating and her mind kept flashing on something she had seen many times before—a fiery red handprint. There were times when she thought she couldn't take another step, but she couldn't go back. Charming had to know what happened to Snow.

"What's wrong with you?" Puck said. "You're starting to look a little green."

"I'm just tired," Sabrina lied.

Puck spun around on his heels and transformed into a donkey. Bunny helped Sabrina climb on his back, but not before examining the jagged slash on her arm where the piece of magic mirror had cut her skin. Bunny's face looked worried, but she didn't say anything.

The front door of the mayor's mansion hung open, and all the windows were broken. When they stepped inside, it was obvious that it had been looted. There were huge holes in the floors and graffiti covered the walls. Sabrina hardly recognized the place.

The group climbed the once-grand staircase and found Charming asleep on the floor of his old office, just as in Sabrina's strange, painful vision. His weapons and maps were gone, as was the portrait of Snow he kept on the wall, and the poor man looked and smelled as if he had been drinking.

"Wakey wakey, eggs and bakey," Puck said.

Charming lifted his head as if the motion hurt him. He groaned and closed his eyes. "I told you to leave me alone."

"That's not an option anymore," the Wicked Queen said. "Atticus has Snow."

Charming strained to focus his eyes. "What? When?"

"A few hours ago," Sabrina said.

"We would have come sooner, but we weren't sure you were finished feeling sorry for yourself," Bunny said.

Charming growled. "How dare you, Bunny? You meddled with my life—my memories, my identity—and you think I should just snap out of it? You try to be a fictional character for a minute!"

"I've been a fictional character just as long as you have, William. I had to rewrite myself to keep Snow safe. I had to give up my daughter! I had to make her believe I was evil. I had to make her fear me, not to mention every Everafter I've encountered since. Do you think that was easy, being the scorn of an entire town for hundreds of years? I had to take on a completely different persona for centuries."

"That was your choice," Charming cried.

"So you were edited! It's not like I made you into a fool. I gave you courage and strength. I made you the heir to a fortune and I gave you a girlfriend who is the most beautiful woman in the world. Was it really that intolerable?"

"This fighting is stupid," Sabrina said. "We need a hero, and Billy, that's you."

"Bunny should open her magic book and write herself a new one," William said.

"You know what? You're not fictional at all and you never have been," Sabrina cried. "Because you're a jerk!"

"What?"

"She just said you're a jerk," Puck said. "I know because she calls me one all the time."

"Bunny remade you into the ideal man: brave, strong, and clever. What she did not make is a grouchy, impatient, and arrogant crybaby."

"She's right, William. You really are an insufferable boor, which proves you are not a toy that I wound up and let loose. I wanted you to be dashing and romantic and ever-smiling. I wanted perfection."

Charming slumped back onto his makeshift bed. "OK, I've heard enough insults for one day."

"You don't understand," Sabrina said. "You constantly turn from perfect into a sour old lemon. So if Bunny didn't write that into her daughter's story, it must be coming from you. You're a real person, William—warts and all."

Charming sat up and looked them group for a long time. "This is the worst pep talk in the history of the world."

Puck laughed. "It really is."

"Is it working?" Bunny asked.

Charming nodded.

"So are you ready to put away the sad face so we can go save the love of your life?" Sabrina asked.

Charming snatched his sword off the ground. "I am."

"Great, we got the band back together," Puck said. "Now, where do we find Atticus?"

Once again, Sabrina's mind was ripped open. She staggered and fell as visions of Atticus flashed through her mind. He was camped in a house that overlooked the river. It was perched on a rocky edge, probably the home of one of the humans who had abandoned the town when the trouble began. Atticus was hitting Snow White. She tried her self-defense techniques, but he was too strong. Nottingham stood nearby, watching as if amused.

Puck helped her to her feet. "What is wrong with you?"

"I know where he is," Sabrina said. "We have to hurry."

• • •

The road that led to Atticus twisted upward toward Devil's Peak, running parallel to the choppy river below. To get to the house where he was camped Sabrina's army had to take a steep path that cut back several times. Charming insisted on leading the group and demanded that everyone walk as quickly as possible. Canis stumbled forward as fast as his old bones would allow. Though his body was failing him, his eyes were confident, and for the first time in many days he was not depressed or beaten. He walked with purpose.

On the other hand, the Queen of Hearts wasn't exactly in a hurry. Her wounded leg was still hurting her and she whined incessantly.

"This is a very steep road," Heart complained. "Perhaps I should stay here and wait."

"We've heard enough of your whining and wheezing, Mrs. Heart. If you don't want to go, then stay here," Pinocchio snapped. The boy now walked with determination, a simmering desire for justice keeping his feet moving forward.

Sabrina was sure her uncle would lash out at the mayor as well, but again he treated her with patience. "I would probably recommend you stay behind if Nottingham weren't still around. I'd hate to be too far away if he were to show up. I know it is physically demanding, but I do think it's safer if you stay with the group."

Heart grumbled but continued the climb, wheezing like a tired pig all the way to the top.

And that's when they heard the screaming.

"Snow!" Charming cried, and raced ahead.

"Charming, no!" Bunny said. "We need a plan!"

Sabrina's brain buzzed with possibilities. There were so many different options, all laid out to her like the strands of a spiderweb as big as the world. Each strand led to a possibility—some sort of final outcome—but there were so many. She couldn't follow all of them to their conclusions. There were thousands of them and each one branched into another thousand paths.

So many ended in the deaths of people she loved. She followed one particular strand as far as she could—and found it ending in blood. Still, it seemed like the right choice, but there were so many others swirling and spinning her thoughts into mush. How did she know such things?

"We need to circle around, try to get behind Atticus," Sabrina said. "It may be the only way to help him and save Snow."

"How can you know?" Henry asked.

"I can't explain it. I just do," Sabrina said. "And we have to do it now."

Everyone scurried through the bushes, circling around the house. All the while Sabrina watched Charming in her mind. Even though they were many yards away and hidden by foliage, it was as if he were standing right next to her.

"I am here, Atticus!" Charming shouted. Every word spun the web inside Sabrina's mind in a new direction.

"Billy! Don't come any closer. He's going to kill you!" Snow shouted from somewhere within the house.

"Shut up!" Atticus roared, and there was a wicked slap.

"It's a cowardly man that beats on a woman, brother," Charming said.

"So you remember me now, do you, William?"

"No! But from what I understand, that's for the best. I suppose if I did remember you, I would have stolen your wife anyway. You aren't worthy."

Suddenly, an arrow flew out the window and pierced Charming in the leg. He fell over, clenching the wound and cursing. There was blood everywhere and the strand of the future reflected its crimson color.

"You should not be so insulting, little brother."

Sabrina watched Charming pull the tip out with his bare hands and get to his feet. It was clear he could barely move the leg, but he walked the best he could.

"So once again you prove you have no honor," Charming shouted. "Sending arrows from the safety of a house. I was told you were a brave man."

Atticus stepped outside, dragging Snow behind him. Nottingham followed, with his dagger drawn. Snow's face was bloody and her clothes torn. "I have no problem being seen, William. Now that you are satisfied I suggest you leave while you still can. I have my wife and I'll mark up your little indiscretion as the crimes of a drunkard."

Charming drew his sword.

"So you want to fight, baby brother? I promise you this will be more than the roughhousing we used to do on the castle lawn.

Father and Mother are not here to attend to your bloody noses and boxed ears."

"Have your fun, Atticus," Nottingham said. "I have my own vengeance to win."

Atticus pushed Snow to the ground and rushed at Charming, his sword held high. Their blades met with a savage crash, and Atticus kicked Charming in his wounded leg. The prince fell to one knee with a cry but quickly hobbled back to two legs. Atticus attacked again. When he went for another kick, Charming stepped out of the way, only to get a punch to the side of the head. Charming stumbled but kept standing. He swung wildly but missed his brother completely, and Atticus took another ferocious swipe with his sword. This one sliced Charming's shirt open and blood seeped into the cloth. He fell down and clutched his wound.

Atticus looked down at him in disgust. "You were a fool to come here. This is hardly worth my time," he said. Then he returned to where Snow had fallen and dragged her to Charming's body. "Look at him! This is what you chose over me? He's a runt. My father should have taken him out back and drowned him in the river. Don't you fools understand? No man can kill me while I wear this armor."

Mr. Canis stepped out of the woods with his pack in hand. "I have a friend who might be able to help with that." He opened his pack and reached inside, then turned back to the group with surprise. "It's not here. The jar is missing."

And that's when Sabrina saw Red with the jar in hand, unfastening the cork that kept the monster inside. She had seen this but she had seen so many versions—so many ending in terror. Before Sabrina could stop her, the black spirit that resided inside zipped out and flew into the little girl's open mouth.

"Oh boy," Puck said, and quickly stepped out of the little girl's path.

"Red, what did you do?" Daphne cried.

But the girl did not answer. She was going through a horrifyingly familiar and unsettling change. Hair sprouted from every pore, claws grew where fingers once were, and a long bushy tail sprouted. When the terrifying transformation was complete, the creature towered over everyone at a staggering nine feet with a coat of red.

"Look who's back," the Wolf howled. "What's for dinner? Oh, I know. Him!"

It leaped at Atticus, knocking him to the ground.

"I think we have to get this crab out of his shell," the Wolf taunted the evil prince. The monster reached over and snatched

Atticus's breastplate, ripping it from his body and throwing it into the woods.

Atticus shrieked in fear and backed away from the creature.

"Is that all that's inside?" the Wolf complained. "Why, there's hardly any meat on him."

Atticus swung his sword in desperation, managing to slash the Wolf's arm. The wound only made the beast laugh. Without a pause he leaped onto Atticus, knocking him to the ground. He climbed on top of him, yanking the rest of the armor off and tossing it aside. Soon, the magical defense was completely gone, and Atticus was just a man.

"Atticus is mine!" Charming said, struggling to his feet.

"No, he's mine!" the Frog Prince shouted.

"Get in line!" Pinocchio shouted.

"NO!!!!" the Wicked Queen boomed, and with a clap of her hands the entire army fell to the ground. Bunny floated into the air and hovered over Atticus, her eyes white like stars and her hands red as magma. "I told you not to touch my daughter, son-in-law," she said, her voice like thunder. "I told you what I would do."

"She's my wife! My property!" Atticus cried, climbing to his feet.

"You should have stayed inside the book, Atticus Charming,"

she said as the energy built up in her hands. Sabrina could see she was going to unleash something wicked on the villain.

But before she could attack, the end of a sword pierced through Atticus's chest. He looked down and squirmed like a worm trying to free itself from the fisherman's hook. Behind him stood Snow White. Her face was bloodied and bruised, but she had the hilt of the sword in her hand.

"No," she said. "He's mine."

And then Atticus fell forward and never stood again.

Snow rushed to Charming and helped him to his feet.

"William, you and I are getting married. No arguments," Snow said.

Charming grinned.

"That was a lovely appetizer," the Wolf said as he licked his lips. He turned toward the crowd and stomped forward only to have spindly Mr. Canis block its path.

"Well, look who it is," the Wolf growled. "Step aside, old man."

"No," he said defiantly.

"You old fool. I'll tear you apart."

"Red! Red, can you hear me?"

The Wolf laughed. "She's not listening."

"Red, it's time to come out of the darkness. You're in charge. You can do it. Just follow my voice," Mr. Canis said.

The Wolf let out an angry protest and doubled over as if in pain. Then he transformed back into Red Riding Hood. She stood before Canis, trembling and crying.

"I didn't know it was like that," Red sobbed. "The demon that controlled me wasn't so angry. It was just crazy. This thing . . . it's so vicious."

Canis pulled her into his arms. "I'll help you."

Suddenly, Sabrina's head was filled with an insistent buzz. It felt like there was a little man pounding on a door in her mind, and when she opened it she saw images flashing before her eyes: Uncle Jake's face; serpentine blades glinting in the sun, slashing at arms and legs; cliffs over a rocky beach. She looked around at the gathered crowd. Jake was not there. Where was he? And worse, there was someone else missing too.

"Nottingham!" she cried.

Henry rushed to her before she could fall to the ground. "Sabrina, what is wrong with you?"

But she couldn't answer. The images had taken over and all she could see was her uncle watching Mayor Heart and Sheriff Nottingham stabbing at each other with daggers. He wasn't in any danger at all, but the two villains were trying to murder each other.

"You betrayed me, Heart, and that is something I will never forgive," Nottingham said as he poked at his former ally.

The queen shrieked and slashed at him. "Stay back, you lunatic. Can't you see the writing is on the wall with the Master? He can't open the barrier. Isn't that why we were doing all this? The Grimms offered us an alternative. Since when do you turn down an opportunity?"

"An opportunity! One you no doubt planned to keep to yourself. You'd happily leave me here."

"Please, don't fight!" Jake said, reaching into his pocket. He took out a folded piece of paper and held it out to the villainous duo. "Here, just take the spell."

Nottingham snatched the paper from Jake's hand and tried to unfold it, but Heart seized it from his grip.

"Give it to me!"

"It's mine, you fool!"

Nottingham grabbed it, but Heart tackled him. They rolled on the ground, fighting and cursing and slowly rolling down the hill to the edge of the cliff. They were too busy struggling over the paper to notice.

"I should never have cast my lot with you," Nottingham said. "The Master told me you couldn't be trusted."

"You and your precious Master. He cares nothing for you or anyone else."

The two stopped their fighting as they neared the edge of the cliff. The queen held the spell.

"What is this?" she cried, when Nottingham snatched it from her with his free hand. He searched one side of it and then the other, and then crumpled it into a ball. "It's a blank piece of paper. This is a trick!"

Uncle Jake took two daggers from his pocket and approached the edge of the cliff. "Yes, it is. I knew the two of you would turn on each other if you had the chance. I should have thought of it earlier. Maybe Briar would still be alive."

"You manipulated us?" Nottingham said. He reached back to toss his blade at Jake.

The world slowed to a crawl as the strands of time forced their way back into Sabrina's mind. She saw her uncle's death a thousand times. "Stop it," she cried. "What can I do about it?"

And then the webs were gone and she was seeing her uncle once more. Just before Nottingham could release his deadly missile, the ground beneath him and Heart crumbled and the duo cried out in fear as they fell off the edge of the cliff.

Uncle Jake rushed to the edge. Below him, Nottingham and

Heart clung to roots in order to keep from plummeting one hundred feet to the rocky and jagged beach below.

"Killing us won't bring her back, Jacob!"

"No, it won't," Uncle Jake said as he knelt on one knee. Sabrina hoped he was about to hoist them onto safe ground, but instead he reached into the pocket of his shirt and removed the white rose he had taken from Briar's grave. Despite many days in his pocket, it looked as fresh and alive as if it had just bloomed. With his fingers he dug a tiny hole in the soil and set the severed stem inside. Then he gingerly packed it with more earth.

"What are you doing, you fool?" Nottingham shouted. "This is no time for gardening. We're going to fall. Help us!"

Uncle Jake gazed upon the rose lovingly. As before, the flower quickly sprouted a twin. It pushed its way toward the sunlight and bloomed like a tiny exploding firework. Then came another rose and another and another until the entire cliff side was churning like a sea with new blooms. The roses sprouted around Jake's feet and down the cliff and through the desperate fingers of Nottingham and Heart. The blooms wove through their arms and torsos, ran down their legs and around their feet. Soon, there were hundreds of flowers, then thousands—and each flower blossom moved a tiny portion of earth. Combined, the tiny portion became a ripple, then a wave, then a churning, bubbling sea of soil, making it impossible for the villains to hold on any longer.

Nottingham and Heart fell with little white petals fluttering alongside them. The rocky beach where they landed rapidly transformed into a garden of flowers that reached right to the shore. Soon their bodies were swallowed up, as if the earth demanded that something ugly be replaced with beauty.

Uncle Jake looked out over the edge for a long time, saying nothing, and then he leaned down and took a single rose from the abundant garden at his feet. He gingerly placed it into his pocket for safekeeping.

And then a fever swept over Sabrina that felt as if her very blood was on fire. The last thing she saw before she collapsed was the worried look on her father's face.

11

abrina Grimm was no stranger to nightmares. Long before she came to Ferryport Landing, she had spent many nights tossing and turning as her imagination fought off Ms. Smirt and her endless supply of crazy foster families. When she found herself surrounded by real monsters, they invaded her dreams as well. But her mind had never concocted a terror quite as horrible as Baba Yaga. What was worse, the old crone wasn't a dream. She was real, and now she was peering into Sabrina's mouth and tugging on her tongue.

"The child is infected," Baba Yaga said to her family and friends.

"With what?" her father said. He looked panicked.

"Magic, of course," the old crone said dismissively. "Did you think I was giving her a checkup for chicken pox? This thing you love so dearly has the sickness."

"You mean there is magic inside her?" Daphne asked. She placed her hand on her sister's and nodded. "Yes, I can feel it."

Sabrina shook her head, which made her dizzy. "When the mirrors exploded, a piece cut me. I guess some of it got under my skin. I haven't felt like myself ever since, but I'm OK. No one needs to worry."

"This is not good, Henry," Mr. Canis said. "Your daughter is magic intolerant."

"Yeah, I sort of get power hungry around it, but I'm fine, really," Sabrina said as she tried to stand unsuccessfully. They were still at Atticus's hideout. They needed to get to Mirror and were wasting time. "I have that under control. I just feel like I've got the flu or something."

"You should lie down, honey," her mother said.

"Let her stand," Baba Yaga said. "She'll be dead soon."

"She could die?" Veronica said.

"Didn't say could," the old crone croaked. "Said will."

"Then we have to get it out of her," Puck demanded.

"Leave her be, I said. It's inside her—in the tissue. It isn't coming out."

"Then what?" Bunny said. "We just let her die slowly? That's our only choice?"

"It's no choice at all, poison maker," Baba Yaga said. "Best thing to do is put her to work. She's got the stuff mirrors are made of floating around inside her. Can't you feel the power coming off of her? It rivals that of your monster, the First. If you're wise, you'll send her out to kill it. We have nothing that can stop that thing, and she might be our only chance."

"You're saying my sister has power like Mirror?" Daphne said.

"Not like him!" Baba Yaga snapped. "He's out there somewhere enjoying himself. Her magic is killing her. But yes, they can do the same things. Bah! Enough talk, we're wasting time."

"Sorry if you're on the clock, Old Mother," Charming said, "but we're going to sit here until we find a way to help her."

"There's a chance she could burn herself out," Bunny said.

"A slim chance," Baba Yaga argued. "You do these people an injustice giving them false hope. I've seen your handiwork. Even the tiniest splinter is enough to destroy a hundred worlds."

"What are you talking about?" Puck demanded. "What do you mean burn herself up?"

Bunny sighed. She explained to Sabrina. "If you could use it all up, just give in to its power and let it take you over, you might be able to expel enough so that you run out. You do only have a tiny piece inside."

"So all you have to do is just get crazy with the magic," Daphne said.

"OK, we've got a plan," Uncle Jake said. "Just use it all up. Let it all out on him."

"I can't. That's Granny Relda's body. I might kill her," Sabrina said. Her words seemed to suck the hope out of the room. "I don't want to die, but if that's what's going to happen anyway, I should do what I can to help Granny, not hurt her. But I need your help getting to him. He's waiting on Route 9 near the barrier. He's calling to me. He knows I can see him. He's demanding I bring him the spell."

"Then give it to him," the Scarecrow said.

"Just let him out," the Lion agreed.

"You don't understand what he'll do," Daphne said as she took the real spell from her pocket.

Sabrina could see the webs and all of their possibilities—she could see the future that Mirror owned. She watched him step outside of town once the barrier fell. She watched him sweep across America, then Europe, Africa, and Asia, sitting on a throne held up by the broken bodies of men and women. She watched the stampede of panicked people running from giants and fiery dragons in the sky. She saw all manner of monster running amok. "Dad, I think you and Mom and Basil and Uncle Jake should leave the town. Take the spell with you. If it's here, he'll never stop and he may try to hurt you to get what he wants."

Canis stepped forward and set a book in front of her. It was the Book of Everafter. "You can't leave the town."

"You had the book?" Daphne said. "Why did you take it?"

"I'm sorry to have made you worry about its whereabouts, but I had to have it. I had made some changes and—"

"What kind of changes, Canis?" Bunny said sternly.

"When your grandmother was taken by Mirror, I knew he would be able escape the barrier in her body. I also knew we were powerless to stop him, but the book offered an opportunity. It was an emergency. Something had to be done."

"What opportunity?" Henry asked.

"I had hoped it would be a temporary solution while I made changes to Mirror in his original story. But every time I wrote a word into Snow White and the Seven Dwarfs, the story would erase it, like it was protecting itself."

"The stories don't like being tampered with," the Wicked Queen said. "You shouldn't have been playing with it, old man."

Canis's face flashed rage. It was nearly has angry as when the Wolf had control of him. "Who do you think you are, woman? I'm not some retirement-home-bound burden. Wolf or no Wolf, I have been an important part of everything that has happened to this family for twenty years and you will not talk to me like I'm feeble and senile. This kind of nonsense is exactly why I took the book without asking. While you people are trying to wrap your head around what to do with old Mr. Canis, he was working to stop the end of the world!"

Sabrina flipped through the book. At the very end was a short story. She scanned it quickly—there was hardly anything to it—but she spotted her name, and her heart sank.

"He wrote us into the book," she said, then read aloud. "'Once upon a time there was a family called Grimm. They were detectives and lived in a town called Ferryport Landing. Relda, Henry, Veronica, Jacob, Sabrina, Daphne, and Basil were their names. The end.'"

"You turned them into Everafters," Bunny seethed.

"He did what?" Veronica cried.

"I did what needed to be done. I couldn't risk the chance that Mirror would just jump out of Relda and into one of you, so right after he took over Relda, I found the book and made you all Everafters. That's why he can't get out of town. He's not inside a human being anymore."

"So we're fairy-tale characters now?" Daphne said. "Cool!"

"I thought it would take the fight out of Mirror when he realized he now had no chance to escape, but then Jake appeared with his infernal magic spell, and Mirror had a new goal."

"I had no idea," Uncle Jake said.

"Why didn't you tell us?" Veronica asked. "We could've helped."

Canis's eyes flashed with anger. "This was something I could do myself. I didn't need anyone's help."

"So now we're stuck here with him," Henry said. "We can't leave the town, either."

"What are we going to do?" Uncle Jake asked.

"We fight," Sabrina said.

She was too ill to walk, so she would have to be carried. Puck spun around on his heels to transform. She expected him to become something disgusting—a camel, a giant chicken, a farting bear—but instead he became a majestic white stallion. After Uncle Jake helped her up onto his back, she quietly thanked him. Daphne joined her on Puck's back. Charming was too hurt to walk as well, so Poppa Bear offered him his back, and once everyone was settled, they began the march down the hill to the road that would lead them to Mirror.

Sabrina did her best to present a strong face like Puck had told her to do. Fake it until you make it, she reminded herself, but the power inside her was eating her alive. Twinges of pain soon became gut-searing agony, but she bit her lip and gritted her teeth. There were a few times when she was sure she would black out and fall off the horse, but Daphne wrapped her up in her little arms as if trying to bear her sister's pain. Her father walked alongside them with his hand on hers. Uncle Jake was on the other side. Veronica and Basil followed closely, as did Mr. Canis and Red. No one spoke, not even Puck. It was as if Sabrina were already dead and her friends and family were taking her casket to its final resting place.

She was too tired and hurt to be afraid. In fact, during the long journey she didn't think once of what might be at the end. Spotting her grandmother in the road, madly contorted by the creature controlling her limbs, was almost a relief. The magic was building. She needed to let it out.

Mirror stood in a wide stance with his arms outstretched in a mocking welcome. It made Sabrina angry. He wasn't taking her seriously. She could see in the expression he forced on her grandmother's face that this confrontation was nothing more than the last annoying thing on his "to do" list.

Sabrina asked her father to help her and Daphne down. Puck transformed back into a boy and seized his wooden sword from his belt.

"You stay here," Sabrina said.

Daphne shook her head. "We stick together. We are Grimms. This is what we do."

"But—"

"We're all going," Goldi said.

"Now let's go kick his butt," Puck said.

The rest of the crowd shared his stubbornness. Only Veronica stood back to shield baby Basil from whatever might be coming. She offered to look after Red and the other children, but they refused. Mirror had damaged all of their lives, and they would stand with the girls to confront him. Everyone surrounded Sabrina and Daphne and took each painful step with them, until they were standing before the Master.

"There's something different about you, Starfish," Mirror said through Granny's mouth. "Did you change your hair?"

"Don't call me Starfish," Sabrina said. "That's a name a friend gives another. You have never been my friend."

"Fair enough," he said. "I see you brought your family and friends. I suppose that means Atticus is dead. Can't say that bothers me much. He was a bit of a lunatic, that brother of yours, Billy—always shouting and carrying on with his threats. 'I'm going to kill my brother! I'm going to have my revenge!'"

"He's gone," Snow said.

Mirror cocked a curious eye. "So our little schoolteacher stood up for herself. Is that why you're all here? Did she inspire you? Do you plan to kill me?"

"I don't want to kill you," Sabrina said. "I don't want to kill anyone. I'm not like you. But I have to stop you somehow. I gave your thugs the same offer I'm going to give you. Stop this. Let my grandmother go. Bunny is here. She might be able to give you a body of your own."

"Oh, Mother is finally going to help out her baby, is that it?" Mirror sneered. "She abandoned me, Sabrina. She gave birth to me and then turned her back. No thank you. I think it's a little late for a mother and child reunion—but enough whining, right? Do you have the spell?"

"I'm not giving you the spell."

Mirror's fingers exploded with light, and suddenly from behind the group Veronica and Basil were dragged by an unseen force. It held them hovering over the crowd.

"Now, Sabrina, you know I can kill them. Just give me the spell."

"Don't do it, Sabrina," Veronica cried as she struggled to console Basil's fright.

Another blast of light and Henry joined his wife and child floating in the air.

"This doesn't have to get ugly," Mirror said. "Just hand me the paper."

"Let them go, Mirror," Sabrina said, her voice quaking from the tremors that rocked her from inside. She felt like she might explode—that her body might break in half and release a torrent of violence on Mirror and everyone around her. She turned to Daphne, who gave her a brave smile.

"Sabrina, do not give him the spell!" Henry shouted.

A moment later, Uncle Jake was jerked off the ground and floating helplessly with the others.

"Our lives are not worth the whole world!" Jake shouted.

"A simple snap of my fingers will end them," Mirror said. "It's that easy, Sabrina. But you can have them back for one little piece of paper."

"Daphne, give it to him," Sabrina said.

Daphne shook her head. "Sabrina—"

With a wave of her hand, Sabrina commanded the paper to leave her sister's pocket. Before the little girl could stop it the spell floated into Mirror's hand.

"NO!" Henry cried.

"I can't let you die!" Sabrina said. "I lost you once. I can't let it happen again!"

Mirror's face twisted into a smile as he gazed down upon the paper. With a laugh, he recited the ancient words, each growing with sound and fury.

There was an odd tinkling sound, and its great, ancient magic evaporated into the sky. The barrier was gone. Such a simple act for such powerful magic.

Mirror turned to the Everafters and smiled. "You're free. You are all finally free!"

The crowd shuffled uncomfortably, as if unsure of what to do.

The Frog Prince was the first to try. He gingerly searched the air for the wall, but it did not stop him. He stepped through, suddenly free.

"It works," he cried, urging his daughter to join him. She went with her father out into the free world. The Scarecrow and Cowardly Lion were next, followed by Cinderella and her husband, as well as the Three Blind Mice.

Mirror reached his hand through where the barrier used to be, and he grinned and laughed. "Finally!" He giggled.

"Don't get too excited, pal," Daphne said. "As long as we're alive, we're going to be on you like bedbugs. We won't stop until your back in your mirror and our granny is safe and sound!"

Mirror turned to the girls, his eyes aglow and his hands exploding with flames.

"Leave them alone!" Henry shouted.

"Sorry, Hank, but the little one is right. As long as there is a Grimm, you will always manage to find a way to ruin the party." He pointed his flaming finger at the girls, and a powerful force sent them flying through the crowd.

Just before they slammed into the ground, Sabrina felt a

bubbling explosion inside her, as if the top of a soda bottle shaken by a mischievous child was opened inside her belly. When they landed, instead of feeling the agony of tearing skin and broken bones, a metallic shell appeared, covering the girls and sending orange sparks zipping in all directions as they skidded down the road. When they came to a stop, they helped each other up as the hardened skin faded away.

"Neat trick," Daphne said.

"Thank you," Sabrina said.

"Any idea how you did that?" Daphne asked.

"Not a clue."

The girls walked back through the crowd to where they started.

Mirror saw them coming and surprise spread across his face. He snarled and blasted the girls again. This time Sabrina's hands reacted, and a shield of pink light pushed back against his attack. With another wave of her hand the earth broke open like an egg beneath Mirror's feet and swallowed him whole. At once, her family also fell to the ground. It was a miracle that no one was hurt, though baby Basil started to cry.

Sabrina reeled from her power. On the one hand, it felt good to let some of it out. It made her feel strong and a hundred feet tall. But on the other hand, she felt the desire to hurt Mirror again. She wanted to stand over his broken body and laugh.

That was when she knew how truly sick she was. She had to end this fast. She took Daphne's hand and together they ran to the crevice and peered into the darkness.

"Mirror!" she cried.

"You can't attack him," Daphne said. "You're attacking Granny."

"I know," Sabrina said. "I . . . this power isn't good for me. There's too much."

Daphne nodded and gestured for Baba Yaga and the Wicked Queen. The crone's horrible house lumbered behind them.

"Sabrina can't attack," Daphne said. "She can only defend, so it's up to the coven."

"But the coven is broken!" the Wicked Queen cried. "We'll try, but without a third—"

"I have solved one of our problems," Baba Yaga interrupted. "We will rebuild our coven stronger than before. We need to choose a third, and a more appropriate third this time. I am the crone. Morgan was the temptress. Bunny was the innocent, which was laughable at best. What we had was one crone and two temptresses. It diluted the magic, so we never could reach our full potential. What we need is a true innocent."

Sabrina looked around the crowd, but there was no one else with any real magical abilities who might be right for the coven.

Baba Yaga may have had a point, but there wasn't much they could do about it. "Who do you have in mind?"

The old witch turned to Daphne. "You will do."

"Me?" Daphne said.

"She's just a little girl. She doesn't know any magic!" Henry argued despite being suspended in midair.

"She tolerates the arcana well," Baba Yaga said. "Can you not see how it moves through her, Henry? Look how their dog stands by her. He is her familiar."

"He's just a dog!" Sabrina cried. "He probably thinks she has a sausage in her pocket."

Elvis rushed to join them and sniffed at Daphne's pockets.

"House! Jacket!" Baba Yaga cried.

The door of her hut opened and there was a terrible coughing sound. Then a long trench coat flew out of the doorway and landed at the old crone's feet. Sabrina recognized it immediately. Many months ago, Uncle Jake had traded it to the witch for her help; its pockets were filled with magical items beyond imagination. Baba Yaga scooped it up in her gnarled hand and helped the little girl into it. It was hardly a perfect fit. It dragged on the ground, and Sabrina had to help her roll up the sleeves so she could use her hands.

"I absolutely forbid this!" Henry shouted, but Bunny had

already reached out her hand and Daphne took it. Baba Yaga reached out her weathered claw and Daphne took that as well.

"NO!" Henry cried, but it was too late.

"We are bound by coven," the two older witches said.

"We are bound by coven," Daphne said.

Daphne's hair stood on end and her hands turned to stone. A moment later she returned to normal except for the unusually large smile on her face.

Then from deep in the abyss Sabrina saw her grandmother's hand pulling her body back to the surface. Mirror's eyes glowed and the ground bubbled. Geysers exploded around the crowd, sending steam into the air. A silver ooze gurgled out of the holes and collected in pools, from which an army of creatures then rose. Each was about the size of a large man, but made of what appeared to be mirrors. The second they were solid, the creatures attacked the crowd, forcing everyone to join the fight.

"Now, where were we?" Mirror said as flashing strands of electricity blasted from his hands. Daphne reached into her pocket and removed an amulet and the girls vanished, only to appear directly behind Mirror. There the little girl kicked him in his backside.

Mirror roared and his hands flew upward as if he were conducting an evil orchestra. The ground beneath the army's feet shot into the air, twisting into a knotted pretzel of earth, trees, roads, and people. The earth grew higher and higher, almost to the height of Mount Taurus, and took everything with it. Sabrina and Daphne both lost their footing and tumbled down, slipping right over the edge. Sabrina managed to snatch on to the roots of a broken tree and Daphne clung to her leg. Together, they hung there, struggling to catch their breaths and pull themselves up to safety.

Sabrina could fix this, she knew, she just had to let a little magic out. She tried and they soared to the top of the new mountain like rockets, landing on the lonely peak. Once they were on solid ground they scurried to the side and looked over. The wind was whipping in Sabrina's ears, and the temperature at this height was markedly lower. It did nothing for the fever inside Sabrina, and sweat dripped off her face like rain.

"Do you see Mom and Dad?" Daphne said.

The visions came like a thunderstorm, booming in her head. Her mother and Basil were safely on the ground, having taken shelter in the woods. Her father was on a ridge below them, still fighting one of the mirror men. Uncle Jake was pulling himself up to the top, branch by branch. Puck was flying to meet them. The rest of their friends were alive and fighting.

"Everyone is fine," Sabrina assured her. "For now."

"Can you see Mirror?"

Sabrina felt tremors shaking through her. "I can feel him. I can't explain it, but he's down there and he's coming up."

"Are you OK?"

Sabrina shook her head. There was no more faking it.

"Where are you, Sabrina?"

Sabrina peered over a ridge. Her grandmother was below, hovering midair on a cone of wind. "I'm done with this. I've held back until now."

"We're not going to let you destroy the world!" Sabrina shouted over the roaring wind. Puck fought the unearthly forces battling his wings but eventually joined the girls.

"I'm not going to destroy the world, kiddo. Where would I live? No, I'm just going to put it back the way it was meant to be. Everafters ruling everything. We're stronger and smarter than humans. You think I'm arrogant. But shouldn't the most powerful be in charge? Would you stay silent if you woke up one day to find dogs controlled the world?"

"Is this the part where the villain tries to explain his stupid way of thinking?" Daphne shouted.

"That's a rookie move," Puck said.

"Then let me explain something that you can relate to," Mirror said as he floated up to the peak and set himself down before them. "Anger. Betrayal. Abandonment. These are things you know. These are things that have made you want to strike out and smash and destroy."

"I don't know them," Daphne said.

"Because she protected you from them, but your sister knows them all too well," Mirror said, turning to Sabrina. "You know what it's like to have people you care about turn their backs on you."

"I'm not angry anymore," Sabrina said shakily.

"Then let me remind you what it's like," he said, and with a wave of his hand, Daphne was sent sailing into the air over the edge of the cliff.

"Daphne!" Sabrina cried.

"I'm on it," Puck said, sprinting to the cliff's edge and leaping off the side.

"Now you know what it's like to be alone," he said.

Sabrina stared into her grandmother's eyes, knowing that it was not Granny looking back at her. What she saw was hundreds of years of pain and uncertainty. The look reminded her of the day she arrived at Granny Relda's house. She had looked into a mirror and seen that same expression on her own face, and she remembered what it was like to wonder if she would ever feel loved again. But in the months that followed she had felt love: from her sister, from her grandmother, from her uncle, and from Puck. She felt it when her parents were found and from the dozens of new friends that had become part of her family. It had saved her and she knew that her father had given her excellent advice some days before. *Look for your enemy's weaknesses.*

She grabbed Mirror around the shoulders and hugged him. "I'm done fighting you, Mirror. I understand how you feel and I'm sorry that you didn't get the love that I did. But I am not like you. Let me show you."

She placed her hands on her grandmother's face and let loose all of her magic, but it wasn't an attack or an act of destruction and hostility. It was love—the love she had been given—and it was pure and brilliant and strong. She sent him every moment of kindness and concern she had ever received. She gave him her memories with her friends. She gave him the feelings she had for Mr. Canis and Red and her uncle. She gave him her father reading a bedtime story and her mother giving her a wink. She gave him her grandmother's hugs and the tiny, almost imperceptible smiles Mr. Canis sent her that let her know he cared. She gave him the softness of her baby brother's cheek nuzzling into her shoulder. She gave him Elvis's happy kisses. She gave him the love that she had once felt for him—all of it opening like an overstuffed jewelry box into his heart—and then she gave him the surprise of Puck's first kiss, and then her want for another, and the odd, fluttering feeling inside her whenever he talked about their future together, even when he was teasing. And then she gave him Daphne—sweet, loving, hilarious Daphne. She gave him her sister's warm hand in her own and the joy she felt when Daphne laughed. She gave him their nights asleep together, their many escapes and daring rescues. She gave him every meal with Daphne stuffing her face. She gave him her sister's frustrating and yet miraculous sense of right and wrong, and how the little girl could see the good in everyone. She gave him every day that her sister made Sabrina feel stronger, braver, and happier. She gave him an hour of Daphne brushing her hair. She gave him their secrets and inside jokes and silly giggles. She gave him every single new word Daphne ever invented. She gave him what had saved her own life—her sister's love. She wrapped it all up and slipped it into whatever Mirror called a heart.

And then the mountain was sinking back into the earth, twisting back into the land it once was. The mirror men dripped back into the soil and the wind disappeared. With the last of her magic, Sabrina created a cushion of air that caught her friends before they collided with the ground.

When it was over, Sabrina was still hugging Mirror, and he was hugging her back.

Mirror looked down into her face. Granny was more present, just beneath the surface. He was letting her go. "I didn't know it was like that."

Mirror and Sabrina stood silently for a long moment.

Bunny approached, and Mirror's eyes lit up with happiness. "Hello, Mother," he said, without scorn and rage.

Bunny flashed Sabrina an uncomfortable look, but Sabrina just nodded.

"Meet your son," Sabrina said.

Bunny hugged him tightly. "I'm sorry."

"It's time to give me back my grandmother. I love her very much," Sabrina said.

Mirror nodded. "Sabrina, would you do me a favor? I know that you have no reason to, but . . ."

"What would you like?"

Mirror reached out his hand. "Before I go, will you tell me that I'm your friend?"

Sabrina took his hand and held it tightly. "Mirror, I am your friend."

He smiled and sighed and winked at her. Then Granny Relda's mouth opened and the black spirit of Mirror slipped out and fell to the ground. Granny Relda collapsed. Bunny helped the old woman revive while Sabrina watched the dark mass flopping about like a fish unable to return to the sea. Sabrina caressed him and told him that everything would be OK. Then Mirror melted into a puddle of glistening silver. His remains leaked into the soil and were gone.

There was the sound of fluttering wings. Puck landed at her feet. He had Daphne with him, safe and sound.

"You know, as many times as you two get tossed off of tall things, you would think you'd start wearing parachutes," he said.

Sabrina swept her sister up into a hug.

"How are you feeling?" Daphne asked.

"It's gone," Sabrina said. "The magic is gone."

Granny stirred, and Sabrina helped her to sit up just as Uncle Jake, Daphne, Henry, Veronica, Basil, and Elvis rushed to join them. The old woman blinked and looked around.

"Welcome back, *liebling*," Sabrina said.

Granny Relda smiled and gave her a hug. "Have you girls been up to shenanigans?"

"Hey, that's my word!" Daphne cried, and hugged her so tight Sabrina worried the old woman might break. Elvis pushed his way in to shower her with happy licks.

Henry and Jake helped their mother to her feet. She wobbled a bit but finally found her balance.

"How do you feel, Relda?" Veronica said, embracing the woman.

"I suppose I should be tired, but I'm actually very hungry," Relda said with a laugh. "Oh, dear, I've lost my hat."

"We'll buy you another hat, Mom." Uncle Jake laughed.

Basil squirmed in Veronica's arms. "Who is this, Mommy?"

Veronica smiled as a tear escaped her happy eyes. "Honey, this is your grandmother. She's part of your family."

"Do you have a boo-boo?" he asked.

Granny wrapped him up in her arms. "I do! But I bet a kiss would make it feel better."

Basil gave her a big kiss on the cheek.

"You look just like your *opa*," Granny cooed.

Puck stepped forward and the old woman nodded at him. "Just so you know, I pretty much saved the whole world," he said.

"Oh, I have no doubts."

"Mom, look," Henry said, pointing to the Everafters who were all bravely stepping on ground they hadn't been able to reach in hundreds of years. "The barrier is down."

"Oh dear," Granny said.

"It's going to be OK, Granny," Daphne said.

And then they walked to the edge of town with the rest of the Everafters following behind them. Sabrina could see their faces, uncertain if their greatest wish also frightened them.

Sabrina turned to them and smiled. "You're free."

Charming, Snow White, the Cowardly Lion, Baba Yaga, Red, Mr. Canis, Boarman and Swineheart, Pinocchio—so many faces. They all took a step forward and stood with the family on the other side.

Everyone stood silently until Snow White spoke. "It's too big."

"What?" Sabrina asked.

"The possibilities," the beautiful teacher said.

Red helped Mr. Canis forward. He leaned against his cane and gaped at the horizon. Beauty and Natalie joined them, as well as Mr. Boarman and Mr. Swineheart. The Pied Piper's eyes filled with tears while his son stood grinning. The Frog Prince held his daughter in his arms. The Scarecrow's burlap face displayed a wide, painted smile.

And then Puck pushed through the crowd. He rubbed his hands eagerly and grinned.

"Have I got plans for you!" he crowed, flying into the air with his wooden sword in hand.

• • •

A week later, many of the Everafters were gone. The Frog Prince and his daughter left, as did the Scarecrow, the Cowardly Lion, all of King Arthur's remaining knights, and Little John. Daphne and the coven worked with some of the talking animals in hopes of creating disguises that would allow them to look human.

Veronica held a seminar on the basics of modern life, including how to use a computer, apply for a job, and get an apartment. She was very surprised to find that nearly everyone in town came to hear her. It looked as if Ferryport Landing would be all but abandoned soon.

But not everyone was ready to give up on the town. Sabrina marveled at those who decided to stay. Boarman and Swineheart hung up their deputy caps for good and reopened their construction business. They were convinced they would soon be the richest Everafters in town. The former sheriff Mr. Hamstead and his wife, Bess, showed up not long after. It was good to see their friends' happy faces. He and his wife were over the moon with happiness, as they were expecting their first child.

Charming held an emergency election for mayor but lost to his girlfriend, Snow, who was surprised to find herself a write-in candidate. Charming graciously conceded. Mayor White said her first order of business was to finally rebuild the school. She also hired Goldilocks to be the new city planner, after the woman argued that much of the town's troubles were a result of bad energies and flow. She promised the new Ferryport Landing would be designed with feng shui in mind and would prove to be the most balanced and serene little town in New York.

Despite Henry's hourly begging, Granny Relda decided to stay and rebuild. She couldn't bear to leave the town that had been her home for so many years, though she did promise to come to the city for frequent visits with her grandchildren. As always, Mr. Canis stood by her side, now with Red. He and Granny would raise her, and they offered the same to Pinocchio. The kindness overwhelmed him and he sobbed into Granny Relda's dress. Later he would discover that he had grown a half an inch for the first time in a hundred years.

As the founders of the new Ferryport Landing made their plans, Goldi took Veronica aside. Sabrina couldn't help but listen in.

"I know it has been very hard having me around," she said.

Veronica shook her head, though Sabrina wasn't convinced of her sincerity. "You were a big help."

"I just wanted to say that you're good for him. Better than I would have been," Goldi said. "You make Henry happy . . . which is hard to watch. I still—"

"I know you do," Veronica said. "He's kind of awesome, but I think that if you open yourself up, and take a chance, you might find that you will love someone else."

The women hugged and parted as friends.

One night, with nothing left for them to do, Sabrina, Daphne, Puck, and Red walked down the road toward the marina. The dock, surprisingly, was not damaged, so they took off their shoes and dipped their feet into the chilly Hudson River. They sat for a long time contemplating all that had happened and guessing at what lay ahead. Finally, Puck broke the silence.

"Your uncle is leaving town," Puck said. "He says there's magic all over the world that needs to be wrangled. He asked me to go with him."

Sabrina felt a lump in her throat. "What did you say?"

"I'm probably going to go. This is no place for the master of mischief. There's nothing left to break in this town."

"You could come with us to New York City," Sabrina said hopefully. "I'm sure your mom would like to see you around the kingdom."

He seemed to understand what Sabrina was thinking. "Don't worry, I'll swing by and harass you all the time."

Sabrina smiled. She knew this boy would be in her life always. Then she laughed. *Whether I like it or not.*

"Wait, what is that?" Puck said, looking down the river. Sabrina squinted and made out a boat sailing toward the marina. It was the kind of ship that could have drifted from the pages of a pirate novel. Its huge masts snapped in the wind and a fluttering flag smeared with a skull's grin flapped in the air. The children watched as it drifted down to them and then dropped anchor. Moments later a boy in green pants and shirt climbed onto the rail of the ship and leaped off into midair. A moment later, he was flying toward them. Sabrina looked over to Daphne. The little girl was biting her palm with excitement.

"It can't be," Sabrina said.

"It is," Daphne said.

"Who is it?" Red said.

Puck huffed and scowled. "I'll handle this."

The flying boy in green stopped short of the dock and hovered in midair. He had a wooden sword much like Puck's shoved into his belt and a little green hat. "Hey, you!" he cried. "Sorry to spook you with the ship. My lost boys and I sort of borrowed it from a few scurvy pirates back where we come from. The place is overrun with them, so we've decided to start someplace new. We're looking for a town called Ferryport Landing. We heard it's a place for folks like us."

Sabrina eyed Puck closely.

"Never heard of it," he said.

The flying boy frowned. "It's got to be around here somewhere. I hear it's filled with magic and fun."

"I think someone gave you some bad information, kid," Puck said. "This town is as boring as it gets."

The flying boy shrugged. "All right, well, thanks." Then he flew back to his boat.

"That wasn't very nice," Sabrina said.

Puck stuck his tongue out at her. "I hate that kid."

Sabrina looked up the road at what was left of Ferryport Landing, the once-sleepy river town nestled on the banks of the Hudson River. There was hardly anything left of it. Sabrina felt like she was mourning the loss of another dear relative. But maybe one day it would live again.

"Is that it?" Daphne said. "Is that the end?"

Sabrina nodded and took her sister's hand. "Yes, and it's about time."

The children sat on the dock for a long time, looking out at the rolling waves as they moved on to the sea.

"Wait. If we're Everafters now, does that mean we're going to live forever?" Daphne exclaimed.

Puck eyed Sabrina. She could almost see his mind working on the millions of pranks he would subject her to now that he had all the time in the world. She felt sick to her stomach when he giggled mischievously.

"Shenanigans," he said.

DAPHNE ZIPPED UP the back of Sabrina's gown while she studied herself in a full-length mirror.

"Well, that makes it official," Sabrina said. "I'm getting married."

"The wedding dress is a big tip-off," her mother said, adjusting the train. "You look like a princess."

"Which one?"

Daphne laughed. "I don't know. I could go out into the church and bring a few back to compare."

"No Everafters in the changing room," Sabrina said. She looked at herself in the mirror one more time. The ivory dress seemed to glow in the light. If she didn't know better, she would suspect it was enchanted. "I hope everyone is wearing their disguises. Bradley is still not super-comfortable with them, and his folks don't have a clue about the family business."

"Everyone looks like a human," Daphne said. "Except Hamstead's boys. They brought their rocket packs."

Sabrina sighed. "All I need is a bunch of teenage pigs and cows flying around the Church of St. Paul's."

"Nothing is going to ruin this, Sabrina," Red said from the doorway. Looking at Red, now a lovely young woman, as close to Sabrina as her own sister, no one would ever know she had a monster living inside her. Apparently, the yoga and meditation were working as well as ever. "I hope the 'no Everafters in the dressing room' rule doesn't apply to me."

"Get in here and help me," Sabrina said.

"Are all the guests here?" Daphne asked as she took a brush and started combing her sister's hair.

"Baba Yaga is here," Red said as she eyed the bouquet of white roses. "She's wearing a fur coat. At least I think it's a coat. I could have sworn I heard it hiss at me."

"Wow," Veronica said. "Uncle Jake made it. Goldi's here with her fiancé, too. Snow and Billy are there with the kids, Wendell and his girlfriend, Bunny—you know, the regular bunch—oh, Pinocchio."

"Pinocchio! He came? We haven't seen him in a million years," Red said.

"I saw him. He grew up very nice," Veronica said.

"He's hot," Daphne said.

Everyone looked at her in disbelief.

"What?" she cried defensively. "He is!"

Sabrina nodded. "Anyone else?"

No one said anything. Sabrina thought she saw a look pass between her mother and sister. "There was no way to find him."

"Who?" Sabrina lied.

"You know who I'm talking about. I tried," Daphne explained. "He's just hard to track down. I tried every spell I know."

"Well, I don't want him here anyway," Sabrina said. "He'd just make it all about him and ruin it for me. He'd probably toss eggs at me. It's for the best."

"Sabrina, you're not thinking about him, are you?"

Sabrina hadn't seen "him" in almost five years. She did not want to think about "him." She certainly didn't want to talk about him.

"No!"

"Good, because you're marrying Bradley today. You need to be sure," Daphne lectured.

"Oh, you're giving me relationship advice? How many boys have you broken up with this year?"

"I break up with them because they are not right for me," Daphne said. "Most of them are too—"

"Normal? Daphne, there's nothing wrong with normal. I love normal. With an office full of Everafters needing legal help every day, it's nice to go home to something normal."

Daphne giggled. "That's the price you pay for being a fairy-tale defense attorney."

There was a knock at the door and then it opened. Henry entered, smiling and crying at the same time.

"Dad?" Sabrina asked.

"You look so beautiful," he blubbered.

"He's been like this all day," Veronica said, wrapping her arms around her husband's waist. "I love it."

Sabrina hugged her father too, but Veronica broke them up. "No tears on the dress!" she said, which made everyone laugh.

From the open door, the sounds of a pipe organ floated into the room.

"It's showtime," Daphne said, handing Sabrina a bouquet of white roses.

Sabrina checked herself one more time in the mirror. She did look as beautiful as a princess—not all of them, but a few. She took a deep breath and smiled. Today was the start of a new adventure. Bradley was exactly the big, beautiful, grounded thing that she wanted, and together they would build a big, beautiful, grounded life.

"Honey?" her father said. "It's time."

"I wish Granny were here," Sabrina said.

Her father intertwined his arm into hers and together they walked to the back of the church. "I'm sure she's watching wherever she is. She's probably made a big dinner for your grandfather—all kind of weird blue food made from squids and daffodils. They're sitting back taking it all in."

Sabrina smiled at the thought. She shook off her nervousness and took a deep breath. *Bradley is a good man. He is kind and loving and sweet and handsome and normal. Oh so wonderfully normal. He's the kind of man that makes me want to throw off immortality and grow old with him. I need him. He keeps me sane.*

And then she walked into the church and through a sea of smiles. There were many faces she hadn't seen in thirteen years, and new faces she suspected masked more familiar faces. One man sat quietly licking his hand—ah, the Cowardly Lion. Mr. Swineheart and Mr. Boarman, Snow and Charming sitting next to Bunny and her seeing-eye wolf—even the Scarecrow had made it back from Oz, and there, with his shock of white hair, was Mr. Canis. As she passed, he smiled and said, "Relda would be so proud."

And on the other side of the church, there were real, honest-to-goodness people—glorious people—who had no clue that they were at a wedding filled with magic. And at the altar was Bradley, blue eyes gleaming. He had shaved his goatee for the day. It was odd to see him without it. She barely recognized him.

The minister smiled down at her. "Who gives this woman to be married?"

"I do," Henry said, and placed Sabrina's hand into Bradley's. It felt warm and comforting. Henry kissed her cheek and joined his wife and Basil in the front pew. Her brother, who was no baby any longer, standing nearly six feet tall, grinned and winked at her.

"Marriage is a journey," the minister said. "A walk down a long, twisting road. Some days the path is clear and bright, and others, murky and mysterious. There are many bends in the road and more than a few crossroads. Today, the two of you take that road together, hand in hand, promising to all here and God himself that you will not let go of each other. Before we start, it is customary to ask the congregation to witness this union. I ask those gathered here, do you promise to support this marriage, in good times and bad, to help this couple down their road whenever possible?"

Sabrina turned to look at the audience just as they all said, "We do."

The minister smiled. "Very good. It is also customary to ask those gathered if anyone can give cause or reason that this union should not take place. If anyone objects, speak now or forever hold your peace."

Sabrina cringed and looked out to the crowd once more. But no one rose. No one spoke. No one threw an egg. He was not there. He was not going to ruin her wedding. So why was she . . . disappointed?

"Very well," the minister said. "I believe the bride and groom have written some vows they would like to share with one—"

His voice was drowned out by wings flapping like thunder above the crowd. Everyone craned his or her neck to see what the commotion was, but Sabrina didn't have to look—she knew. When Bradley's side of the church gasped and screamed and rose from their seats, she sighed. When Henry and Veronica scowled, and when Daphne bit down on the palm of her hand, Sabrina did not have to look up.

"It's—it's an angel," the minister said, falling back in shock.

"Hardly," Sabrina muttered.

And then "the angel" was floating down before her, the light from the stained-glass window silhouetting him in color. He was a man. No longer a boy. And he was beautiful.

"Hello, stinky," he said with a wink that infuriated Sabrina, but not enough to stop her from grinning.

August 16

I love my backyard. It's small and not much to look at—just a few flowers, a stone path, a birdbath, a hammock, and a shed for tools, but it is my heaven. I can spend hours here, reading, relaxing, and practicing the yoga Red and Mr. Canis have recommended for my stress. (Well, I don't actually do that, but someday I could!)

In my backyard there are no headaches. No lawyers or judges, no negotiations, petitions to the court, bail hearings, and hung juries. There are no meetings with the mayor, no reporters digging for a story, no campaign dinners, and no elections. Lying in my hammock, I can forget about how the brownstone needs a new roof, and the neighbors are making me crazy with their construction, and how our dogs, Bono and Edge, need a bath. And best of all, for a brief moment, I can forget that I am the mother of two lovely but extremely difficult girls.

The younger, Emma, is a lot like Daphne at that age—funny, kind, precocious, but unlike Daphne, Emma enjoys antagonizing her sister. They don't have the relationship that Daphne and I had. Most of the time they can't stand to be in the same room. Admittedly, Alison is a handful—a total Grimm! Six months ago she turned fourteen, and along with the presents came a surprising change in attitude. Suddenly, my sweet, loving, happy child has turned into a teenager—headstrong, rude, impatient, and forever embarrassed by her parents. It was as if sometime in the night goblins had snuck in and replaced her with one of their own.

Daphne says I was exactly the same way, but I don't remember myself being so self-centered. Well, Daphne will be a lot more sympathetic soon enough with her twins. Basil's the smart one in this family. He says he's going to be a bachelor for life. I just have to laugh. Love does not allow you to make plans. I remember what I used to say about marriage, but—

Suddenly, there was a scream. Sabrina threw down her journal and reached under the garden table, where she had duct-taped a dagger. Yanking it free, she dashed into the house. If it was them, she would make them pay. They had made threats lately. She had seen their mark in the streets. She would not let them harm her family.

She dashed up the stairs two at a time, then darted around the corner, running as fast as she could down the hallway. Emma was waiting by her sister's bedroom door.

"The spaz won't open up," Emma said.

Sabrina tried the doorknob but found it locked. "Allie, open the door!"

But Alison didn't open the door and the screaming didn't stop.

"She's probably just got a zit, Mom," Emma said. "You know how dramatic she can be."

"Alison! I'm coming in right now," Sabrina shouted, then kicked the door, ripping the lock out and sending it flying open.

"Wow!" Emma said. "You have to teach me how to do that!"

Sabrina charged into the room fully prepared to face a monster, but all she saw was Alison, looking right at her, tears streaming down her face.

"What? What happened?" Sabrina said.

"Mom!" Alison cried. "Mom! I need you!"

Sabrina peered around the room for intruders, then quickly hid the dagger in the pocket of her shorts. "What is it, honey?"

"It's horrible!"

"Did Parker break up with you again?" Emma said.

"Emma, stop teasing her," Sabrina snapped. "And Allie, stop crying and tell me what's wrong!"

Alison turned her back on her mother. Sabrina saw something begin to poke out of the back of Alison's shirt. There was a loud pop and then there were wings—huge, glorious, pink insect wings. They fluttered at a fantastic speed and lifted Alison off the ground. She hovered in midair awkwardly, elbows and head slamming into the ceiling and walls.

"That's no zit!" Emma shouted.

"Mom? What is going on?" Alison sobbed.

"Honey, I know you are a little freaked out right now—"

"A LITTLE? I'm turning into a bug!"

"I bet you're going to grow pinchers next," Emma said.

"You're not turning into a bug!" Sabrina said. "Now both of you calm down. I promise everything is going to be fine. Your father will be home soon from the castle and—"

"The castle?" the girls cried.

Sabrina sighed. She wanted to go and hide in her backyard. "He'll be able to tell you what you are."

"What am I?" Alison cried.

Sabrina cringed. "You're a fairy princess."

Alison burst into tears. "I don't want to be a fairy princess!"

Emma's eyes were as big as full moons. "Wait, if she's a fairy princess, that means I'm one, too, right?"

Sabrina nodded.

"OMG," Emma said, then did a little tap dance on the bathroom floor.

"Girls, I need to tell you some things about our family," Sabrina said. "Have you ever heard of the Brothers Grimm?"

THE END

ABOUT THE AUTHOR

Michael Buckley is the *New York Times* bestselling author of the *Sisters Grimm* and *NERDS* series. He has also written and developed television shows for many networks. Michael lives in Brooklyn, New York.

This book was designed by Melissa J. Arnst, and art directed by Chad W. Beckerman. It is set in Adobe Garamond, a typeface that is based on those created in the sixteenth century by Claude Garamond. Garamond modeled his typefaces on those created by Venetian printers at the end of the fifteenth century. The modern version used in this book was designed by Robert Slimbach, who studied Garamond's historic typefaces at the Plantin-Moretus Museum in Antwerp, Belgium.

The capital letters at the beginning of each chapter are set in Daylilies, designed by Judith Sutcliffe. She created the typeface by decorating Goudy Old Style capitals with lilies.